# A Detective in Love

H. R. F. Keating, a Fellow of the Royal Society of Literature, was the crime books reviewer for *The Times* for fifteen years. He has served as Chairman of the Crime Writers' Association and the Society of Authors, and in 1987 was elected President of the Detection Club.

He has written numerous novels as well as non-fiction. He is perhaps best known for his Inspector Ghote series, the first of which, *The Perfect Murder*, was made into a film by Merchant Ivory and won a CWA Gold Dagger award, as did *The Murder of the Maharajah*.

*A Detective in Love* is the second in H. R. F. Keating's Harriet Martens series, following *The Hard Detective*. The latest Harriet Martens mystery, *A Detective Under Fire*, is available in Macmillan hardback.

# By the Same Author

# H. R. F. Keating

# A Detective in Love

PAN BOOKS

First published 2001 by Macmillan

This edition published 2002 by Pan Books
an imprint of Pan Macmillan Ltd
Pan Macmillan, 20 New Wharf Road, London N1 9RR
Basingstoke and Oxford
Associated companies throughout the world
www.panmacmillan.com

ISBN 0 330 48897 X

Copyright © H. R. F. Keating 2001

The right of H. R. F. Keating to be identified as the
author of this work has been asserted by him in accordance
with the Copyright, Designs and Patents Act 1988.

Grateful acknowledgement is made to William Heinemann for
permission to publish copyright material from *The Heart of the Matter* by
Graham Greene

Grateful acknowledgement is made to William Heinemann for
permission to publish copyright material from *The Tree of Pearls*
by Louisa Young

1 3 5 7 9 8 6 4 2

A CIP catalogue record for this book is available from
the British Library.

Printed and bound in Great Britain by
Mackays of Chatham plc, Chatham, Kent

# Chapter One

'Right, how was it for you?' Detective Superintendent Harriet Martens asked, if with a hint of mischief in the snapped-out demand.

John gave a grunted chuckle at her well-worn joke.

'One hundred per cent satisfactory, thank you, ma'am,' he answered.

Silence for a time in the tumbled bed.

Then John sent a reflective thought up towards the ceiling.

'Just think, I've been away more than six months, and it all goes as well as it's done at any time in the past – what's it? – twenty-two years.'

'You been keeping in practice with Brazilian whores?'

'In accordance with our long-standing agreement? But, no, I really put that success just now down to what old Tolstoy called *the feeling of amorousness that has the greatest power over human beings.* Words you may have heard from me before. And that power doing its stuff for you too?'

'Well, something was. I think in the circumstances I could say *Wow.*'

'*Wow*, it was. But then perhaps you, too, have been taking advantage of that agreement?'

'You know me better than that. Had the occasional *amorousness* twinge, of course. When I happened to

1

see someone of your build, actually. Nice and lithe. So sometimes in bed there was a bit of masturbation.'

'Uh, oh.'

'However, being the Hard Detective, as the media loved to call me, plainly took up more of my energies than you expended negotiating away out there for Majestic Insurance.'

'Okay, I'll grant you the more demanding time. But don't get to thinking you can always escape. Brazil or Britain, *the greatest power* is always there. I see it as a huge hovering cloud, over the whole wide world. And tense with lightning that can strike at any time.'

'You don't need to tell me. A police officer knows all about rampant sex.'

She let loose a little giggle.

'Pun not intended. But,' she went on, 'everybody who can read a newspaper knows how rampant sex is.'

'Ah, but that's where you're wrong. Oh, yes, you might say we're all media-immersed in sex. But, in fact, I doubt if most people actually realize how totally ubiquitous the sex impulse is. And always has been.'

'Oh, come on. We do. The vast majority of us. Nowadays.'

'No, no. All right, in that mythical Victorian piano-legs-in-pantaloons era people, at least in the respectable classes, may have convinced themselves sex was something that manifested itself only when a baby had to be made. But in fact it's us, the sophisticated, we-know-it-all generation, who still don't really acknowledge how we're all in every way all the time at the mercy of that louring cloud.'

'No, listen, where I don't go along with you – and, God, what are we doing discussing what Tolstoy said at this hour of the morning? – where I don't go along with you is in believing your great cloud is as looming as all that. I still think, however much you say we're thinking of sex all the time, it's actually something that' – bare-armed, she made quote-marks in the air – '*rears its ugly head* just from time to time.'

'No, no. I—'

'No, listen, I certainly don't believe I'm thinking of sex morning, noon and night. I've got better things to do. And you actually? Joking apart, how often did you really resort to your Brazilian whores?'

'Oh, I suppose only a couple of times, when it was just a matter of *alivio*. Of, as the jargon here has it, *relief*. You know how it is. There you are, deprived of what they call conjugal rights but seemingly getting along fine, until suddenly something starts it up. Often something ridiculously trivial or unexpected. Remember my favourite Graham Greene quote? *A hunchback, a cripple – they all have the trigger that sets love off?*'

'Number five hundred and forty-three from the John Piddock collection of pithy remarks.'

'Touché, Mrs Piddock, touché. Or should I say, Miss Martens?'

'I answer to both. Or – hey, my quotation, my quotation, *The Hunting of the Snark* – I answer *to Hi or to any loud cry*. And, d'you know something? When we first met I nearly went right off you when I heard what your surname was.'

'Oh, yes? But you didn't, did you? Know why? Because two were playing at the game. Not that it's really any sort of a game, much more charged than a game. No, what it was on both sides with us then was *Amor vincit omnia*, as Chaucer neatly put it. Right?'

'Chaucer now. Love conquers every—'

The phone was shrilling out.

'For God's sake,' John spluttered. 'What time is this? Damn it, half-past six.'

Harriet turned on to her side, lifted the receiver, listened.

In a moment she put her hand over the mouthpiece and, twisting half-way round, muttered, 'Bloody Chief Constable.'

Then, back with the phone, she said, 'Bubbles Xingara? The tennis star?'

A jabbering from the far end.

'And you say murdered? You're sure you – I mean, how did you learn about this, sir?'

More quacking from the far end.

'Right, I'll switch it on as soon as you—'

Now a more prolonged jabbering.

'Very well. But I'd better have one of our own cars. Could you possibly arrange one, sir? I'll need all my time here.'

Quack, quack.

'Thank you, sir. And I'd better take someone with me, a DI for preference.'

She put the phone down, reached further over, snapped on the radio.

The newsreader's voice, still urgent with excitement: . . . *stabbing is thought to have taken place while Bubbles was out for her early morning training run. Adam and Eve House, which the nineteen-year-old tennis star bought about a year ago, is a remote property on the banks of the River Leven. It is believed to have cost a sum in excess of three-quarters of a million pounds. A statement, issued a few minutes ago, from Leven Vale Police headquarters said that inquiries are being pursued with vigour. Meanwhile speculation is already growing about how the death of the favourite for the Ladies' trophy at*

*Wimbledon will affect the tournament. More news on the hour every hour. You're listening to Greater Birchester Radio, 98. 4 FM.*

Harriet clicked it off.

'Bubbles?' John said. 'Bubbles Xingara's been murdered?'

'She has, and all hell's breaking loose.'

'But didn't the radio say the Leven Vale Police? So what's it got to do with you?'

'I've been seconded,' she said, scrambling out of bed and looking for clean underwear. 'That's what the Chief was on about. Leven Vale's CC feels they can't cope. And I can see why. They're a tiny force policing a big rural area. So, as they abut on to Greater Birchester territory, I'm to take charge. A car'll be here in a few minutes. I must shower, get some clothes on. Grab a bite, if there's time.'

'I'll go and make some coffee.'

'Okay. But instant.'

'Instant, it is. And I suppose this means I shan't see you till late this evening?'

'You'll be lucky if you see me at all today, or tomorrow. This looks as if it's going to be a major, major inquiry.'

'You're right. I dare say I know more about that girl than you do. You were never one for the gossip columns.'

He was calling now through the open doors into the bathroom.

'Bubbles Xingara's not just the next new tennis Number One, she's wildly pretty as well, and she's – she was, oh, God – fun. That's what got to people. When she won a point she gave a great big smile, and when she lost one, even unfairly, it was just a wry grin. Bubbles by name and bubbly by nature. God's gift to the media – *from China to Peru*, as Sam Johnson neatly puts it.'

'Number five hundred and forty-four.'

Driven through the gates in the high wall surrounding Bubbles Xingara's Adam and Eve House and on round the sweep of its drive, Harriet found herself – all that the investigation meant she would have to do laid out in order in her mind – in a poles-apart scene.

Peace lay like a blanket over a wide stretch of lawn running down to the River Leven. In the quiet sunshine of the early morning all the scents of the countryside came drifting in, a waft of sweet orange from a big untidy syringa bush at the corner of the house, a heavier, acid-edged odour from a long row of lavender bushes, a smell of gently rotting plants from the edge of the trickling Leven, and, distantly, the rich tang of cows and cowdung blown on the gently shifting air from fields stretching away as far as the eye could see. A cuckoo was calling somewhere in the distance. The faded red brickwork of the old mansion, straggled over by ancient creepers, made it seem as if nothing had changed here over all the years and that nothing ever could.

But something had.

Just a few feet from the river's edge, cut off from the rest of the wide lawn by a drooping Scenes-of-Crime tape, a staringly blue plastic tent was concealing what must be the body of the dead girl. A Leven Vale constable, already looking overheated, was standing guard beside the entrance to the secured area.

Pausing only to pull out her mobile and log herself on, Harriet went over to him.

'Detective Superintendent Martens, Greater Birch-ester Police,' she said. 'Who's in charge here? Where are they?'

The constable, with some haste, saluted.

'It's DI Brent,' he said. 'He – He's in the Incident Room. It's been set up over there. In what they call the Boathouse, only it isn't one any more. It's – Well, it's Bubbles' sort of gym really.'

'Miss Xingara, Constable.'

'Yes, ma'am. Yes.'

'Right, get Mr Brent. Now.'

The constable went at a heavy trot across to a lichen-stained, shed-like brick building projecting over the baked-hard mud of the river bank, and a moment later the Leven Vale inspector emerged. Someone much as Harriet had expected, not totally a yokel but not far from it. Stocky in build, though still in his early thirties, his face under a thatch of fair hair burnt by sun and wind to the dull red of a flowerpot and lit by a pair of observant forget-me-not blue eyes. In place of the sharp suits senior detectives in her Greater Birch-ester force affected, there was, dangling half-off broad shoulders, a well-worn jacket in dull orangey tweed and heavy grey trousers straining at solidly muscular thighs. As he came close she caught the tang of the drying sweat at his armpits. None of your poncy deodorants here.

Ah well, she thought.

But, in answer to her shot-out questions, DI Brent, voice laced with a country burr, provided answers quickly enough.

Yes, he had managed to get here within half an hour of the murder being reported. Mr Peter Renshaw, the victim's stepfather and coach – Harriet noted with a quantum of pleasure that the DI had avoided familiarly talking about *Bubbles* – had called Levenham police station shortly after six a.m. when, coming out as he always did to check his charge's blood pressure after her morning run, he had found her body lying on the grass beside the river.

'Death been certified?'

'Yes, ma'am. Police surgeon came out with me.'

'But the pathologist hasn't seen the body yet?'

'No, ma'am. Someone's coming from Birchester for that.'

'I take it you haven't found a weapon?'

'No, ma'am. I organized as much of a search as I could. But no luck.'

'Whoever it was took it away with them, no doubt. Or hid it, if we're looking at an inside job. Try the river when you've got the manpower, if you can call that trickle down there a river. And callers? You checked on them? Milk van? Post? Papers?'

'They fetch their milk from a farm about half a mile away, ma'am, and the papers are delivered by a schoolgirl on a bike. Post came shortly after we got here. Van driver gave a pretty good account of himself. I put in a radio check on him, and back came *NCR.*'

'Right. I suppose most postmen will register *No Criminal Record*. But check whether he saw anybody unusual about. And with that paper girl. Then the minute you've got the personnel I want a full-scale search for the weapon. Find that, and perhaps we'll make a quicker job of this than looks likely.'

'Yes, ma'am.'

'And now you can show me the body.'

\*

Yes, Harriet registered as DI Brent lifted away one side of the blue tent. Yes, Bubbles Xingara had been pretty. Wonderfully pretty.

Even in death she seemed to have kept the liveliness of a face framed in a cluster of dark curls with cheekily tip-tilted nose and full, ready lips just parted as if in surprise. Somehow as outgoing and even cheerful as she must have been in life. Cheerful, even with blood from the wound in her throat, round and almost an inch across, that had spurted all down her white running singlet. Cheerful, even lying in the drying puddle of her own suddenly voided faeces escaped from her white shorts, flies buzzing round and down on to it in lazy summer circles.

Hardened as she was, Harriet felt a stab of sharp regret. That someone, something, so pulsingly alive should have been in an instant transformed into nothing but putrefying flesh . . .

Faintly again came the cuckoo's call, a requiem.

'At least it isn't likely she was raped,' Harriet said. 'I can't see her attacker pulling those shorts up again afterwards.'

'No, ma'am. And anyone trying to get near her would have had a hard time of it. Look at those arm muscles. You know, in the States she's called *the Brit with the hit.*'

'I didn't know. Not much of a sports fan. But you're right. She'd have made a fight of it. Hey, wait, her hand. The right one. All those calluses on it. What can she have been doing to have got it into that state?'

DI Brent turned and gave her a quick blue-eyed, shyly come-and-go smile.

'She's been playing tennis, ma'am,' he said. 'Day

in, day out for four, five, six years, I'd say. Or more. I play a bit myself, so I know. Look.'

He held out his right hand, palm uppermost.

Glancing down, Harriet saw reddened skin dotted with yellowy-white calluses, the broad masculine palm innocently held up for her inspection as if it was a child's being checked before a meal. And, in a sudden jolt that seemed to run from the top of her head to her very feet, she felt one single outflame of sexual arousal.

*Amorousness . . . that has the greatest power . . .*

# Chapter Two

Harriet, astonished and embarrassed by the sudden rush of plain desire she had felt, inwardly shouted at herself *No*. No, no, no. No bloody *amorousness*. Christ, I'm on an investigation. And one, damn it, that's going to make demands, even if I get to the heart of it in the next couple of hours. Bubbles Xingara. The media will go crazy. Are already, no doubt. Cameras, reporters here almost as soon as the bloody Scenes-of-Crime team, if they ever turn up. And if I don't detect this in the next few hours, and it's almost certain I won't, then I'm going to need all my energies day and night, day after day too. So, no, no. Not another sodding thought about DI Brent's calloused palm. Nor any other part of his anatomy.

'Yes,' she said, as the Leven Vale DI let his hand fall to his side, 'I should have seen what the thickened skin there meant. But I haven't played tennis since I was at school. And – And –' Why do I feel obliged to say this? To tell him I'm married? 'And my husband isn't much interested in sport either.'

She choked out a sort of laugh.

'He's a terrible bookworm,' she torrented on, forcing herself not to look directly at the DI in case he might see how still she longed just to touch him. 'Always jotting down things he's read. Or heard.

Pockets full of little notes. Quotations, bits of verse. On restaurant napkins, old envelopes, matchbooks, anything.'

She brought herself to a halt.

God, what will he be thinking of me? Going on and on about John, the casual references to the big-city life he leads, restaurants, literary talk. And it's not even as if that's really the true picture.

But, no, I am not, not, going to look at DI Brent any differently than I look at any male I come across. Well, if I do just occasionally . . .

'Right, DI,' she snapped out. 'By the look of it we don't need to wait for any forensic nonsense to have a pretty good idea of the time of death. I gather she finished her morning run just before six at this time of year.'

'Yes, ma'am. Or that's what her stepfather told me.'

He seemed unaware that anything out-of-order had gone shooting through her mind.

'And he seemed kosher?' she asked. 'Kosher at least as far as you could tell? No blood flecks on his clothes, nothing like that?'

'No, ma'am. He was still in shock when I got here, but more or less normal.'

'All right, we'll assume he was giving you the facts straight. So, if he found her just after six, and judging by the state of the blood, not all of it quite congealed, plus still-damp sweat on that singlet – under the shade in the tent it's been slow to dry off – she must have been killed only a few minutes earlier. He didn't say anything about seeing anybody out here, I take it.'

'No, ma'am.'

She glanced back at the big house, still as set in its summer stupor as when she had arrived.

'There are windows overlooking here,' she said. 'Have you spoken to anyone bar the stepfather so far? If someone was awake earlier they might have seen an intruder.'

'No, ma'am. I haven't had a chance to talk to anybody yet, except Mr Renshaw.'

'No? Well, you've done a lot already. Good work.'

Why – Why am I giving the fellow credit like that? Is it because . . . No, damn it, he has done well, and I should tell him so. But . . .

'Right. So, the work of some outsider. Unless I find different when I talk to whoever's in the house.'

'The mother, a secretary, cook and gardener couple, plus Mr Renshaw. That's all. I've got a list of their names.'

'No boyfriend for Bubbles Xingara?'

'No, ma'am. In fact, going by what I read in the paper, she hasn't got anybody and hasn't had anybody.'

'You can't believe everything you read in the papers, DI.'

That's better. Treat him just as I would any other glib-thinking subordinate.

'No, ma'am. But they always say about her that she's too busy with tennis to have any what they call social life. And it seems down at the Eastbourne tournament the other day some fan shouted out to her, *Who's your boyfriend?* and she just turned her head and shouted back, *Who's yours?* Sparky, I say.'

Abruptly he looked down at the girl's body in its ugly mess of blood and faeces. 'Poor kid,' he said.

'You're right. So we're going to find whoever it was who killed her. Whoever it was.'

*

13

Harriet went back to the car, where the officer who had been found to drive her, Sgt Grant, snatched from night duty at the Rape Unit, was waiting. Seeing her sitting there placidly with the door beside her standing open, she thought suddenly of what they had talked about as they had driven out of Birchester, across the Leven at Levenham and on to isolated Adam and Eve House.

It had been ironically amusing. Because Sgt Grant, with whom she'd long been on friendly terms, had learnt that the detective inspector assigned to her, a DI Anderson, recently arrived trailing clouds of London glory from the Met, had most probably been chosen to shunt him away from Birchester's B Division, where he had been creating nothing but trouble. Not in his work. But in his so-called social activities.

'I don't know how true this is,' sturdy Sgt Grant had said. 'But the gossip is he's made it his target to have every woman in B Div. Handy Andy, the WPCs call him.' She had given a bark of a laugh then. 'He'll have his work cut out if he ever gets round to me. In the Unit, I see too much of the trouble random sex brings about.'

'So what's the man's great secret?'

She had put the question idly enough.

'I dunno really. Of course, he's a handsome sort of hunk. But you have to be more than that to score the way he does. Total self-confidence is probably it most of the time. Golden tongue, and not afraid to use it to get what he wants. Something like that.'

'Well, he'd better keep his prick in his trousers while he's under my command.'

'If anybody can keep that there, you could.'

The sergeant had glanced across at her then, as if

wondering whether she had gone too far. And had there been, too, a glint of speculation in her eyes?

'Okay, thanks for waiting,' she said to her now. 'But no need for you to stay on.'

'Thank you, ma'am. And best of luck with the investigation. Eyes of the world on you.'

Then as she started up the car she tossed out one more word.

'Oh, did they tell you? You won't be seeing Handy Andy till tomorrow. He's had to be called back from leave.'

Handy Andy, Harriet thought. Will I find bloody sex complicating my investigation at every turn?

And, more to the point, has it in Bubbles Xingara's life complicated the case already? All right, apparently she didn't have an acknowledged boyfriend. But here at Adam and Eve House can there be some other sexual entanglement? And, worse than that, there's all the sexual interest from outside that the poor girl's bound to have aroused. Men everywhere making her the object of their fantasies. *An unhealthy interest*, isn't that what they say? Women, too, come to that. A woman could have had the same thoughts about her. God, there'll have been dozens of people who've gone to tennis tournaments just to see her in the flesh. And stalkers. Little doubt that she'll have been followed at times, followed by stalkers thinking at least of seizing her and, as they say, enjoying her.

And all of them lost to view. If it turns out in the end that one of those hundreds did this, the investigation's not going to be a matter of hours, nor days or weeks, but of months and months, even years.

On the other hand, it could still be some nasty close-knit family business. It could be.

So, go inside and do some talking.

Again she became conscious of the cuckoo, sending out its maddening call time and again into the still morning air. A male, if I've got my orni-what'sit right, seeking a female. And didn't John once tell me that a cuckold was named after *cuckoo*? How someone whose wife was being unfaithful must have hated in those days hearing that silly bird's repeated and repeated call.

But through French windows, left just ajar, she could see the man who must be Bubbles' stepfather, and coach. He was sitting hunched in a deep chintz-covered armchair staring down at the floor at his feet. Green-and-yellow striped cotton-knit shirt, tan-coloured shorts revealing legs matted with coarse black hair, feet in trainers topped by thick white socks. Aged forty-five or so, slicked-back black hair, well built with broad shoulders.

At present bowed down.

She stepped inside.

'Mr Renshaw? Mr Peter Renshaw? I'm Detective Superintendent Martens, leading the investigation into this sudden, appalling death.'

'Yes?'

He seemed to have nothing more to say. But after a moment or two he roused himself and looked up. A strongly handsome face, heavy unshaven jaw darkened with black bristles, tangled eyebrows descending in a frown of bemusement.

'I – I'm sorry, Superintendent. I – I – This – It's left me stunned, to tell you the truth.'

The truth. But is he telling it? Or is this man, this evidently sporting type, intent on concealing what, in place of taking blood pressure, he had done to his stepdaughter just two hours ago? A macho figure, clearly. So what had been his relations with pretty, extrovert Bubbles? Father figure and acquired stepdaughter? Coach and pupil? Or . . . Or what?

But a roundabout approach.

'Tell me,' she said, 'how long have you all lived here? In Adam and Eve House?'

'Oh, eighteen months. Or more. More.'

The dulled voice. But attempting to play the suddenly bereaved stepfather? Was this a mind in turmoil after a sudden burst of rage, at maybe some sexual rebuff, had made him thrust that weapon into the girl's throat?

And – this had been itching away at her mind from the moment that she had set eyes on the wound – what sort of weapon could it have been that had caused that unusual injury?

'Adam and Eve House,' she said. 'It's an odd name. Was that what attracted you?'

He looked up at her, slightly less dulled.

'Oh, it was Bubbles who wanted the place,' he said. 'Teenager's romantic notion, really. The name made her absolutely set on it. Apparently, there's a story behind it. The house was built – it's eighteenth century – by a man called Adam Something for his new wife, an Evelina. And in the first flush of marriage he linked their names together.'

Love. Sex, Harriet could not prevent herself thinking. Was this whole business going to be infused with Tolstoy's *amorousness*? John would claim it was bound to be. But would he be right?

'So it was your stepdaughter who actually made the purchase?' she asked, keeping her voice casual.

'Oh, yes. She's the one with the money. She's been

a corporation in the States ever since she was fifteen, you know. A tennis star makes a hell of a lot. Not from prizes so much as with sponsorships, spin-offs, endorsements of a hundred and one unlikely things from cars to wristwatches.'

'But she must have had – what? – trustees, when she was fifteen. Does she still have them today, or not?'

Was it going to be money, after all, lying at the root of this? Not, for once, sex?

'Well, yes, she does,' Peter Renshaw answered, seeming to be slowly coming back to the world as it had been before he had found Bubbles' body down by the river. 'I'm one of them. Or . . . Or I was. It was to be until she reached twenty-one. That's in a couple of years' time. Her mother is the other. But we neither of us ever stood in the way of her spending what she earned on what she wanted. Word of advice, maybe, but when it came down to it she was her own woman.'

'So – I have to ask you this – who monetarily will benefit now?'

He looked up in bewilderment. Or false bewilderment?

'I – I suppose . . . Well, I presume Bubbles' mother will. I'm sure Bubbles never made a will. But – But you're not saying – Look, that's ridiculous. Aimée couldn't possibly have done – done what happened. She – She was in bed asleep. I had to wake her up to tell her. And how would it have benefited her? Or me? We both depended on Bubbles' career being successful. We couldn't – No, Superintendent, this must have been some maniac. Some sex maniac.'

He shunted himself up towards her.

'No. It was a sex maniac. And I hope to God you catch him.'

'I hope so, too, Mr Renshaw. But what I'd like to know now is whether anyone in the house was up early enough to see any—'

The French windows, which Harriet had all but closed as she had come in, burst open with a clatter. A constable stood there, panting hard, his face glistening with sweat. From far away, now that the doors were open, came once again that sweetly irritating *Cuckoo, cuckoo.*

'Ma'am, ma'am,' the fellow managed to gasp out, 'DI Brent's compliments—'

'Yes? Yes, man? What is it?'

'Ma'am, they've collared someone. Come. Come quick, he said.'

# Chapter Three

Hurrying out, Harriet saw coming round the corner of the house a cluster of irrepressibly grinning Leven Vale Police officers. DI Brent was in the middle of them, with his hand – that hand, she could not stop herself thinking – gripping by the elbow a shambling, roughly dressed man of sixty or so, who was making his way forward, head hanging, as if each step was more than he could manage.

As soon as he saw her, DI Brent handed his captive over to the nearest uniformed officer, a hefty-looking sergeant, and came across.

'Look what we've found, ma'am,' he said.

'Well, who is he? Do you know?'

'I certainly do. He's an old friend of ours. Name of Rowley. Tim Rowley. Layabout we've known for years in Levenham, always in and out of work and – and this is what you'll want to hear – a long, long list of convictions for – words of the Act – *wilfully, openly, lewdly and obscenely exposing his person.*'

'And more serious offences?'

'Well, nothing he's ever been done for, ma'am.'

'So, where did you find him?'

'About a quarter of a mile away, just off the lane that leads to the house. Fast asleep under the hedge.'

'Drunk?'

'Breath still smelt of it.'

'Anything to say for himself?'

'Not much, ma'am. Surly bugger, really. Way he always is when we pull him in.'

'Blood on his clothing?'

'Nothing to see. But what look like semen stains on the trousers.'

'No sign of the weapon, I suppose.'

'We looked around but didn't find anything.'

'We've got to have the weapon. If only to see what it actually was. But, first things first, we'll have to question this fellow under proper conditions. I imagine you haven't got a recording machine in that boathouse you've taken over.'

''fraid not, ma'am.'

'Right. We'll have him taken to Levenham then, and you'd better go there with me since you know him of old. Anybody out here now you can leave in charge?'

No sooner had she said this than she felt a dart of disquiet. Without a car of her own here, she would have to go in the DI's, putting herself in close company with the man who had aroused that jab of desire in her. Was that stupid? Well, had to be done, stupid or not.

'Yes, ma'am,' DI Brent said now. 'Sgt Wintercombe's well experienced.'

'Very well. Brief him. Tell him to get every man and woman he can spare looking for that weapon. Number One priority. And, wait, no doubt the media hordes will be here any time now. He's to keep them well out of the way. And to say nothing, nothing at all, to any of them, right? Now, is that the pathologist down there with the body and the Scenes-of-Crime people?'

'Yes, ma'am.'

'Then I'll have a quick word, and you can drive me over to Levenham as soon as I've done.'

'I'll get my car.'

Less than an hour later Harriet was standing outside Levenham police station watching Tim Rowley, Old Rowley as everyone seemed to call him with half-affec-tionate contempt, being hustled inside in advance of the media. DI Brent, who now, against her better judge-ment, she knew as Anselm, was beside her. Under the euphoria of the capture, as they had driven together in his cramped little VW, he had produced, turning towards her with a sudden shy smile, that somewhat odd forename. And she had seen it as churlish, in informal circumstances, not to use it.

'Name's a sort of family tradition,' he had said. 'Lev-enham parish church is St Anselm's, and I don't know why but that name's been handed down in our family, father to son, for as long as there've been Brents in the place.'

'So you're solidly local then?'

She had a suspicion that it might have been better not to let herself get on such friendly terms with the man who had shown her that triggering right hand. She had been conscious, too, as they sat side by side, all too conscious, of his faintly sweat-smelling male presence. But, if they were about to get a result here and now, if Old Rowley really was Bubbles' murderer, then it was surely safe enough to allow herself to be aware of that presence. It was hardly likely, after the committal, that she would see very much of DI Brent of Anselm.

'Yes, we've even a sort of family tradition of serving in the police,' he had answered then. 'Going right back to the days when it was just the Levenham force, before anyone had thought of Leven Vale.'

'So your father was a police officer?'

'He was. Ended up as custody sergeant at the station here. And I dare say my young nephew Jonathan, who's next in line, seeing as I'm not married, will be joining one day.'

Not married? Free, she had thought. And had at once suppressed the thought.

'Oh, yes? So how old is Jonathan now?'

'Eleven. First term at Levenham Grammar. Bright little chap, though I say it.'

'But won't you be providing someone in the direct line yourself one of these days?'

Damn it, why am I asking him things like this? Probing into his private life. Surely to God, I'm not asking once more *Are you free sex-wise?* It's not what I want to know. I do not want to have sex with a junior officer, different force or not. I don't actually want to have sex with anyone bar John, despite our agreement. That's okay for him, with his long stints abroad, but I don't need it. Not even while he's away. Bloody, bloody sex.

She had taken a deep breath then.

'Tell me,' she had said, keeping her voice even and only mildly interested, 'Levenham, don't you find it rather – well, quiet?'

His answer had surprised her. Or, rather, it was the look he had given her, turning aside from the wheel. There was the smallest hint of mockery in the forget-me-not blue eyes, and perhaps the very slightest of smiles on his lips.

'Oh, Levenham's quiet all right. There never has been much to do, but I'm happy about that. Used to be a cinema once, but it closed down when everybody got the telly. So now there's what? The municipal tennis courts, of course, where I go almost every day, and what they like to call the Water Sports Centre on the Leven. One of my neighbours is the bailiff there, so I sometimes take out a kayak and paddle up and down a bit.'

Yes, she had thought. He's been quietly putting me in my place, telling me not to be bloody patronizing. Good for him. I like it. Yes, I like the way he did that.

And it was at this point, as they stood on the pavement outside the heavy old, formidably impressive Victorian police station waiting while Old Rowley was hustled out of the van that had brought him from Adam and Eve House, that Anselm turned to her.

'Could you do me a little favour, ma'am?' he asked.

She stopped. A favour? What was this? Had he somehow guessed that favours were what she wanted to give him? And were they? Were they? No, they were not.

'Yes?'

He smiled then, his occasional, devastatingly straightforward, bashful smile.

'That lad hovering there,' he said, nodding towards the corner of the building. 'That's young Jonathan. Well, on my way out this morning, crack of dawn, he was up – we live in the same house, you know, his mother joined us when his Dad died – and I mentioned where I was off to. Said my boss most like would be the famous Hard Detective. Well, thing is – Well, he'd love to have your autograph, ma'am.'

'My autograph? I'm not a pop star, for God's sake.'

'No, I know, ma'am. It's cheek really. But it'd mean a lot to the kid. Future detective himself perhaps.'

She thought for an instant.

'Oh, well, future detective. All right.'

Anselm Brent gestured the boy forward, autograph book already open with a choice of virgin green or virgin pink page. After she had signed – she chose the green page – he suddenly blushed.

'Hope you get whoever killed Bubbles,' he said hoarsely. 'The whole school's mad on her.'

Then, overcome, he silently pushed forward another boy wearing what must be the grammar school blazer, a heavy-built, red-faced lad, who had been lurking behind him.

'And could you sign for him too, miss?'

'Nothing to write on,' the boy muttered.

'You got a piece of paper in your pocket. Saw you stuff it there.'

Reluctantly the lumpy blob pulled out a sheet, evidently torn from an exercise book. He thrust it forward.

Writing awkwardly on the unsupported sheet Harriet contrived to scrawl down her name, and then on an impulse added *Join the Police*.

The boy snatched back the sheet and turned at once to go.

Leaving Anselm to have a word with his young nephew, Harriet mounted the steps up to the station, puzzling for a moment about the incident. Had Anselm, in some not altogether clear way, taken advantage of her in demanding his *little favour*? Had he been setting up, from having somehow intuited that sudden gust of sexual interest of hers, a chain of quiet moral blackmail? Of other favours to be sought? Or was he just a naïve innocent?

And, more, in allowing him that favour, had it been because her own judgement had been affected? By that sudden sight, beside Bubbles Xingara's vandalized body, of a broad reddish palm dotted with calluses?

Brushing it all aside, she decided it would be best to let Anselm, as the local officer, begin questioning Old Rowley. Most likely the shambling mess of a man would more readily let himself be teased, admission by admission, to a final confession by someone he had known for years than by a stranger, and a woman. But, she warned Anselm, he was not to let himself be influenced either by his prejudices or by any contemptuous fondness for the old recidivist.

'All right,' she said, 'Rowley's got a long record of offences. But just because he's always liable to succumb to sexual pressure by exposing himself, it doesn't mean he's committed a savage sexual killing. So, go carefully. I don't want there to be anything on the tapes that'll give the Defence a loophole when we get to court.'

She was pleased to find her warning being strictly heeded as inch by inch the questions approached the crucial time.

'All right, Timothy,' Anselm said for the ninth or tenth time, 'so just what were you doing out there?'

'Feller can have a kip, can't he?'

'You've told me that. But why there? Why out in the middle of the countryside?'

Old Rowley took longer to answer this time. Is he trying to concoct some sort of reason now for being out at Adam and Eve House, Harriet asked herself. But at last there came a muttered reply, little different from anything he had said earlier.

'Like it in the country. Bit o' peace. No blurry policemen. Blurry chasing you night an' mornin'.'

'But we weren't chasing you, Timothy. You went out that way all on your own. Didn't you?'

'Why shouldn't I?'

'But why should you, Timothy? Why go out to just that part?'

'What's it to you where I go?'

'Well, it has been in the past, hasn't it? It's been plenty to us when you've gone where you put yourself in the way of girls coming back from the Grammar sports ground, hasn't it?'

'Just 'cos once or twice couldn't help meself . . .'

'More than once or twice, Timothy. A lot more. And was it for the same reason you were out there this morning at Adam and Eve House? You wanting to show someone new what you've got inside your trousers?'

'I wasn't nowhere near that place.'

Indignation in every growled-out word.

'Oh, but you were, Timothy. We found you sound asleep not a quarter of a mile from the house.'

'What if you did? Free country . . . Nothing to me, some big house there. I got as much right . . .'

But each time that the questions got nearer that savage act down beside the mud-cracked bank of the Leven, Old Rowley backed away. Quietly persistent, Anselm, from time to time chewing the end of a pencil he had picked up – like a damn schoolboy, Harriet had thought in a little blaze of irritation – would begin again.

Fighting off Old Rowley's pingingly sharp odour that had come to permeate the whole interview room, she felt a growing admiration for her fellow questioner.

All right, my first impression may have been of a country clodhopper risen up by default to detective-inspector rank, but he – but Anselm's bright enough under that countrified exterior. And I like –

No, no, no. He's interviewing our prime suspect. Listen. Listen to him, listen to the replies he gets. Be ready to jump in.

'Look, Timothy, all I want to know is: why were you out there, all that way from Levenham, at that time of the morning? Come on, tell us that, and then we'll know where we are.'

'Don't see why I gotter.'

Then abruptly Harriet saw there was something – my occasional lapses of concentration? – which she had failed to take into account. Wasn't it quite probable that no one out at Adam and Eve House had actually told the old man that Bubbles Xingara had been murdered? So was he being obstructive, not out of fear of incriminating himself, but simply from the long-established pattern of his relations with the Levenham police?

She leant forward across the bare wooden table.

'Timothy, do you know who Bubbles Xingara is?'

She watched him for the least flicker of guilty response.

'Bubbly what?'

'Bubbles Xingara, Timothy. She's a big tennis star.'

'Tennis? Don't know nothing 'bout that.'

Could that be so? Yes, it could. But . . .

'Listen, Timothy. Bubbles Xingara lives, lived, at Adam and Eve House. It was her house. And early this morning she was found dead there. Murdered.'

It was difficult to make out what exactly Old Rowley's reaction was. Certainly, there was nothing to indicate he was trying to hide that at six o'clock that morning he had thrust some sharp-pointed instrument

– what was it? what could it be? – into the throat of the young woman whose name he claimed not even to know. Nor was there any obvious sign of a subnormal man not realizing what all this was about. He had blinked once or twice, let his tongue for a moment protrude between his lips. Nothing more.

At last he produced a few words.

'Don't know anything 'bout that.'

'Don't you, Timothy? Weren't you there? First thing this morning? There at the back of the house, down by the river?'

'No, no. Wasn't.'

'But you were quite near the house when Mr Brent here found you asleep.'

'Got a right.'

So it's back to the beginning, Harriet thought.

What to do? Advance the interrogation to an altogether tougher level? Batter the man towards that confession?

But, before she had come to a decision, there came a heavy tap at the door. A constable put his head in, looking somewhat scared.

'PC Morton has just entered the room,' Anselm said into the microphone.

'Yes?' Harriet turned to the apprehensive-looking constable.

'Ma'am, sorry. But there's a pack of journalists outside, up from London some of them, photographers too. And TV cameras. Inspector Smithers said I should tell you, ma'am.'

She sighed.

It was to be expected. The full might of the story-hungry media. *Bubbles Xingara Stabbed to Death*. The pretty, wonderfully lively star of the much-hyped tennis world. Alive she had been good for column after column, photos splashed across half-pages, hints about boyfriends, speculation about an unflaunted love life. Dead now, what wouldn't these greedy sex-exploiters do?

No wonder Leven Vale's Inspector Smithers was feeling unable to cope.

'Interview suspended at 11.27,' she said.

She turned to the waiting constable.

'Take him back to a cell.'

'Very good, ma'am.'

'We'll let him stew,' she said to Anselm as soon as Old Rowley had been hustled away. 'He won't be used to being left in suspense. I imagine with his other offences you used to get a pretty quick cough, yes?'

'You're right, ma'am. His efforts to get himself out of trouble don't usually last more than fifteen or twenty minutes.'

'But if he's got something a lot heavier to hide it's no surprise he's hanging on. Still, off to the paparazzi. And I think you'd better make yourself scarce. Nobody should have to submit to a battering from that lot, not unless they have to.'

She thought, as he pocketed his much-chewed pencil, that he looked a little disappointed, though it didn't seem likely that he was the sort of officer who loved the limelight. Perhaps it had been unnecessary to protect him.

And why did I do that? He's not, he absolutely must not be, any special concern of mine. Or . . . is it that he's aware, damn it, that there's something there between us, for all he's shown no direct signs recognizing it? Can he be thinking that he's the one who should be coming, Sir Galahad, to rescue me from the media dragons?

Blast all sex.

Protection was, when she faced the hounds crammed into the station foyer, what she might well have needed. Their questions came banging at her from every side, shouted out one on top of the other, and angled – those she could clearly make out – from every sort of catchpenny direction.

*Was Bubbles raped?*

*Can you tell us what injuries there were?*

*Where? Where?*

*This the work of a sex maniac?*

*A well-known pervert's been brought in, when are you going to charge him?*

Damn, she thought as she caught this last yelled-out inquiry. Been some leak to a local reporter from inside the station here. Wouldn't have happened in Birchester, not if I'd had anything to do with it. Must make it bloody clear it's not going to happen again here. Some crafty sod thinking he can earn himself a few drinks dishing out some nice sexy details. Or, be fair, some crafty female sod thinking she can do it. But damage done now.

'Ladies and gentlemen,' standing a couple of steps up the stairs, she sent her voice carrying over the hubbub. 'I have a statement for you. And it is all you are going to get. So, listen. I am Detective Superintendent Martens, of the Greater Birchester Police—'

'The Hard Detective,' a voice called out.

She ignored the interruption. A splutter of photoflashes went dancing across the faces below.

'I have been seconded,' she went steadily on, 'to

the Leven Vale force to give what assistance I can in what may well prove to be a long and difficult investigation into the death early this morning of Miss Bubbles Xingara.'

'But you've got a suspect inside,' came a strident woman's voice.

'We have not yet established the full circumstances,' Harriet continued, 'and until we do so we will have no other information to give you.'

'Come on, what about old Tim Rowley?' One of the Levenham reporters.

She paused then for a moment.

'Very well, I think I can say that among the many people we may have occasion to interview in the course of our inquiries, we have at present one individual answering some questions. I will not tell you his name.'

She turned on her heel and marched up the stairs behind her, wondering in fact where they might lead to.

# Chapter Four

The stairs, it turned out, brought Harriet face-to-face with the Leven Vale Chief Constable. He was there, in all the splendour of his much-braided uniform, looking down at her as, having tramped past framed photograph after framed photograph of his predecessors in, first, the Levenham force and later the Leven Vale Police, she came within sight of the top landing.

'Superintendent Martens,' his briskly clipped voice greeted her. 'Mr Tarlington, Chief Constable. I came down here from our headquarters to have a word, and I happened to hear you putting the media in their place. I'd like to say I thought you did it admirably. We don't want any half-cock publicity until we can say we've charged this fellow.'

Looking up, Harriet saw a neatly small man, tightly embraced in his uniform, his narrow face distinguished by a pair of sticking-out red ears and a sharp smile that revealed a hotch-potch of this-way-and-that teeth.

'A charge, sir?' she said, mounting up higher. 'I'm not sure that it's come to that yet.'

'Oh, come on, Superintendent. DI Brent's just been telling me the circumstances. First-class job, bringing this fellow in. Well done.'

'Not much of my doing, sir. Except that I saw the importance of making a search of the area as soon as possible. But I think Mr Brent may have given you to understand rather more than our questioning has so far established.'

Or you, she said to herself, have jumped too quickly on the straight facts Anselm gave you.

'Oh, come, Superintendent, don't belittle your own quick work. Or Brent's. It's plain we have the right man. Found drunk near the scene, known sex offender of the nastiest sort, low intelligence. It all fits.'

'Yes, sir. But I'd rather wait till we've had another crack at him. Without a confession I hardly think charging him would be justified. Not unless other evidence comes to light. I'd give a lot, for instance, to put my hands on the weapon used.'

'Well, quite right to be cautious, of course, though I must say that's hardly the approach I expected when I asked for Birchester's famed Hard Detective. But I don't think from all I've heard we shall have much trouble getting that confession out of Rowley, or finding more evidence. Could well be something under the fellow's fingernails.'

'I don't think so, sir. There were no scratch marks on the girl's face or anything of that nature. Otherwise, of course, I'd have had samples taken. The killing was effected with just a single blow from some sort of spiked instrument. It's hard, in fact, to say just what. I'm having a new search of the whole area made, and if we come across whatever it was and find Rowley's prints on it, then we may have a case we can safely take to court.'

'Well, perhaps Brent should go back out there and see that progress is being made. Or both of you, if you see fit. I want that man charged before nightfall. We can't have the station here besieged by those wretched reporters. The public will be up in arms, too, unless we show we're on the way to getting someone sent down for this.'

'Very good, sir.'

Harriet thought rapidly.

Should I send Anselm on his own out to Adam and Eve House and stay here myself? Side benefit, putting temptation at a safe distance. Plenty to do here, if I do stay. I'm going to have to get a proper Incident Room set up. Whatever happens with Rowley, there's going to be a hell of a lot of paperwork generated.

Or, I could leave Ans – leave DI Brent here to establish a proper Incident Room. He's well up to it. Out there myself, I could see that the weapon search is being properly thorough, and, as important, I could talk to the people in the house. If in the end we get nowhere with Rowley, they'll have to be questioned. And the sooner the better.

Yes, that's the answer. And temptation kept at bay.

'I think I'd better go out to the scene myself, sir,' she said. 'I'll leave Mr Brent here. I can come back and have another go at Rowley later. If he's going to cough, he'll do so all the more easily for having sat in a cell for a few hours.'

Deciding against an early lunch as too much of a complication, after a quick visit to the female toilets, stuck like an afterthought in the car park behind the grave Victorian building – scrawled graffiti: the work of police officers? – she drove swiftly out of Levenham in the Leven Vale Police car she had been given.

Soon she found herself thinking with a smile about something Anselm had said after she had briefed him. With an unexpected touch of sly humour, he had told her that, precious to his nephew though her autograph was, the future detective's sullen friend, as soon as her back was turned, had scrunched up the sheet she had scrawled on and dropped it in the gutter. Bit of a lesson for the famous Hard Detective, she thought.

Never mind, Hard Detective or just plain Detective Superintendent, it's got to be full focus on the investigation now. Doing what I'm here to do.

But at once, like a sudden urge to vomit, the thought of Anselm, of his quick smile telling her the story, hit her. I want him, she thought. Just that.

But why is it like this? Why should I have to fight against what – admit it – I actually want so much at this moment? I want to be with that man. With Anselm. And – how strange – I want this however much I ought to be satisfied, if not with that first quick hugger-mugger mating with John, at least with our prolonged love-making this morning. Was it only at break of day this morning? Yes, it was.

But John was right to talk about the lightning flashes from his louring cloud. Because, by God, one came shooting down and struck me. Struck when a country detective inspector I'd never seen before, out of mere friendliness, showed me his right hand marked by hours of wielding a tennis racquet.

And now I somehow want to be existing without anything tugging me away to different loyalties. Why can't that be?

The lilting words of a once-popular song, just remembered from the radio music of childhood, came reverberating into her head.

*You and I, alone in a world for two.*

Back at Adam and Eve House, she found the picture

of quiet repose she had come upon when she had first arrived had gone. As if it had never been. The full noontide sun was bleaching the faded red brick of the old building into dazzled nothingness. Even the monotonously calling, mate-seeking cuckoo had been silenced. Much as she herself – a wry internal smile – had succeeded now, just, in silencing that part of her mind that kept calling *Anselm, Anselm, Anselm.*

Instead the whole place was alive with Leven Vale and Greater Birchester officers searching like so many cumbrous bumblebees for something to feed on. Without, however, any success so far, as Sgt Wintercombe lugubriously informed her.

'No, ma'am, I've had the grounds searched again by your team from Greater Birchester, and my chaps have fanned out half a mile into the fields. But nothing at all to show for it.'

'And down by the river? Any signs at all there? Whoever we're looking for may have actually come from across it. From Greater Birchester Police territory into yours, Sergeant.'

'No, ma'am. I've had them down there on hands and knees, but the mud at the river bank's so hard, what with there not having been any rain for weeks, it's not surprising they found nothing.'

'Right. But in the house itself?'

'I didn't like to send anybody in there, ma'am. Not without direct orders from DI Brent or yourself. I mean, there shouldn't be anything to find, should there?'

Or shouldn't there, she said to herself. Isn't it just as likely that Bubbles Xingara was killed by an intimate, by one of the family, as by someone from outside? And that person could well have concealed the weapon somewhere indoors. But what the devil is that weapon anyhow?

Giving orders to put some of the Birchester squad into going over the big house, she made her own way inside, thinking which of its inhabitants she would tackle first. Eventually she chose the live-in gardener, Arthur Fairley. After all, she thought, a handyman would be the likeliest to have access to some large spiked tool. And, as day after day he had seen butterfly Bubbles flitting round the house, or athlete Bubbles running through the dawn mists, he could well have become prey to the sexual call. Have attempted this morning to force himself on her.

She found him in the kitchen. He was sitting at the big deeply scrubbed whitewood table, with above him a cluster of ancient ceiling-hooks for, she thought, long-stored winter hams. At the far end, the big open fireplace had its iron spit still in place, and an ancient dresser had equally its shelves lined with bright pieces of old delftware. But, in contrast, round the rest of the walls there were up-to-the-minute cookers, big refrigerators, a long freezer cabinet, and painted built-in cupboards, all bought no doubt by that corporate-at-fifteen millionaire, Bubbles Xingara.

Arthur Fairley, who seemed to be just finishing a solitary midday meal, teapot in its padded, flower-decorated cosy in front of him, got to his feet with the easy action of a man always in good physical shape. A deeply tanned face with a pair of keen-looking brown eyes, a big, generous nose, a mouth straight and firmly set. Aged forty-five or perhaps fifty, his dark hair grey at the sides. Open-necked workshirt, grimed-over cord trousers, heavy rubber boots. Smudge of handyman's black grease on the back of his hand.

'Mr Fairley?' she said. 'I am Detective Superintendent Martens, in charge of the investigation here.'

'Good morning, madam. Or afternoon now, isn't it?
Just, anyhow.'

'Yes. Yes, I suppose it is. But your wife, Mr Fairley,
is she not eating with you?'

'Ah, no. Betty takes her dinner later, so she can
serve the family their lunch. Not that much'll be eaten
in the dining-room today.'

'No, I suppose not. They must have all taken it
pretty hard.'

'They have in their different ways, what I've seen
of them, and what my Betty's told me.'

'Oh, yes?'

Gossip going to flow? Or not?

He seemed to be asking himself the same question.
For as much as half a minute he stood where he was,
eyes steady in thought. But then he spoke.

'Takes all sorts different ways.'

'Yes. Yes, it does. At least that's what I've always
found. And I've learnt, too, not to place too much
reliance on first impressions.'

It worked.

'But take a seat,' Arthur Fairley said. 'And there'll
be another cup in the pot, if you'd like that.'

'I certainly would. I've been too busy since first
thing this morning to think about refreshment.'

'Then I dare say there'll be a biscuit or two in the
tin.'

He went across to one of the built-in cupboards,
opened its door and, stooping easily, brought out a
colourful old biscuit-tin. He put it on the big scrubbed
wood table – how long has that been here in this very
room, Harriet asked herself – pulled off the lid with

its picture of two countryfolk lovers, arms entwined under an archway of roses, and inspected the contents.

'Plenty there,' he said. 'Help yourself, and don't feel obliged to go easy. Miss Bubbles wasn't ever one to spare.'

'Did she take charge of the housekeeping herself then?'

Suddenly ravenously hungry, with the sugary, crisp-baked smell of the biscuits striking her nostrils, she dipped a hand in, took whatever her fingers first grasped.

'Ah, no, not really,' Arthur Fairley said. 'That's all done nowadays by Miss Diplock. Secretary, they call her, but from what I've heard she's just a friend of Miss Bubbles from that posh school they were at before Miss Bubbles went to America.'

'I see. It must have been nice for Miss Xingara to have been able to give her a job.'

'Well, nice for Miss Bubbles, of course. But not so nice for Miss Diplock, her having been what you might call a rich kid when Miss Bubbles was at that school only because of her tennis. I'll say this, though: Miss Bubbles was never one to crow over someone she'd outpaced, as you might say. Whatever Miss Fiona felt about it herself.'

Something here? The jealousy of someone who, once having seen herself as higher up the tree, was now reduced to – call it secretary, call it friend – something of an object of charity? Not the most obvious of motives for murder, but to be borne in mind. Stifled hatred behind more than one case I've investigated.

'So how long has Miss Diplock been here?'

'Oh, just about a year. Ever since Mrs Renshaw found the house too much for her.'

'She's not been well, Mrs Renshaw?'

'Not for me to say.'

The set mouth tightening. All right to gossip about a fellow employee, but a line to be drawn at disloyalty to an employer.

So withdraw. But only a little.

'But, Miss Diplock – Fiona, did you say her name was? – how does she cope with housekeeping? Or being a secretary, come to that?'

'Well enough. The wife and I know what's to be done, far as the house goes, and how to do it. I don't know about secretary, but she spends long enough fiddling about with that computer. Keeping everything up to date, she told me once. And the number of letters she has to answer. What you call the fanmail . . .'

'Yes, I suppose there'd be a lot of that. And I dare say we'll have to go through it all before we're done. If it turns out we're looking for a stalker of some sort. Somebody out of nowhere. You didn't see anyone out of the ordinary, did you, hanging about first thing this morning?'

'I have to say I didn't. I was up by five all right. Like to get something done on the tennis court, in the old kitchen garden, soon as it's light. But that's well shut-off by its walls, so I wouldn't have seen anybody if they were lurking about. And I didn't hear anything either.'

'Not any sort of scream, when she . . .?'

'No. No, but then it's likely I wouldn't have. You don't hear much inside there, bar an aeroplane or two going over sometimes and that cuckoo singing away fit to bust.'

'I see. And your wife, is she generally up as early

as five? She didn't mention seeing anybody about by any chance?'

'Well, no. No, she gets up at seven when the alarm rings, plenty of time to get the breakfasts then. So I don't suppose Betty would've seen anybody. When I slip out of bed myself she's always sound asleep. Sleeps like a log till that clock goes racketing off, summer and winter alike.'

'But how about you in the day or two before this? Anybody hanging round who'd no business to be?'

'Well, no, nobody I can recall. Unless you count Old Rowley.'

'Old Rowley? He was here?'

'Oh, yes, the silly old fool. He was here yesterday morning, not in the house but hanging about a couple of hundred yards down the lane. I know what he was wanting. But he has his fits of being scared, and I dare say he shied away when he caught a glimpse of me.'

'But what was it he did want?'

'Oh, just to be given an odd job, if one was going. I'd found him bits of work once or twice in the past. More out of kindness, really. He was never up to much.'

'But, when you were employing him, he would have seen Miss Xingara about the place?'

'No. No, he wouldn't have done that. This was before the Renshaws came, while they were still in America for Miss Bubbles' career. I mean, Old Rowley must have been remembering he'd had odd jobs here. I suppose he's out of work just now, out of gaol, too, I dare say, and was hoping he'd get something from me again.'

'I see. You know we found him this morning sleeping under a hedge not very far away?'

'Oh, yes. I saw your chaps bringing him in. But

don't get it into your head he's the one you're looking for. Doubt if he's strong enough. And he's certainly not vicious enough, ask me.'

'Yes. Yes, I think you may be right. Well, thank you for your help.'

As much as I'm likely to draw out of Arthur Fairley, at least for the time being. So who now? The ex-school-friend secretary? Or the mother who's given up looking after her rich daughter's house?

Yes, her. Mrs Aimée Renshaw.

Harriet found her in her sitting-room upstairs, next to the large husband-and-wife bedroom, belonging once no doubt to Adam and Evelina, love-birds.

*Whore's parlour* were the words that came into Harriet's head as, her knock answered, she stepped inside, well though she knew prostitutes' premises were decidedly different from this soft room, cloyingly full of perfume. Its flowered wallpaper with even more roses on it than had sheltered the lovers on the kitchen biscuit-tin. Curtains in the same pattern, all but closed against the bright outdoors sunshine, leaving every-thing in dimness, the large mirror over the empty fireplace, the baby-blue carpet, two chintz-covered armchairs. In one of these, pinkly plump Aimée Renshaw was sitting, silk summer dress in a pattern of mauve indeterminate flowers, short-sleeved and cut very low to show an expanse of blooming, if faintly crinkled, flesh.

Harriet put her age down as something over fifty, though every effort had been made to take off ten years, or more. But liberally applied make-up, however soft in tone, can always be seen through by eyes prepared to look, and golden-dyed hair will fool only males prepared to be fooled.

She introduced herself formally.

'But – What – What does a police officer want with me? Who are you anyway? How am I to believe you're – what did you say? – a detective superintendent? You could be anybody.'

'Mrs Renshaw, I've shown you my warrant card.'

'Oh, how should I know what that was? It might have been somebody's driving licence, anything. And in any case I haven't got my glasses. How can you expect . . .'

'I could show it to you again. Let you have a longer look at it. Even hunt for your glasses, if you like. But really none of that should be necessary. All I want is to ask you a few questions about your daughter. To help us find whoever it was who did that to her this morning.'

'Bubbles. My poor Bubbles. Inspector – Superintendent, whatever you are, you can't have any idea what a darling that girl was. It – It's too cruel. No one should have . . .'

'Yes. Yes, Mrs Renshaw. No one should have taken her life. But someone did, and I am determined, however long it may take, to bring that person to justice. So, please, will you listen carefully to what I ask, and do your best to answer as fully as possible.'

'All right. All right. You think I'm a silly old fool, don't you? But I'm not, you know. I haven't lived through two marriages and heaven knows how many – two marriages, and not known which way is up.'

'I'm sure you do. So, can you tell me first whether you were up and about early enough this morning to see someone, a stranger of any sort, anywhere near the house?'

'Up? At dawn? Or whenever it is Bubbles goes for those runs of hers? No, no. No, I have to have my beauty sleep. A girl needs that. To be at her best. So, no. No, I've no idea who was prowling about round the house at that sort of hour. Who was it, Inspector?'

'We don't know, Mrs Renshaw. We don't know whether there was anybody. It's just that I thought you might have been out of bed, if only for a few minutes. A call of nature, perhaps. And you might have looked out.'

'No, no, I wasn't. I didn't. Thank goodness, I've not got to the stage yet of having to wee-wee every hour of the night. What if I'd had someone in bed with me? Not that I did, you know. But, well, I might have done, mightn't I?'

'You mean your husband?' Harriet said, though she knew perfectly well that, real or imaginary, that bed visitor was not supposed to be a legitimate spouse.

Aimée Renshaw smirked.

'Well, it would have to be my husband, wouldn't it? Not that he spends much time in my bed these days. Goes off to the spare room, accusing me of snoring. As if I would.'

So, Harriet thought, there's Peter Renshaw, in the full vigour of life, as I saw him earlier, and not sharing his wife's bed, if what she's been burbling about means what I think it does. So, was he sharing some other bed? Was his interest directed towards his pretty, effervescent stepdaughter? Or towards someone else? Like perhaps the secretary, Bubbles' friend? And, if so, is that relevant to my inquiries? Well, Peter Renshaw was definitely up and about at six, so Fiona Diplock, if they are lovers, may well have been about at that hour too. And have seen someone?

'Well, if you weren't awake first thing this morning,' she said to Aimée Renshaw, 'you weren't. I may have to come back and ask you other questions. But, for the present, thank you for your help.'

Thank you for precious little, she thought, closing the door of the too sweet-smelling, prettified room behind her. What have I learnt, besides the patent fact that, whatever age Aimée Renshaw is, she still sees herself as some sort of man-eater, man-devourer?

But, on her way to see if the search teams had now had some success, either in the house or out of it, Harriet almost bumped into a tall, milk-fed young woman in a boldly yellow summer dress, massed very blonde hair held in a tight chignon that contrived to highlight a pale pink, bow-shaped mouth and wide blue eyes. Fiona Diplock, she thought, recovering. Must be.

She had been coming out of a room next to the one where, earlier, Peter Renshaw had been sitting, slumped forward in his chair.

'You must be Miss Diplock. The very person I want to see.'

'And you're the woman in charge of finding out who – who killed Bubbles. The famous Hard Detective.'

'Well, never mind about that. Hard or not, you're right that it's my business now to track down that murderer.'

'Or murderess.'

What had made her say that? Is she some mad-nut feminist, anxious to claim anything for our sex, even murder? Or is it just that she seizes on any chance to assert her superiority?

We'll see.

'Right, can we go back into this room? What is it? Your office?'

'My office.'

Fiona Diplock preceded her into the room, something of a stately yellow-vibrant swan. It looked office-like enough, computer screen glowing, long wall-to-wall desk-top covered with print-outs and rolled-up faxes, two differently coloured phones, tall executive chair in black leather. On one wall there was a chart for Wimbledon with the Bubbles Xingara name highlighted. Now to no purpose, Harriet thought with a pang of sharp regret.

'Tell me,' she said, as Fiona pointed firmly to the room's second chair, 'why did you say just now that your friend's murder might be the work of a woman?'

Up-tilted chin.

'Well, it could be, couldn't it? Women are just as capable of killing people as men. I should have thought you'd know that.'

Yes. Determination to be the one in charge.

'Well, as a police officer I'm frankly more inclined to believe I'm looking at present for some sex-dominated male stalker.'

See if I can let her believe we've no interest in anyone in the household.

'There are women stalkers, you know.'

'Yes, I do know. But at this moment I'm here to find out what I can of the circumstances of Miss Xingara's death. And, if there's anyone in the house who can help me, it's you.'

For a moment, a fraction of a second, it looked as if Fiona Diplock was going to contest that. But she took a deep breath – Harriet watched the rise and fall of

her full breasts under the bold yellow linen dress –
and changed tack.

'Very well, if I can help in any way, I shall be only
too glad.'

A little cold, that response? Another assertion of
superiority? Or were the two girls not as friendly as
might be expected? And how deep had that gone? We'll
see.

'Right, first of all, I'd like to know if by any chance
you were up at round about six this morning. Looking
out, did you see anyone strange?'

'I wasn't.'

'No? You're certain? You weren't up spending a
penny or anything? You might have forgotten that for
the moment. Did you glance out, without thinking,
and see something you haven't remembered till now?
What room do you have? Does it look out towards the
river? You might have just glimpsed the murderer.'

'No, no. No, I didn't. I was asleep. Of course I was.
Sound asleep in my own bed.'

A note of protest? But why? If this young woman
has nothing to conceal she has no need to protest.
Something to watch.

But the young woman was going on in full flow.

'For God's sake, wasn't it six in the morning? It's
all very well for Bubbles to be up at that godforsaken
hour, but I was never that sort of a person, even at
school.'

'Where you were together, I understand. Where was
that?'

Another proud chin-raised look. And isn't she
taking Bubbles' death extraordinarily calmly? But some
people do react like that, refuse almost to admit what's

happened. So, is she transferring feelings she's bottled up into an urge to take it out on me? Anyhow, answer.

'It was a place called Grainham Hall. If you've ever heard of it.'

'I have. I work in Birchester, so it's not all that far away. Famous for all sorts of athletic activities, yes? Scholarships for boys and girls likely to boost the sporting record, or, like your friend, bring in publicity when they did well afterwards?'

'Yes, that's about it.'

A somewhat sullen reply. So jealousy there? Extending possibly to hatred? Go carefully.

'But you weren't one of the sports scholarship girls?'

'Good God, no. Daddy had money— But you don't want to hear about that. What can I tell you to help find the person who killed Bubbles?'

'Well, if you weren't up at six and didn't see any stranger outside, then I don't think there's much you can tell me at the present time. So I'll leave you to get on with your work. I've a notion you'll have floods of inquiries now, so— Oh, wait. Yes, there is one thing. Bubbles Xingara. I suppose she's gets the Xingara from a former marriage of her mother's. But what about the Bubbles?'

'Oh, she's always been called Bubbles. At school we used to tease her unmercifully about that when she first came, until she began to win all the cups. But her actual given name is Barbara, though hardly anyone knows. And, you're right, the Xingara comes from the man Aimée was married to when Bubbles was born. Or, I'm not actually sure, she may not have been born until after Mr Xingara had disappeared from the scene. You know how it is in that sort of world.'

'That sort of world?'

A look of dismay, or mock dismay.

'Oh, I shouldn't have said that. She is the mother of my employer. Or even my employer itself now, I don't know. But I suppose it's the truth about her, after all. Put it this way. She comes from a very different world. Always talking about King's Road, Chelsea, in the sixties. You know, anything-goes time.'

'I think I know what you mean. But I won't keep you now. If you do remember seeing somebody who shouldn't have been there outside this morning, you will let me know, won't you?'

'Of course. Yes, of course.'

The door shut, Harriet echoed that *Of course* in her head. Of course, she won't, she added. She won't tell me anything she doesn't think I'm fit to know, that stuck-up voice, stuck-up attitude. I wouldn't be at all surprised if she actually was up and about at six this morning, even if she has nothing to tell me. Up and about, leaving Peter Renshaw in the spare room and making her way quickly back to her own. Or had he been in her room? And when he left did she wake?

Or, had he just perhaps said something at that near-dawn hour that had suddenly caused her resentment of Bubbles to burst, like a pus-compacted boil? Could she have gone then, hurrying out before her lover was there, and let that suppressed venom have its outlet at last? The girl who had humiliated her by offering her a well-paid job after her father – *Daddy had money – but you don't want to hear about that* – came financially unstuck, perhaps when all those Lloyd's Names were caught wrong-footed. It could have been. Wasn't there that word *murderess*? Perhaps not so much an intended put-down but a tiny Freudian slip?

Timing a bit dodgy, though. Who had got up first? Peter Renshaw or Fiona? Who had gone to a bathroom first? But at that early hour no one would be carefully consulting their watches. Dodgy, but perhaps just possible. But what was the weapon she had used? And where was it now? Will the searchers in the house here bring the case to a conclusion in the next half-hour?

Was I, in fact, hearing a half-hidden confession just now? And should I have seized on it? Followed it up? Pressed for an answer? For answers?

But, no. No. What's that Sherlock Holmes thing old John's always quoting at me? A mistake to theorize without the data. No, *a capital error*. Well, perhaps it is. However much we're inclined to do it. So wait to find concrete evidence. If it's there somewhere to be found.

# Chapter Five

Sgt Wintercombe's bumblebee-buzzing searchers came up with nothing, neither outside the house nor in it. Nor had there been a single useful report from a necessarily belated alert Harriet had had put out over a wide area round Adam and Eve House on both Greater Birchester Police territory on one side of the Leven and that of the Leven Vale force on the other.

Well, she thought, neither search was all that likely to have brought a result. Can't expect miracles. So now – how many hours is it since someone thrust that thick spike into Bubbles Xingara's throat? – it looks as if in all probability the long, long haul really does face me now. There's the possibility, of course, that Fiona Diplock's odd behaviour means Bubbles' death was a strictly personal affair. But as for Old Rowley, I can't believe, especially after what I learnt from Arthur Fairley, that he's our man, however much toothy Mr Tarlington would like a quick result. May have to box a bit clever there, but I'll be very surprised if ten minutes in the interview room with Rowley later on won't bring to light whatever comparatively innocent reason he had for being out here this morning.

Then, like a jab of pain from a troublesome tooth that had seemed to have cured itself, the thought shot into her mind of Anselm Brent and how he would be at her side while she questioned the old layabout. And with it a bright, horribly bright, picture of Anselm himself. Of that calloused right palm of his, that thatch of fair hair, those somehow innocent forget-me-not blue eyes. And, yes, of the tangy smell of his sweat.

Anselm. What has happened to me? And why, why, hasn't it gone away? For God's sake, I'm his superior officer. I've got a job to do, and one that's going to make the fullest demands on me. And he's younger than I am. Ten years younger, even. I've no right to be thinking of him. No right whatever.

And that pencil, chewed in the disgusting way it was. He's like a schoolboy, really. And, God, he's sweet. Sweet.

So, when I've driven back to Levenham, am I going to say he shouldn't sit with me when I interview Rowley? Right, in fact it might even be better if he didn't. He's got that streak of sympathy for the bumbling old pervert. Something I know all about. I've felt something similar for dozens of pathetic or charming criminals in my time. But I haven't ever let it influence me. Criminals are criminals. Yet can I say the same for Ans – for DI Brent, comparatively inexperienced, a Levenham man dealing with another Levenham man?

So, yes, get hold of somebody else to assist me.

Taking her place in the interview room beside Anselm – why did I change my mind? – Harriet felt as if she, too, was one of those pathetic, plainly guilty criminals she half-wanted to get lucky and survive her questioning. As they never did.

In a moment Old Rowley was brought in. Anselm set up the recorder, recited the preliminaries.

She leant forward and looked the stinking old reprobate full in the eye.

'Now, let's get this business of what you were doing out at Adam and Eve House this morning over and done with.'

'Please, I wasn't doing nothing.'

The defiance of that first interview was no longer there. It was plain any truculence he had managed to summon up then had been leached out of him by his hours in a solitary cell.

'All right, perhaps you weren't doing anything. But you'd had odd jobs at the house there in the past, hadn't you?'

'How d'you know?'

A rheumy glint of something in the old man's eyes. Of relief?

'I know because I've been talking to Arthur Fairley and he's told me about you.'

'About a job?'

'A job? You wanted a job from him this morning, didn't you?'

'I never . . .'

'You never? You're saying you never went up to the house in the end?'

'No. I didn't, not never. I mean . . .'

'You thought Mr Fairley would be angry with you? You made a mess of whatever he'd given you to do last time? Was that it?'

All right, I'm making it easy for him, practically putting the words into his mouth. If somehow it turns out after all that he did kill Bubbles, I'll look a total fool. But he didn't kill her. Just looking at him now, it's easy to see the shaky old idiot wouldn't have had the determination to plunge in that missing weapon. So the quicker he's cleared out of the way the better.

'Now, why don't you tell us everything? Take your time, and just say bit by bit what happened.'

'It were her.'

What's this? What the hell is he saying? Not Bubbles? Oh, no. Surely not Bubbles. God, this isn't going to be the confession?

'Her? Who are you talking about?'

'Her. Maggie.'

'Maggie who?'

'Where I got a room. When I'm not in the gaol.'

Now Anselm, uninvited, joined in.

'You mean, Mrs Appleyard, Tim? That widow lady? The one whose address you give when we have you in?'

'Yeah. She told me. She told me last night. I couldn't . . .'

'Couldn't what, Tim? Come on, cough it up.'

'Couldn't have no nice time wi' her. Not 'less I got work. Wasn't right I got me dinners, an' – an' me that, if I never had no work.'

Harriet gave Anselm a quick nod to say *Get him to spell it out.*

'Let me get this straight, Timothy,' he said. 'You sometimes sleep with Mrs Appleyard? Sleep with her? Is that right?'

''s nice.'

For a brief moment Harriet allowed to enter her mind the thought of the disgusting, high-smelling old man engaged in the sex act with a widow, of whatever age. What was it John said this morning, all those hours and hours ago? *A hunchback, a cripple – they all have the trigger?*

She swallowed.

'So,' she said to the now-revealed unprepossessing lover, 'you went over to Adam and Eve House to get a job because your landlady had told you that you had to. But when you got there, you were afraid to go in. So you went and sat in the shade of that hedge to think about it, and you fell asleep. Is that what happened?'

'Yeah. 'course.'

'And you never entered the grounds of the house? Tell us the truth. If you don't, we'll find out, you know.'

'Jus' didn't want ter go in. He mighter kicked me out, Mr Fairley. He mighter done.'

The slack-bellied old man looked all round him, staring-eyed, as if peaceable Arthur Fairley was there with a blackthorn cudgel raised in anger.

'All right, all right. Calm down. Now, let's get this finally right. You're now telling the truth, the whole truth, about everything you did out near Adam and Eve House this morning? Yes?'

'As God's my.'

Harriet let out a sigh of exhaustion.

'All right, you can go now.'

Leaning forward, Anselm gave the old man a smile that Harriet would have liked for herself.

'And you can tell Mrs Appleyard,' he said, 'you did your best to get a job this morning, and you're going to go to the Job Centre tomorrow and say you want work. All right.'

Old Rowley heaved himself up, with a good deal more vigour than he had shown so far, and shuffled hurriedly out.

Anselm turned to her as she gathered her notes together.

'Well, ma'am,' he said. 'Young Jonathan's friend

may not have thought the Hard Detective's autograph worth keeping, but I've got a different view. I thought I knew Old Rowley through and through, but I'd have never sussed out why he didn't go into Adam and Eve House, never for a moment. But, well, I reckon you've saved us a lot of useless work.'

Compliment indeed. And one only a fellow as naive and as nice as Anselm here would pay me.

But I wish he had not.

He's right, though, about work saved. We're all the better for not pursuing a lead like that. In all probability the signs now point to murder by a stranger. But how exactly did it come about? Someone by chance down there by the Leven at that early hour this morning? Not impossible, of course. But surely more likely that the killer had some link with bright, carefree Bubbles. Did she somewhere, somehow say something that had so enraged someone, someone lost now behind those successive misty screens of *somewhere* and *somehow* and *something*, that they tracked her down to Adam and Eve House? Thrust home that spiked tool, there beside the summer-shrunken Leven?

And, God knows, will we ever hustle into a cell this unknown person?

Then, yes, she answered herself. Yes, we'll get him, or perhaps we'll get her. Police work will do it. Unrelenting, never-give-up police work. The efforts of dozens, scores of detectives, examining every possibility untiringly, eliminating, correlating, questioning, filing and cross-filing. In the end that will do it.

Right. Next step, hold a briefing.

But an unexpected interruption greeted her as she made her way through the station's wide entrance-hall to the small top-floor office that had been put at her disposal. There, standing looking quietly about, was her husband.

'John. What are you doing here?'

He smiled.

'The bearer of good tidings, I hope. Or, to be exact, fresh clothes.'

He glanced across to the row of benches lining the wall opposite the duty sergeant's counter. On one of them was her own soft green-leather suitcase, still with smears of dust on it from where it had been kept on top of her wardrobe.

'Trust you to be thoughtful. But how did you know I'd be here?'

'Phoned around. Not difficult.'

'I suppose it wasn't. Listen, bring the case up to my office. I've got to hold a briefing in a bit, but we can talk for a minute or two.'

Up to the office on the very top floor of the heavy old building.

'So how's it going then?' John asked.

'Oh, you know what it is at the beginning of a case. You're totally occupied finding out just what's happened, just who the people involved are.'

'Not much different from me, arriving in Rio or Johannesburg or wherever. You getting any useful help from the – what's it? – Leven Vale force?'

And suddenly she found herself faced with a temptation. Tell John what had happened to her, there beside Bubbles Xingara's body, when the *useful help* from the Leven Vale Police had shown her his calloused right palm? After all, John was the great theorist of *the feeling of amorousness* coming like a thunderbolt out of the all-covering cloud. See what he makes of an up-to-the-minute example?

But she drew back.

'Oh, yes,' she answered. 'As a matter of fact the DI I've had assigned to me seems very much on the ball. Bit clodhoppy, I thought at first. But, no, he's a good man.'

Then, to her internal fury, she found herself anxious to change the subject.

'But – But, you,' she said. 'All well with you? You haven't felt the need for the – what was the word? – *alivio* of a Birchester whore or two?'

John chuckled.

'Hardly. My needs were thoroughly dealt with first thing this morning. With the best will in the world there's hardly been time for the great god Eros to have whizzed down a sex-bolt from his hovering cloud.'

'Eros?' she said. 'What's this now?'

'Oh, just another way of looking at my theory of the ubiquity of the sexual impulse. It's the way the ancient Greeks, who knew all about ubiquitous sex, chose to view it. To put it all down to a god.'

'Apt quotation coming up? Or is there something in one of your pockets copied from somewhere?'

'Pockets empty. Suit from Brazil went to the cleaners, which was what made me think that, if you're not coming home till tomorrow or the day after, you might be glad of a change of clothes. But let me tell you about Eros. The Greek god, not of love, as is often said, but actually of simple lust. Those old fellows had got it pretty well taped, you know. First, Eros strikes. You suddenly feel a crude desire for sex.'

God, she thought, he's actually describing that moment, Anselm's hand. Has he somehow . . .? No, he can't have done.

But John, in full spate, was tumbling on.

'And in the general way it's after Eros has struck that on occasion Aphrodite, risen from her sea-foam, comes coiling in.'

Head-deep in her suitcase seeing what clothes John had selected, or to save herself from admitting to the thoughts that had plagued her ever since she had seen Anselm's hand, Harriet just grunted, 'Sea-foam?'

'Yes, yes. Aphrodite was imagined as having been born in that way, the sort of way Greeks always appeared on the scene. You know that Botticelli painting, naked lady standing in a big shell, sort of balanced on the sea? Well, that's her. Only Botticelli called her by her Latin name, Venus.'

'Oh, yes,' she said, surfacing not so much from the sea as from a man-selected jumble of clothes in a sea-green suitcase. 'Yes, know the one you mean. Pale body and long, long hair, gracefully concealing the private parts?'

'Yup. That's her. But, I was saying, get caught in her coils, or, if you like, in those impossibly long golden tresses, and you're in real trouble. Ah, wait. I have got one quote in one of my pockets, now I think of it. Scribbled it down while I was driving over here. Hang on.'

Left-hand pocket of his old fawn summer jacket. Right-hand pocket. Inside pocket. Then, at last, two scissoring fingers into the handkerchief pocket. And half a card-bookmark pulled out.

'Yes. From a book I actually bought just this morning. Pretty cover, pretty good book, too, so far. Let me see. Yeah, *The Tree of Pearls*, someone called Louisa Young. And this is what she makes one of her characters say. *The trouble with fucking is it leads to kissing*. Not bad, eh? Because that's what happens often enough. A bit of quick sex, and another and perhaps another, and then before you know it you're in the coils of Aphrodite.'

Should I tell him now, she thought abruptly, that I've been struck down by his Eros, even if there's been no fucking that could – yes, that's a shrewd observation – that could lead to kissing. To Aphrodite wrapping all that down-to-her-vulva hair round me?

But, mercifully, John was bringing his fanciful theories down to reality.

'You know, from what little I've gathered from the radio since first thing this morning, old Eros may very well be at the root of your current case.'

'Well, yes,' she said, sobering up. 'Sex does seem likely to be there, and in every aspect of it. With the possible exception, actually, of poor dead Bubbles herself. From all I can make out, what she was obsessed by was tennis and nothing else.'

'So ubiquitous old sex not the absolute key to it?'

'Oh, I wouldn't say that. Far from it. But sex in some other head than Bubbles''.

'So you think she may have just walked into some sex maniac?'

'Well, yes and no. She wasn't raped, or I'm pretty certain she wasn't. Should get confirmation at the p.m. But in every line of inquiry sex is there.'

'No rape? You've probably got doubly big trouble in that case.'

'Why's that? I'd have thought I'd got trouble enough as it stands.'

'Not if what's at the heart of it is love, what I've just been talking about, Aphrodite's amorous coils. That's the one that can cause real danger. But, look, I must go. Didn't you say you'd got to hold a briefing?

You'll need a moment or two to sort yourself out. Mustn't keep you idly chatting. See you when I see you.'

'Yes. 'fraid so.'

*Real danger*, she thought as John went, tramp-tramp-tramp, down the narrow uncarpeted stairs outside. He's right, though. Think of all the great love tragedies, in life and literature, Romeo and Juliet, Jane Eyre and Mr Rochester, Anna Karenina. Tragedies enough there.

But – But, more, was John in fact giving a veiled warning to me? Has he – we know each other that well – guessed something? From the tiniest wrong note in my voice? One word not quite right?

No telling.

Arriving for the briefing, Harriet found what had been the Parade Room in the days of the old Levenham Police had been transformed under DI Brent's initiative into a full-scale Incident Room ready for all that a major inquiry might give rise to. Computer monitor screens lined the walls to send e-mail demands for information to any and every corner of the country. Twenty or more telephones were set at intervals all the way down a long central table, piled, too, with neat stacks of wide Action Sheets. A pair of fax machines stood in a corner, one already chattering with an incoming document. Cabinets full of new-looking box files seemed hungrily to be demanding the mass of papers they were bound to collect. Big pinboards stood blankly awaiting the sheets of information, the memory-jogging photos that would soon be placed on them. And clustered at the far end of the room were detectives she recognized from Birchester, glancing with hints of suspicion at a smaller band of Leven Vale detectives and a bunch of uniformed officers.

Good man, Anselm, she said to herself. I was right. Under that countrified exterior of yours there's brains and determination. Something more, too, a quick ability to see the other side of the coin, as witnessed by that little story about what happened to my *Join the Police* autograph.

She stopped herself. No, he's a good officer, and thank goodness for that. But that is absolutely all I'm going to think about DI Brent.

Swiftly she counted the officers standing there. Leven Vale and Greater Birchester. Forty-four. Good enough, at least to begin with.

She mounted the platform at her end of the room, and was pleased to see that merely stepping up on to it had secured her a hushed silence. Some benefit, then, from that absurd, media-donated label *the Hard Detective*.

'Right,' she said. 'The murder of Bubbles Xingara, tennis star, media darling, known from one end of the world to the other. You and I are facing what may well become one of the biggest and most scrutinized murder inquiries any of us will ever see. And it's going to be an inquiry that brings a result. It will bring a result because every one of us in this room, and every other officer it may be necessary for me to call in, is going to work flat out for however long it takes to get that result. Six months, a year, more than a year. You're going to have that name Bubbles Xingara so branded on your minds that for the rest of your lives you'll always remember this moment. You're going to be able to think of nothing else until we can point the finger squarely at whoever it proves to be, man or woman, who killed that girl. You'll be working every hour of the day, and as and when needed far into the night. You're not going to see your loved ones for more than the shortest of times. You're not going to have a minute to think of girlfriends or boyfriends. You're going to work, work, work.'

Looking down, she saw that what she had said had brought about the reaction she had hoped for. Faces were tense, thoughtful, even here and there a little hostile.

And myself? Have I taken to heart the words I have been speaking? *Not a minute to think of girlfriends or boyfriends.* Of the ubiquitous sex that John talks about. Will I stamp out those thoughts I have had? But, John himself, how much am I actually going to be able to be with him during this spell of his in Birchester before bloody world-spanning Majestic Insurance sends him off somewhere else?

I'll have to see. I'll have to see. And as for Anselm, that must be over. Over now, over for ever.

Leaving no time for the impression that she hoped she had made on her team to fade, she went on to the details of how the investigation was to be conducted.

With a jab of irony she found herself, when it came to allocating someone to make inquiries back at Adam and Eve House into Bubbles Xingara's love life – 'We know precious little about it, but did she really not ever have any boyfriends?' – thinking that Anselm seemed to be the obvious choice for the task. Had the apparently notorious DI Anderson, Handy Andy, been available she might have seen him as better able to deal with this aspect of the inquiry. But the task needed an officer of some seniority if his questions were to get full answers. So Anselm it has to be.

*

Then began a long period of sheer slog. Harriet divided her time between the Incident Room, where messages and reports had begun to pour in, and her top-floor office. At some point in the long day Anselm came up to report on his inquiries about Bubbles' possible sexual entanglements.

She found, to her inward relief, that he was being strictly formal.

Can I keep it that way? Can I from this moment on begin to forget, to push aside, all those thoughts banging at me since . . . that calloused hand. Oh, God.

'Ma'am, I've spoken to the mother, the stepfather and that secretary of hers, who's an old friend so she said, as well as to both Betty Fairley – I can't see how she can be the killer, not in a million years – and Arthur Fairley, hoping I might get something from them the family didn't know about.'

'Good thinking. Any result?'

'Can't say there really was, ma'am. Both the Fairleys had nothing but good to say about Miss Bubbles, as they call her. She can do no wrong, far as they're concerned.'

'And having boyfriends is doing wrong?' she asked, stepping into possibly dangerous ground before she could stop herself.

He looked embarrassed. Delightfully embarrassed, she thought.

'No. No, ma'am. I didn't mean that. I meant . . . Well, p'raps the Fairleys, or Mrs Fairley anyhow, might think sleeping with a boy was wrong. That's all.'

And – the idea stealthily crept into her head – you, Anselm, don't believe, as you very well might have done, that it's wrong to sleep with someone of the opposite sex when you're not married to them.

But, no. Think of the investigation. Get on with the job.

'Well, I can understand that,' she said briskly. 'So, what else did you learn? The stepfather. Anything from him? He hasn't been playing around with his step-daughter, has he?'

'No, ma'am. I'm pretty sure he hasn't, actually.'

'Why's that?'

'I reckon he's playing around with the secretary, Fiona Diplock. There was something he sort of stopped himself saying.'

'Yes, good. Talking to her briefly, I got a hint of that, too. And, if we're right, that would put Peter Renshaw almost certainly out of account, together with all the negative evidence about him. How about the mother? You make anything of Mrs Aimée Renshaw?'

Anselm pulled a face.

'You're right,' Harriet said. 'She's a terrible woman. I can quite understand why Xingara ran off all those years ago.'

'You're dead right about *terrible*, ma'am.'

His shy smile flashed up.

What's this?

'She was all set to take me to bed. Honestly. Well, not to bed, I suppose, but to the chair she was sitting in, or the rug on the floor.'

So, yes. Yes, you're ready to envisage the possibility of love-making with someone – with anyone – with – with –

'Go on, DI.'

'Well, it was all I could do to freeze her off, ma'am. But in the end, in a way, I did get something out of her. Or I think I did.'

'Let's hear it.'

'Put it like this then. She's so wound up about sex and all that – her two husbands and the devil knows how many lovers, from all I could make out – that she'd have liked nothing better than for Bubbles to be the same. She was sore at her for not being like it, when it comes down to it. So I reckon that if young Bubbles did have any affairs, her Mum would've made it her business to find out. And have told me about them, every last detail like as not.'

'Yes. Yes, I think we can say in view of that, coupled with what we knew about Bubbles already from the gossip in the papers, that the thwarted-boyfriend line can at least be put on hold.'

Then something occurred to her. If Peter Renshaw was out of account, wouldn't the young woman who had been, in all probability, sharing his bed until just before six be equally out of account? Some careful checking of times needed, but it looks as if one tentative line of inquiry has petered out.

She told Anselm to go over to Adam and Eve House in the morning and find out, dotting the last *i*, just when it had been that Peter Renshaw had got up to go to take Bubbles' blood pressure, and what time Fiona Diplock believed she had left her bed, if it was her own bed she had left. Then she made herself dismiss him.

On and on she sat at her desk, reading her copies of every message that came in, every report made. At some point she realized that outside the office's sole little window it was beginning to get dark, and got herself sent up a canteen meal, though five minutes after the last mouthful she was unable to say what it was she had been eating.

Late into the night, when she found she was hardly

taking in what had been put in front of her, she decided to snatch a quick sleep in her chair. Only to be woken by the insistent ringing of the phone.

Good God, it's John, she thought, shaking the sleep out of her head. I never let him know— No. No, of course, he came over here, when I was glad he left before I blurted out –

But it was not John.

'Superintendent Martens, I'm glad I managed to get hold of you. Sam Porter here.'

A half-second of incomprehension. Then the name clicked into place. Sam Porter, crime reporter of the paper she always privately called the *Daily Dirt*. How the hell . . .?

'Listen, we've just had something from one of our stringers in France.'

'Mr Porter, I don't want to know. It's the middle of the night, I was just catching a few moments' sleep. Nobody should have let you get through to me.'

She was aiming, in the three-quarters dark of the room, to slam the receiver back on to its base when one more brief sentence squawked out.

' . . . said Bubbles was linked with a French gangster.'

She jerked back the handset.

Groping for the switch on her desk lamp, she thought rapidly.

Is this some sort of try-on? We've blocked every press inquiry till now, but perhaps Sam Porter's hit on this way to get some sort of quote out of me. Yet it could be true, this titbit from France. Not actually all that likely as an invention.

'All right,' she said into the phone. 'Tell me what you know.'

Was it a chuckle at the far end, or a throat-clearing?

'I hope you'll remember who was helpful to you, Super. The Hard Detective has never been too kind to us poor gentlemen of the press.'

'Tell me what you know.'

'All right, all right. Now, you ever heard of a man called Pierre le Fou?'

'Frankly, Mr Porter, that sounds like a name you've made up on the spur of the moment.'

A laugh.

'Wish I'd thought of it two or three hours ago, when I'd have had time to catch the last edition. But I didn't. No, Pierre le Fou exists all right. It's not his real name, of course. That's something like Carbonato, Pierre Carbonato. But Pierre le Fou – Peter the Mad – is what everyone in France calls him. Well, all the people who read their equivalent of our paper. He's got quite a reputation. For personally disposing of people he doesn't like.'

'And . . .?'

'And, according to our stringer in Marseilles, when Bubbles was playing an exhibition match somewhere in the South of France shortly before the French Open, which she won as you know, our friend Pierre was present and said something about going to bed with her. And little Bubbles turned him down – in good round French, so our chap said – in front of a whole crowd of tennis writers and God knows who else. So, was P le Fou pissed off? Well, a mobster like that doesn't forget that sort of thing. And, you know, mad's mad in any language. So what d'you think? He your best bet?'

Yes, Harriet thought, perhaps my best bet so far. If all this is kosher.

A French gangster, evidently with a certain amount of public profile, possibly having some link with Bubbles . . . Her well-concealed boyfriend, after all? Then, if things turned sour, a public put-down. And . . . Yes, he might have come all the way to England . . . To Adam and Eve House, intent on revenge. Perhaps.

She managed to have the sense before ringing off merely to thank Sam Porter in as neutral a way as she could. It would do no good at all for the *Daily Dirt* to spread all over its front page next day that the Hard Detective was targeting French gangster Pierre le Fou. As she might be. As she very well might be.

# Chapter Six

At seven next morning, a little over twenty-four hours after that bedside phone call saying Bubbles Xingara had been murdered, Harriet was at her desk once more, showered and breakfasted, and dealing with the remaining overnight messages. But then she found herself thinking of something else.

God, if in an hour or so when Anselm comes on duty I catch sight of that calloused hand, it'll all start up again. I know it will.

But, one thing. Anselm Brent isn't going to have time for tennis for many weeks to come. Not with a murderer that the whole world wants to be hunted down. Or not unless, perhaps, inquiries in France about Pierre le Fou lead to a quick breakthrough.

Interpol must put them in the picture. And the police in Marseilles. Must get old French-speaking Inspector Franklin back in Birchester to contact them as soon as he's at his desk. Could try him before the p.m. at nine, otherwise leave him a message. And I arranged the next team briefing for ten. Hell of a lot to be got through. And, no doubt, I'll have to deal with the bloody media again at some stage. Murder of world's-darling tennis star. With a sex angle like that, they're not going to let go.

But, another thing, even if I get maximum co-operation from the Marseilles police, I'll almost certainly need to send someone to France. One of the DIs on my team, it should be. So which? Anderson sounds as if he'd be able to deal with things there. Experience in the Met and all that. But till I've seen something of him, I've no idea what he's really like. Except that he's rumoured to fancy himself as a stud. I suppose I could make an instant decision when he turns up some time today. But if I can't, what about Anselm? Wonder if he speaks any French. He could have learnt it at Levenham Grammar as well as anywhere. Bright as it turns out he is.

Oh, God, I so like that in him. That sort of – what to call it? – ex-directory intelligence of his.

Christ, I mustn't – I must not . . .

But, wait, if I send him off to France, won't that make my life that much easier? Away for a week in Marseilles, out of my sight. Or longer even, if extradition proceedings come into it. That's always provided this whole Pierre le Fou thing doesn't turn out to be some sort of bloody mare's nest. But if it doesn't, if this is the beginning of the end of the trail, then with any luck I won't need to see much more of Anselm Brent ever.

If I mean *luck*.

For the hundredth time in her life, Harriet found herself once again in attendance at a post-mortem. She could have passed on the duty of being the police presence at it to someone else, to DI Brent perhaps. But, when she could, she had always made this task her own. She felt now it should be doubly so. The more she had learnt about puppy-happy, tennis-dedicated

Bubbles Xingara, the more she had felt her murder as a brutal act that should never have been.

So in the mortuary at the edge of Levenham Police Station car park, next-door to the added-on women's toilets – *Sarge Musgrove's only got one ball AND THAT'S MADE OF RUBBER* – she rapidly hauled on dulled green protective jerkin and dulled green voluminous trousers. Soon Professor Polk, the Birchester pathologist, was descending on his task with all the relishing zeal she had so often witnessed. And, as the smells and the sounds she had long become inured to followed in their accustomed way, there came his detached voice stating what he was doing to *Bubbles Xingara, female, aged nineteen, of Adam and Eve House, near Levenham*. Soon there followed the intermittent click-clicking of the technician's camera as each stage of the intrusive revelation was laid bare, and eventually the screech of the rotating trepan cutting through the skull. While unceasingly – somehow yet more of a strain on the nerves – there was the sound of the steady trickling of water washing away blood from the white ceramic slab.

Yet the human tissue and bones that he's working on, Harriet could not help saying to herself, were, until early yesterday morning, a lively, forward-looking, dazzlingly enchanting young tennis star. Blotted out now, erased.

Escorting Professor Polk to his car when the examination was over, she put to him the one question she most wanted answered.

'That wound in her throat, Professor, what did you make of it? Any indication what the weapon might have been?'

Professor Polk gave a sharp little laugh.

'No, Superintendent, I am not going to provide you with the one clue pointing directly to your murderer. But I will admit that puncture puzzles me, too. I mean, I can tell you how deep it was, how wide at the entrance, where it penetrated to, why it caused instant death, all the details you've heard me dictate and will see in more detail in my report. But, to be honest, I can't tell you anything at all about what sort of object was used, beyond the negative fact that it left no obviously visible traces in the wound.'

'So, something smooth? No great force needed to plunge it in that far?'

'Yes, no great force. But some, perhaps.'

He got into the car, thumped the door closed, tugged down his seatbelt.

'And I suppose the only other out-of-the-way thing I found,' he said, abruptly activating the window-lowering button, 'is that the girl had every appearance of being a virgin. Hymen broken, of course, as it would be with any sports-playing young woman. But certainly no signs of recent intercourse, and all the indications that it did not habitually take place.'

So, Harriet found herself thinking, yes, it seemed there was at least one young female who had escaped the power of that *feeling of amorousness* which John's Tolstoy had slavered over.

By the time she got back to her office two things had happened. First, there was a long fax from Inspector Franklin, more or less confirming from his phone call to the Marseilles police what the *Daily Dirt* stringer had told Sam Porter. Pierre le Fou, according to press reports, had been the victim of a fierce rejection when he had openly suggested taking Bubbles to his bed.

The story had been the talk of Marseilles for weeks. *Les Bulles qui ont smashé le gangster* (*The bubbles or Bubbles that smashed [tennis term] the gangster*, Franklin's fax had over-obligingly explained). The joke had been repeated and repeated, he said, and had soon actually driven Pierre le Fou into hiding. It had been weeks since he had been seen in any of his regular bars in the city.

So, Harriet wondered, can he have crossed the Channel somehow? Any enterprising criminal with money to spare could do that without showing a passport. Could he then have found out from whatever London contacts he might have that Bubbles lived at Adam and Eve House? And could he have made his way through the unfamiliar English countryside, first to spy on the dawn runner, then to cross the ineffectual obstacle of the Leven – he would scarcely have needed to get the bottoms of his trousers wet – and finally to plunge that clean spike into Bubbles' throat?

Franklin's fax had said nothing about whether Pierre le Fou was capable of making the trip, and little about whether he was called *le Fou* because he was in fact a certifiable psychopath. So, yes, a visit to Marseilles still necessary. Especially if, in a day or two now, Pierre is seen in his usual haunts there once more.

The second thing she had been greeted with was the elegant summer-suited figure of Detective Inspector Anderson, Handy Andy. When she had seen the long, curling strip of Franklin's fax on her desk, she had asked him to wait while she dealt with it.

Now she called him in.

Tall, dark and doesn't-he-know-it handsome was the thought that came straight into her mind as she took a better look at him. Lean tanned face, lean figure – just, in fact, she thought wryly, the type I go for – mid-thirties, holding himself well and looking down at her as she sat at her desk with a confident white-toothed smile. Easy enough to understand why all the women officers in B Division in Birchester were succumbing to his charm, if in fact they were. But will he, she asked herself, prove to be a good detective?

By way of testing that out she told him about Sam Porter's middle-of-the-night call and how now Inspector Franklin, talking to the Marseilles police, had confirmed most of what she had been told.

'We're lucky to have Inspector Franklin at head-quarters in Birchester,' she said. 'It's amazing how often someone speaking good French is needed. You speak it at all?'

'I do, as a matter of fact. Like to take the odd holiday in *la belle France*.'

Oh, do you? Smart London detective, all right. But you don't take care to address a senior officer you're meeting for the first time as *ma'am*. I wonder whether you'd call a male senior officer *sir*. I rather expect you would.

Say something? No, let it pass this once, if there's a chance that he'll be on my team for weeks and months to come, no point in antagonizing him at the outset. He'd better earn that reprieve, though.

But – the sudden thought – Anselm had been punctilious in using the *ma'am* right from the start, and he still is. But, no, mustn't think along those lines. Must not.

'All right, you seem to know your France, DI. So what's your take on Pierre le Fou?'

He took a moment before replying, serious thought stamped on his leanly handsome face.

'Well, looks good to me, I must say. You know what that sort of gang boss is like. Always ready to pounce on lack of respect, especially if it comes from a woman. And even more especially if that woman's a mistress.'

'You're suggesting that Bubbles Xingara was that? That what she and this gangster had was some sort of public disagreement between lovers?'

'Well, you never know. I've never even seen a picture of Pierre le Fou, but that type, if he's not positively a goon, always has got a certain power over women. Attraction of the very male, you know.'

And are you by any chance contriving to plant such a situation between *very male* yourself and me? Damn it, I think you are. Already. Sgt Grant was right about you, John's Tolstoyan theory borne out a hundred per cent.

But I don't think you're correct about little Bubbles. No, not for a minute. Not about the girl who produced that quick, crushing retort to the fan at Eastbourne.

'So, ma'am,' – at last a *ma'am* – 'you thinking of sending someone to Marseilles, check up on all this?'

'Yes, of course someone will have to go.'

She saw his eyes light up. Not very good at concealing his thoughts, DI Anderson.

But then he said something that jolted her with surprise, as if she had had a slap in the face.

'But, look here, if we're going to be working together, couldn't you call me Andy or Handy Andy, if you like? It's what everyone does. And if you are sending someone to Marseilles, well, my French is actually pretty good.'

'Thank you for your offer, DI,' Harriet said, almost

without having to think. 'But I'm sending DI Brent, from the Leven Vale force. He's been on the case from the very beginning, well up on all the details.'

Handy Andy managed to conceal his chagrin. But only just.

And I, Harriet thought, have I managed to conceal my feelings about Anselm? I dare say I have. But Anselm away for days, maybe weeks? What I want? Or what I by no means want?

Harriet got on to the Leven Vale Chief Constable straight away, and succeeded in convincing him that Pierre le Fou was a much more likely murderer than trembly Old Rowley had ever been, and that the expense of a trip to France for DI Brent would be justified. With that under her belt, she decided to go back again to Adam and Eve House, where Anselm had gone to check those early-morning timings.

After driving through a small ambush of media cameras outside the gates, she found Anselm round at the back of the old house, where the Scenes-of-Crime officers were busy packing away the glaring blue tent and its surrounding police tape.

'Well,' she said, 'did you find out anything more about the timings of what happened in the house here just before six yesterday morning?'

'Think I have, ma'am. Always provided Renshaw and Fiona aren't in it together somehow and lying their heads off. Which I don't think they can be, really. And, if they're not, what I think occurred was this: Renshaw was sleeping in one of the spare rooms, as I gathered he always does nowadays, saw the unmade bed. Get away from that rampaging wife of his, I dare say. He has an alarm clock, and it went off as usual at 5.45.

He got up, went to the lavvy, washed but didn't shave, put on some clothes and set off to go down to that boathouse gym. But he found the body then, and rang us at Levenham PS. Time fits in all right with that, I'd checked yesterday that his clock was still set to ring at 5.45.'

'Good. Go on. What about Fiona Diplock?'

'Not as clear with her, ma'am. Did her best to avoid saying where it was she was sleeping. And I thought I shouldn't try to make her be definite. Not till it looks as if she's on the cards as a suspect, anyhow.'

'Yes, you did right. So what did she tell you?'

'That she woke, as she usually does in the summer, just after six. She made out she doesn't set the alarm on her radio. But I very much doubt if she was in her own room. She said she'd barely got dressed when Renshaw told her about the murder just after he'd rung us. Seems a reasonable account, apart from that confusion over the rooms.'

'Yes. I think we can pretty safely say Peter Renshaw's interests, if they lie anywhere, are with big Fiona rather than they were with little Bubbles. Sex rearing its head in that spare room.'

And can I ask, *Does it often rear up with you, Anselm?* Of course, I can't. I mustn't. I won't.

'As it so often does, in all sorts of places. As you must know yourself.'

The slow blush. God, he's so fucking desirable. Push for it. Yes, push. I can't help myself.

'I mean, you must put yourself around from time to time, yes?'

The blush conquered, or half-conquered. Eyes looking elsewhere. Anywhere. At the brick of the house, mellower now with no strong sunlight directly on it.

'I suppose I do.'

'String of girlfriends, is it?'

How much longer can I go on like this? What a fool I'm being. This isn't me. But I'm going on. Going on. John's Eros thundering down through me. Unstoppable.

'Wouldn't say a string. No. Just two or three really.'

He's wriggling, actually shifting his feet about in those terrible brown brogues he wears. I must not do this to him.

'So it's hookers, is it?' she said, making herself lightly laugh. 'So far as Levenham has any?'

But he seemed unable to respond to the easy jokiness she had tried to hit on. His mouth tightened. She could see, all too plainly, that he was going to come out with a confession, as if a tooth was being wrenched from the gum.

'Well, Levenham doesn't have any prossies, or not proper professionals as you might say. But, yeah, matter of fact, I went over to Birchester, once or twice, when I was younger.'

Oh, God, he's delightful. Delicious. I'm sunk. Sunk.

No. No, I'm not. I won't be. I mustn't be. I'm – I'm, yes, the Hard Detective.

She swallowed fiercely.

'Well, enough of all that,' she said.

She explained then about Pierre le Fou.

'We've got to find out all we can about a madman like that,' she ended. 'He really could be the one we're looking for. And that means someone's got to go out to Marseilles. And I'm sending you.'

She stopped herself abruptly.

'I – I'm assuming you speak some French,' she said, suddenly realizing that this was indeed an assumption.

'Well, ma'am, I've hardly thought about French since I left school. But I suppose I remember it a bit, though I can't exactly say I *parlez-vous* like a native. Still, we had a horrible French master at the Grammar, Mr Lehane, so I did learn it pretty well. That was in the old days, when the school was pretty academic. It's more interested in sport nowadays.' Then came that smile again, brilliant from blue eyes, and at once gone. 'As a matter of fact I won the French prize in my last term.'

'Right. Then I'm not sorry I preferred you for the task to DI Anderson, who's just arrived from Birchester. So it's off to France for you . . . Anselm.'

Yes, off with him to France. Out of sight. But will it be out of mind? And hasn't he, just in the last few minutes, lodged himself yet more rootedly in my head? That blushing admission that he's been with, if not Brazilian whores, Birchester ones.

So, would he, if it came to it, be as shocked as he was by Aimée Renshaw's advances if it was me making them? As, if he's got eyes in his head, he may have guessed I've already done, if more discreetly than that *terrible woman*.

Oh, why am I sending him away? Why did I tell him I was going to when he had only just let me know he's available? If he did. If he's there, ready. There, to be assailed. Yes, assailed.

# Chapter Seven

Detective Inspector Anselm Brent left for Marseilles immediately after the inquest into the death of Bubbles Xingara. Occupied though Harriet was in checking over her notes of the proceedings – verdict: *murder by a person or persons unknown* – she could not restrain herself from going over to the window of her office and looking down at the street below as he got into the car to take him to Birchester Airport.

The same damn clothes. That dreadful orangey jacket – God, how hot he'll be in sun-scalding Marseilles – those heavy grey trousers, those clomping brown shoes.

Oh, but why, why, why, did I send him off? He could be here, here in this room at this moment, near enough to touch. He might be sitting on that chair opposite, and his hand might be resting on the edge of my desk. Palm up.

And he's so damn likeable, too. Look at the way, when I signed that authorization for him, he flashed me his blue-eyed, somehow direct yet bashful smile and said, *I promise I won't be the one to throw this signature of yours into the gutter.*

No. No, come on. The inquest. The inquest. Anything I ought to have spotted there, however minimal?

She marched back to her desk. But, even at the end

of a hard half-hour she had seen nothing in her notes of any help. The police surgeon who had certified death had given a straightforward account of what he had observed. Professor Polk had told, at complicated medical length, what his findings had been at the post-mortem. Peter Renshaw had said no more and no less than he had after finding Bubbles there by the Leven with that wound in her throat and blood all over her singlet. He had stated that she went for a long run first thing every morning, every day of the week, and had added, in answer to the Coroner's question, that this was public knowledge in that it had been reported in at least the Levenham paper. No, he knew of no one who could have any reason for killing his stepdaughter. Anselm, equally, had given, simply and clearly, his evidence about the situation of the body when he had reached Adam and Eve House. She herself had had to do no more than say, falling back on the familiar pledge, that police inquiries were being 'vigorously pursued'.

So they were. The forty-odd officers in her team were all hard at work. Completed Action Sheets from the hundreds of inquiries being made at every house or shop in a ten-mile radius from the murder scene were being checked, analysed, computer-logged. Reports, all so far negative, had come in from airports and ports all round the country about the possible arrival of Pierre le Fou. Every name had been noted of every fan Fiona Diplock had put into her computer or Bubbles had had in her Filofax – more than 370 cards – and one by one, male and female, they were being questioned, either by team members or in answer to requests to local forces. All their alibis were being checked. Another extra-intensive search for the weapon had been carried out, without result. And over at Greater Birchester Police headquarters the force's computer expert, not to say licensed hacker, one Sgt Downey, was investigating, at the end of his keyboard, any website reputed to hold photos of Bubbles.

Thank God, Harriet added to herself, I'll be able to get home tonight. A long hot shower. A long cool drink. And, if I'm not so tired that I'll snap at poor John, a little easy talk.

But, whatever happens, there's going to be no mention of any personal relations I may or may not have with new members of my team, especially those I have most to do with, DI Brent and DI Anderson. Oh, yes, there's as much danger in saying anything about Handy Andy as there is in mentioning Anselm. Begin to talk about the way ever since he first stepped into my office he's been blatantly giving me the look that, presumably, he was giving with such success all those WPCs at B Division in Birchester, and in no time I could find myself launching into a comparison with modest Anselm. And then . . .

And I haven't the time or the energy now to decide what, if anything, I want to tell John. Yes, in theory I could tell him about Anselm. We have our agreement, occasional sex for the sake of sex not affecting our real relationship. And there isn't in actual fact all that much to tell. Yet.

But, on the other hand, if there is nothing to tell, or almost nothing, and if there's never going to be anything to tell, as I trust after Anselm comes back from France there won't be, then there's nothing to be gained from blabbing out those thoughts that Tolstoy's famous *amorousness* has sent whirling in my head.

So what next? Yes, Wimbledon almost on us. And

there, somewhere among the crowds, may be the person who, in the solitude of dawn at isolated Adam and Eve House, let the screeching red, sex-fired impulse to kill have its way.

All right, one thing to be done. Probably should have been done already. Message to the Met: please detail as many officers as you can spare to work the Wimbledon crowds looking for any individual behaving in any bizarre way. Maybe nothing will emerge. The killer may be far away from any tennis tournament, this individual who murdered the tennis darling of three-quarters of the world. All right, perhaps we'll eventually find it's a man now back swanning it in Marseilles, an insult avenged. Still, combing the Wimbledon crowds is something that should be done. No stone . . . Every avenue . . . As I managed not to say at the inquest, or when the media caught me.

By special request of the family, the funeral service for Bubbles at St Anselm's Church was to take place before Wimbledon got under way. Aware that, if the murder was the work of an obsessed stalker, whoever killed her could be among the hundreds of onlookers expected to watch the cortège or even, just possibly, be one of those admitted to the church by invitation, *family and friends only*, Harriet had been grateful that it was the duty of the senior officer on a case to attend. It would give her the chance of scrutinizing the mourners there. Less likely to bring a result than the large squad of detectives she had tasked to work the crowds, together with a team of video operators from Birchester. But worth doing.

When it came to it, there were even more people round the church and along the road leading to it than she had expected. The walls of the churchyard, too, were alive with television cameras, swinging to and fro like so many this-way-and-that Centre Court tennis watchers.

It was all Harriet, militarily correct in uniform, could do to squeeze her way behind one of the eight-foot-high flower pillars, rotund as barrels, on either side of the porch and make her way in. Momentarily she recognized the flowers as what someone had said were Bubbles' favourite, blue-and-white nigella.

Love-in-the-Mist, she thought, hardly appropriate for Bubbles, dedicating every hour of her time, not like the majority of teenagers to dating and thoughts of dating, but to tennis. Yet nigella, she abruptly recalled marvelling at what the subconscious can suddenly throw up, was once called Devil-in-the-Bush. And under that name the flower was grimly right at the funeral of the girl murdered by an unknown for their dark reason.

Or was that bush devil actually Pierre le Fou? And would it turn out that Anselm, after wrestling with the harsh French of southern France, would come back with something more definite than the rumour passed on by the *Daily Dirt* stringer. Or would he be defeated by the world of Marseilles crooks, surely in a different class from the occasional burglars of Levenham and such odd flashers as stinky Old Rowley?

Standing at the back of the big church, filled to capacity and with its every available surface carrying more huge pots of blue-and-white nigella, Harriet began an up-and-down survey of each crowded pew.

*Family and friends only*, she saw, had been interpreted in a decidedly generous spirit. Only two pews right at the front were strictly family, with Peter and

Aimée Renshaw and Fiona Diplock supplemented by a handful of plainly ill-at-ease 'country cousins'. A little further back the Fairleys sat, stiff in their best clothes, Betty dabbing at her eyes with Arthur's big coloured handkerchief.

But otherwise the congregation consisted of a large number of tennis stars – every now and again there was a face Harriet thought she recognized – taking an hour or two out of Wimbledon preparation to pay their respects to a fellow player always with that spreadingly cheerful smile. Or, perhaps, not so much to pay their respects as to get their pictures on television or in the papers.

But, not only were players there in strength, there were also – she had made it her business to see the final invitation list – all sorts of people from the circus that attends the stars, from officials of the Women's Tennis Association flying in from America, and of the Lawn Tennis Association up from London, right down to coaches and practice partners, even to a would-be player who had the year before acted as Bubbles' racquet carrier. Then there were the agents, both Bubbles' own and those of several other players, and the sponsors' representatives, the sports-clothing designers, the gossip columnists and tennis writers, the sports beauticians and sports hairdressers.

Tennis, after all, Harriet knew now from the rapid reading of newspapers and magazines she had inter-spersed with her other work, was business. Big business. Bubbles Xingara was by no means the only financial corporation due to play on the Centre Court at Wimbledon. And, she thought, with big business goes greed, the desire for money and power that is,

despite John's theories, surely as powerful as that overhanging cloud of sex. Or is it at least nearly so?

A different motive here for Bubbles' death? It could
be. Get the fraud-and-figures people in Birchester on
to it. Some advantage in belonging to one of the big
battalions.

But, more urgently, somewhere among the pews
at this moment there could be someone who had had
some grudge against Bubbles. Or who had been caught
up by sexual obsession for her and come stalking
through the dawn mists rising from the Leven to thrust
that spiked weapon into her throat.

Was anyone looking unduly tense? Was someone
in the rows of fidgeting mourners sitting frozen by
guilt into give-away immobility?

Pew after pew scrutinized.

Then, beside her, through the wide-open doors, the
black-coated, top-hat-carrying, stiffly reverent-faced
undertaker appeared, leading in the flowers-smothered
coffin. The opening hymn rolled out – organ deplor-
ably squeaky, choir valiant – and at last tailed into
silence.

'Good afternoon,' said the Vicar, black cassock,
white surplice, richly coloured academic hood.
'Welcome to this ancient church of St Anselm.'

Oxford hood? Think so. But why must he conduct
the service as if it was some sort of social gathering, a
whist drive, a bun fight? Damn it, when I used to go
to church vicars did what vicars were there to do,
praise God, announce the hymns, lead the prayers.
Doing their job.

But the chit-chat came to an end soon enough, and
then up to the front of the chancel, where a shining

brass reading-stand had been placed, came Fiona Diplock.

'I am going to read to you,' she announced, still seemingly as unaffected as at first by her friend's death, 'a poem that reached us only this morning, sent by one of Bubbles' fans who gave no address and who signed himself simply *Angus*. We don't know who he was, but we think his simple words say all that should be said about – about dear Bubbles.'

Does that pause mean she checked back a sob? Is she really deeply affected by Bubbles' death? Or putting on an act? Bitter about the once despised schoolfriend who gave her a job, better paid no doubt than whatever she had found to do after Daddy's wealth had suddenly evaporated?

No telling. But something to keep in mind.

Then in her water-clear, upper-class voice Fiona read out the poem.

> She was a vision of delight
> Our tennis girl in dazzling white.
> She hit the ball as hard as hard,
> She hit our hearts, got through our guard.
> Never, never shall we forget
> That grin, that laugh that won each set.

Terrible, of course, Harriet thought. Derivative, when it wasn't banal. Who in the family had decided it should be used? Not Fiona, in so far as she was family at all. More like Aimée. Yes, almost certainly her. Her taste. Think pink, think whore's parlour sitting-room.

No, wait. All right, there are dozens of bits of verse I've seen from Bubbles' records every bit as clumsy as those. But they were all sent when she was alive. They were, if you like, just messages saying, *Look at me, look at me*. But this was sent after Bubbles had been killed. And, unless I'm mistaken, it's the only thing of its sort. Yes, there've been letters of condolence that I've got the Renshaws to hand over. But none of them were anything like this. So isn't it possible that *Never, never shall we forget* was written by someone who won't ever forget? Won't ever forget Bubbles because they killed her.

*Angus*, the versifier. Been noted as sending something else earlier by the detectives going through those 370 index cards? Or by whoever's working on Fiona's computer records? Angus not an uncommon name. So what chance of identifying him from either source? And the poem must have arrived at Adam and Eve House just this morning. Didn't Fiona say that? So the envelope? Don't tell me they threw it away. Must check.

But is this really what we've been looking for? Can it be that six lines of jarringly awful verse, however pleasing to pink lady Aimée Renshaw, really point to someone in the grip of too-intense, unhealthy feelings?

Action all this, as soon as I get back. And, damn it all, why am I stuck in the church here? There's work to be done. All right, someone here may, pressured by the moment, give some sign of not being a simple mourner or a not-so-simple publicity seeker. But no one has so far, and with every minute that passes I guess no one will.

So, go? Force my way past the people clustered at the doors? No. No, I suppose not. Senior police officer in uniform, mustn't draw undue attention.

God, what are we getting now? Prayers from the Vicar. Succour sought from above for the bereaved family. Not all that much needed, judging by what I've seen of them, except perhaps shocked Peter Renshaw. Nothing, though, for any devoted staff at Adam and Eve House, yet I rather think both the Fairleys were more hit by the murder than any of those closer to Bubbles.

Prayer now *for all those who followed from afar the bright star* – God, that Vicar – but among the crowds out there listening to the loudspeakers muffledly relaying these muffly words how many will know he's praying for them, the Bubbles Xingara fans? And, if those prayers have any effect, will they touch the one fan who, possibly, possibly, was so obsessed by the bright star that eventually they could do nothing else but take some heavy pointed instrument and thrust it into her neck?

*Hear our prayer, O Lord, for the police. Help its officers with their onerous task. May Thy justice be done.*

Will that prayer help in distant Marseilles one Leven Vale Police officer needing to wriggle his way through the unknown, find the facts that could nail Pierre le Fou . . .? If Pierre's to be nailed. And then come home. Anselm.

Another hymn. *He Who Would Valiant Be*. Fair enough. Except it's a she we're burying. But Bubbles, from all I've learnt, was valiant. A little cheerful fighter.

And the Vicar – get a move on, get a move on – solemnly going up into the high pulpit now. And it's *Barbara was one who was an inspiration to us all*. Nasal hoot.

Barbara. Name on her birth certificate and I dare say a dozen other official documents. But, damn it, she was Bubbles. Bubbles, *an inspiration to us all*. And, yes, she was that, I suppose. Someone who got to the top of her tree, who worked like a demon at her chosen way, worked till her right hand was no longer a girl's pretty palm but a working woman's calloused one – oh, God, Anselm – someone who worked at what she believed she was there to do, even sheltered under that steel umbrella of work, work, work to the exclusion of Eros bolts from that great hovering cloud.

But, me. Am I going to find, after all, that I can put up my steel umbrella? That work, work, work to find the person, man or woman, who put an end to Bubbles' life of work will protect me, when Anselm – when DI Brent comes back, will protect me from— what? – the moment of madness that came over me beside Bubbles' dead body? Is all that I've learnt over the years going to help me, with prayers or without them, to free myself from that?

Vicar hooting on. *Fame and fortune did not spoil her.* Well, that's true enough. *With her sad death a bright light in the world was in a moment extinguished.* A long pause. *Let us pray.*

Heads in front dipped. One or two kneeling, but not many.

Second bout of prayers ended. Last hymn as the coffin is carried out through the side door.

And away.

Enough bods detailed to watch at the cemetery? Think so. And the reception at Adam and Eve House, right to have ducked out of that? To leave it to DI Anderson to keep his eyes on the guests there, Bubbles' killer just possibly among them? Ought to be sharp enough – unless he takes it into his head to chat up some piece of femininity.

Back in the Incident Room, Harriet at once tasked as many officers as she could lay hands on with re-checking all the letters and cards Fiona Diplock had filed over the whole time she had been Bubbles' secretary. *Angus*, that was the signature to look for. Hopefully, it would be found in front of a surname, and with an address at the head of the letter. But find the man who had written that absurd poem they must.

She turned to go. And then, out of the corner of her eye, she saw lying on the big table near her a pencil, its end thoroughly chewed. Before she knew what she was doing, she had picked it up.

Put it down, put it back, she told herself.

But, holding it intertwined between her fingers, she walked briskly out of the Incident Room. A quick run up the stairs to her office, door unlocked, a step inside, door closed with her back, and – yes, the wretched chewed little length of coloured stick put to her lips. To feel for one long delicious moment the tiny craters and hills those teeth had made on the wood.

And a jolt. If . . . If I give way to this Eros amorousness, what will I be caught up in? Will I go spinning, in Aphrodite's coils, into something that goes against all I believe in? Oh, yes, nowadays in theory it's not wrong to have an affair, a fling, and I've a feeling that, if I were to make a move, a definite move, Anselm wouldn't be altogether unresponsive. He wouldn't freeze away from me as he froze from man-gobbling, twice-his-age Aimée Renshaw. He wouldn't smash some rebuff into my face as Bubbles did into Pierre le Fou's. All right, a fling might mysteriously get him out of my hair. But it might not. It might send him deeper in than just my hair? What if – *fucking . . . leads to kissing* – it's not Eros but tangling Aphrodite I get in thrall to? What if in the end I find myself twisting and turning to keep Anselm? To keep him and chuck everything else?

But, think, what could go spiralling down from that? It could even lead to me leaving John. And could I cause the twins, all but fully adult though they are, confusion and division of loyalties? Could it ever come to that? It might. It might. And the job might have to go. Yes, it could come to that. Setting up with a junior officer, that alone would be frowned on, and it might well put a stop to any career I may have ahead of me. It would almost certainly get me shunted away somewhere out of sight at the very least. A detective superintendent going off with a detective inspector. And, damn it all, I'm actually more than a detective superintendent. I'm the famous-notorious Hard Detective. I'd be a big headline in the *Daily Dirt*. Yes, *Soft Side to Hard Detective. Iron Fist but Chocky Heart.*

No, no, no, no, no. I can't let that happen. I won't. I'm here doing my job, and I'll do it. I'm here to find whoever killed Bubbles Xingara, and, if it takes me a year, if it takes more than that, I'll do it. Murderers must be brought to justice, whether they have killed a star of the tennis world or some poor victim in the course of a burglary.

Chewed pencil dropped on to the desk.

At last and very late, home. The promised long hot shower, long cool drink. And John, the book devourer, patiently waiting up, a slim Saul Bellow novel now on his lap, ready for a little easy talk. And with a small piece of news.

The twins coming home, too. Tomorrow, probably. Jaunt to London with a couple of girls gone a bit wrong.

'Nothing to worry about,' John says. 'Not a police matter or anything.'

'All right, I suppose we'll hear more when they arrive. Or most probably not. Not the full story certainly.'

'Yup. I guess there may have been a row with one of the girls, or both, born of disappointment. Though who's to say on which side. But how was your funeral? Funerals always interest me. There's all the deceased's family and friends, they see the coffin being put into the ground and afterwards it's all right to talk about it, say things like *Poor old Tom, he'd be turning in his grave.* But nobody likes to say anything about what's buried in the body in the coffin, the secret thoughts, what really went through old Tom's mind.'

Harriet laughed.

'Trust you to have an idea about everything.'

'No, it's more than an idea. It's a metaphor, if you like. For our really secret lives. For the sexual ideas we all have that no one actually mentions. All right, nowadays it's okay to talk about people going to bed together. But that's just the putting of the coffin into the earth. It's what's buried with the dead man that can't be mentioned.'

'John, I think you're talking through your hat. People now tell each other everything.'

'Oh, yes, there are people, the young adults mostly, who happily talk about every sort of sexual activity, almost. But they're not everyone. In most people's minds there's still a lot that stays buried out of sight.'

'You could be right, I suppose. But you were asking how *my funeral* was before you leapt on your hobby-horse. So let me tell you it wasn't my funeral. Bar one odd thing that emerged, which I'm having painstakingly followed up, it was just one long bore. You should have heard the Vicar.'

'I have. Only too often. Or countless clones of him. But didn't you get any little bits of enjoyment out of it? Funerals and the wakes after them are hotbeds for Eros work, you know. And that's amusing enough to watch.'

Handy Andy, she thought for a moment, I wonder if this afternoon he neglected his duty at the post-funeral reception at Adam and Eve House? Fastened on some luscious piece of prey there?

'And where did you acquire that unlikely piece of curious information?' she asked John.

'This very book, as a matter of fact. Only about ten minutes ago. So it's hot.'

She twisted her head till she could read the title.

'*The Actual?* Is it good? Apart from this not alto-gether credible notion of yours?'

'Oh, it's wonderful, though I don't know whether that'd make the notion any more likely in your eyes. But not only was it written by a man in his eighties – ' he flipped the slim volume over, colour picture of the author sitting in a white plastic chair in a meadow somewhere, and looking, yes, quite aged, though smiling – 'but he has his hero attend, if not a funeral, a re-interment, and sexual attraction does take place.'

'Well, if Saul Bellow says so . . .'

'And he's now something of an authority on what Eros can do even to people in their eighties. His newish wife recently presented him with a child, you know.'

'One up to your big theory. But one up to bed, as far as I'm concerned. I'm just about exhausted.'

# Chapter Eight

On the third day of Wimbledon, with the tennis writers busy speculating, in a sort of ghostly tournament, over how Bubbles' matches would have gone, Anselm came back.

Right, Harriet thought, as, looking out of her office window, she saw down below what must be the car arriving from Birchester Airport. Even if there's no hard news from Marseilles we at least have one other likely-looking line to go on now. The *Angus* line. Nothing found so far, but something may yet be.

But, she thought with a wild bound of hope, Anselm may come thundering up the stairs at any moment. Will he say Pierre le Fou was seen, some time before the murder, perhaps by some fellow criminal, now persuaded to talk, boarding a private plane at some tucked-away airfield? And heading off northwards. For England.

She turned away and sat herself at her desk. There was, as always, a pile of messages to be checked over. She glanced back to the one she had been reading when the sound of what might have been Anselm's car had taken her to the window, the report from the Greater Birchester Police fraud squad. *Inquiries to date have indicated no malfeasance* – Jesus, how they love the long words, the Frauds people – *in the accounts of the Barbara Xingara Trust*. Okay, another possible line run into the sand. But, never mind, a better lead perhaps appearing in a few seconds when DI Brent comes in to tell me what he found out in France.

And then will he be just DI Brent, a nice enough, intelligent enough officer whom I'm lucky to have on my team? In the light of day will that aching want I was gripped by prove to have been lifted, like the mists that hang over the Leven at dawn?

In front of her, almost concealed by the base of the desk-lamp, she saw now a pencil, with a badly chewed end.

She picked it up between two fastidious fingers, dropped it into the metal bin beside her.

Then, as at last she heard steps on the stairs, without pausing to think she leant over the bin, pulled out a big piece of crumpled paper, quickly opened it wide, carefully put it back so that it covered the evidence.

Bounding steps on the stairs? No. No, not bounding. But are they leaden?

Hard to make out.

But, bounding or leaden, they were approaching, the heavy tread of solid brown brogues. A tap at the door.

'Come.'

Detective Inspector Anselm Brent stood there in the doorway, face surely a good deal more sun-reddened than before, thatch of fair hair as hastily combed as ever, orangey tweed jacket perhaps more dust-darkened, grey trousers with even less crease in them.

He said nothing.

'Right,' she managed to bring out.

Her power of speech seemed to have vanished.

Something had happened to her. She hardly knew what. She felt running through and through her, as if just underneath her skin a thin flame was licking at her very blood. In an instant she was bathed in sweat, and cold. Cold to trembling.

Christ, she thought, it's love. It's more, much more than that spout of mere lust at Adam and Eve House, there with the cuckoo calling and calling. My God, what am I going to do?

No. No, it's past *going to do*. It's done. It's happened. It's – It's obsession. I'm lost.

The River Leven mists have not been lifted, far from it. However absurd it is, however unaccountable, the coils of Aphrodite are round me, entangling, not to be broken. Detective Superintendent Harriet Martens of the Greater Birchester Police, called the Hard Detective, is drowned in love for Detective Inspector Anselm Brent, Leven Vale Police.

She did not know what she might have done next, jump up from her desk, rush over to where Anselm still stood in the doorway, seize him round the neck, thrust a violent kiss on to his lips. But, at just that moment, up the stairs where Anselm had just clumped came a set of hurrying feet and DI Anderson pushed through the open door into the room.

'Ma'am, we've got something. Look at these.'

He banged down on to the desk a small pile of papers. Harriet, bemused, still recognized the topmost one. The original text of the dreadful poem Fiona Diplock had read out in her clear, almost aggressive voice at the funeral.

She was a vision of delight
Our tennis girl in dazzling white.
She hit the ball as hard as hard,
She hit our hearts, got through our guard.
Never, never shall we forget
That grin, that laugh that won each set.

'See the writing, ma'am,' Handy Andy said, voice exultant. 'Now look at the other one. That old Leven Vale plodder, Sgt Wintercombe, got it out of the files. Eventually. Sent to Bubbles care of the Lawn Tennis Association, just after the Eastbourne tournament.'

Harriet turned to the sheets below. A letter, on headed notepaper, running to three heavily scrawled sides. She began to read. An outpouring. Half-sensible phrase tumbling out after half-sensible phrase. *You, only you, are my delight – turn my day to wondrous night, or night to day – I love you, my little Bubbles, I love you and love you and love you.*

Christ, she thought, I could have said just those words two minutes ago to Anselm, standing there now looking as if he hardly knows what's going on. I love you and love you and love you. I could have blurted them out, meant them. Except that bloody Handy Andy came crashing in.

And then she acknowledged that, yes, the words she was looking at were in precisely the same handwriting as that of the poem, for all that they were written with the lines rising madly upwards, veering wildly down, while the poem had been set out with schoolboy neatness.

But the same writing. No doubt about it, the poem signed *Angus* and this splatter of emotion had been written by the same man.

She flipped over the sheets looking for a signature.

*Angus*, and no more. But at the top there had been that address.

Have we got him? Is this him, our killer? Angus. It could be. The signs are there. The signs, but not the proof. All right, this fellow, whoever he is, is plainly crazy still about Bubbles. But no more than that. The forensic psychologists' books outline a possible pattern, and our man here, Angus, fits it. But quite probably there are a dozen, a hundred, out there who fit it just as well.

'Have you gone through all this, DI?' she asked. 'Any other clues about the writer?'

'Skimmed it, ma'am. But there's nothing there, just gush about what he calls *my Bubbles*. Plain he'd never got near enough to do anything about her. Wanker.'

'I dare say he is. But it's clear he's the sort of obsessive we ought to be looking out for, especially after sending that poem. Definitely something to look into. And urgently.'

She looked up at the deep-tanned face standing over her, white teeth bared in a grin of triumph.

'But don't think this resolves the case,' she said. 'Hopeful indications, all right. But no hard evidence.'

'Well, ma'am . . .'

'No. There still might be a hundred, a thousand, other answers just as good. Ans— DI Brent here may have a clincher this moment. Do you, DI?'

If he has . . . If he's coped with the Marseilles police, the Marseilles crooks and got hold of some solid facts . . .

She had not dared to look up from her desk and put the question directly to him. She thought that if she let herself look at him again the same extraordinary thing that had happened to her when he had stepped into the doorway would happen again. The thin flame running and running under her skin, the sweat breaking out all over, on her face, on the backs of her hands, the icy cold and the trembling. And Handy Andy, well-practised seducer, would very likely know what was happening. And mock in secret, and perhaps not in secret.

'The clincher, ma'am?' Anselm said, the faint burr in his voice seeming more noticeable than ever. 'No, I must admit I haven't got that. Not anything like it really. They're buggers, those French police, won't give you a damn thing unless you press and press. And, tell the truth, I hadn't got the facts to press with, nor much of the language, come to that. I did get them to row back a bit and admit that tale about Bubbles putting down Pierre le Fou in front of a whole crowd of his mates was a bit of a concoction. And someone did say, at least I think that was what they said, Pierre is back in circulation now. But they wouldn't do anything to help me get to see him. And the criminals were worse, plain and simply anti-police, wherever you came from. Frankly I could hardly understand a word they said either, had to beg for a translation time and again and then learnt nothing. I felt a proper fool.'

'Bad luck, DI,' Handy Andy put in quickly.

Harriet could have struck him to the ground.

But she knew better than to leap to Anselm's defence. She had succeeded, by keeping her eyes fixed hard on the jumbled pages of the Angus letter in front of her, in not giving herself away in a second fit of cold sweat and inner darting fire. But she knew that, if she once started making excuses for Anselm's failure, she could all too easily find herself praising him to the skies, saying how well he had questioned Old Rowley, what a good job he had done in setting up the Incident Room, how quick he had been that first morning out at Adam and Eve House to get a search going for any intruder, for whatever weapon had been used.

Instead, still looking down at the desk in front of her, she muttered, uncharacteristically, something about *not winning 'em all*.

'Listen, ma'am,' Handy Andy pushed in again, 'hadn't one of us – well, I could handle it – better go to that address on the letter straight away? No. 32, Woodlands Crescent, Boreham, Birchester BC4 3AP. I mean, that's fairly and squarely in the Greater Birchester Police area. I could be there in half an hour.'

She nearly agreed. But Handy Andy's pushiness had set up an immediate sharply negative reaction in her. For a moment she actually contemplated giving the task to Anselm.

Hell, no. Offering a sop to an officer who had clearly not succeeded in the major task he'd been given? An utter give-away. And, in fact, a humiliation for Anselm as well.

'No, DI,' she said, giving Handy Andy a direct look. 'No, I think this is something I'll handle myself.'

Something positive to do may clear my mind, she thought. A tough interview with a real suspect. Back to being, all right, the Hard Detective. Antidote to becoming the Chocky-soft Detective. If it'll work. But, no, it won't. It's too late now. I'm adrift. Adrift – will it be? – for ever. But at least it might take my mind off him for an hour or two. Partly off him.

Harriet did not get to the house in Boreham's Woodlands Crescent quite as quickly as Handy Andy had promised to. *Skimmed it*, he had said when she had asked him if he had gone through the *Angus* letter. So before leaving she gave the three scrawled sheets the close scrutiny they deserved, if without finding anything pointing more directly to the writer as Bubbles' killer. Now, with the poem and letter in plastic wallets in her briefcase, she was giving No. 32 a careful look-over from under the shade of one of the big chestnut trees lining the quiet outer-suburbs road.

'Detached, with mature garden, the estate agents would say,' she commented to staid Sgt Wintercombe, whom she had taken with her.

Probably built in the thirties, she thought. Brick-work lacking anything of the eighteenth-century mellowness of Adam and Eve House, and showing signs of deterioration here and there. The white paint of the windows peeling. The garden notable not so much for being *mature* as for the dried-up, patchy state of its wide lawn. Garage to the side, white tip-up door very much in need of paint, pulled blankly down.

'Right, Sergeant, let's see if our *Angus* is at home.'

'Very good, ma'am. Though I dare say, if this is his place, he won't be in.'

'We'll see.'

She opened the low curly ironwork gates and marched along the short length of the gravelled but weedy drive. No sign of tyre marks. So no car behind that shabby white garage door?

A big round bell-fitting at the side of the time-grimed green front door, with a big fat button at its centre. Forefinger on it, and held there. From inside the faint sound of continuous ringing. And silence.

Harriet was on the point of going round to the

back, leaving Sgt Wintercombe where he was, when the heavy green-painted door swung open.

A dapper-looking elderly man stood there, high-veined, skinny, red hand clasping the door's edge. Dark blue, brass-buttoned blazer, crisp white shirt, striped tie, black shoes shining with polish.

'Police,' Harriet said without ceremony, flipping her warrant card open almost under the narrow tanned face with its jauntily thin white moustache.

A pair of bright blue eyes looked up at the two of them speculatively.

'The boys in blue, eh? Or, not to put too fine a point on it, one female of the species in fetching black-and-white linen costume and one really in blue, sergeant's stripes.'

'We need to talk to you,' Harriet said. 'Inside.'

'Oh, certainly, certainly. Come in. Englishman's castle ever open to the forces of the law.'

He backed away from the door, and Harriet moved swiftly forward to occupy the space left, followed more ponderously by Sgt Wintercombe.

The spry little octogenarian led them into a large room, furnished as a study. Panelled walls, perhaps in oak, two long bookshelves filled with gloomy-looking leather-bound works of some sort, four brown-leather armchairs, well scuffed, Turkish carpet more than a little threadbare, writing-table bearing – Harriet had not seen anything like it since she was a child visiting an old uncle – a three-decanter tantalus. By contrast, tucked away in a far corner there was an aged-looking television set on a grey metal stand.

She began without ceremony, riding over the dapper little man's *What's all this? What? What?*

'Give me your name, please.'

'Name? Name? Jolly old monniker.'

'Please.'

'Youngman, as a matter of fact. Youngman by name, and, I always say, young man by nature. Even at ripe old age of eighty-one. Eighty-one, by George.'

'Notes, Sergeant.'

'Taking them, ma'am.'

'Forenames, please.'

'Ah, donated at birth by loving parents. The pater was an archdeacon, believed in dishing out the full complement. Stand by there with that pencil.'

'Just tell us.'

'Right, here goes. Patrick Angus Peregrine. How about that? P. A. P. Youngman, known at school as Pappy. Ruined my life.'

'But what are you called nowadays? Is it Patrick?'

If he is, then is this the end of as hopeful a lead as we've had yet?

'No, no. Not at all. Hate the name Patrick, people thinking I'm Irish, calling me Paddy. Even worse than Pappy, eh? Feller's parents ought to think before they go loading the son and heir with a collection like mine.'

'So what are you known as, sir?'

'Oh, Angus. Aberdeen Angus, what? Bit of a bull. Or was once. And still just a little bullish, on occasion. Can rise to it, you know. Can rise to it.'

And, standing in the middle of his gloomy, somewhat worse-for-wear study, he abruptly broke into a song-and-dance performance.

> Maybe it's because I'm a gentleman
> That I love ladies so,
> Jilly and Milly, and dear little Flo.

My troubles with Bubbles.
My heart's all a-glow.

'Bubbles?' Harriet snapped out, bringing the ridiculous little song drizzling to an end.

Yes, yes, yes. This could be it. It really could be. This little old man clearly an obsessive. Psychologist's pattern might come from a textbook, compulsively putting rhymes together. All right, he's eighty. Eighty-one, he said. But – what was it? – *still just a little bullish*. Sex impulse by no means dead then. John's instancing Saul Bellow, father at eighty-four or five. So that lightning-bolt hurled by Eros, can it have led to the Leven at dawn and the thrust-in weapon? It could, it could. What did Professor Polk say when I suggested no great force would be needed? *Yes*, he said. *Yes*.

It fits. It fits.

# Chapter Nine

Harriet looked at Patrick Angus Peregrine Youngman, writer of a three-sides turbulent love letter to murdered Bubbles Xingara, tennis darling. She took from her briefcase the poem Fiona Diplock had read out at the funeral, enclosed in its transparent plastic wallet, and held it out for him to see.

'You wrote this?'

Dapper little Angus Youngman gaped at the wallet, all the pertness abruptly sucked out of him.

'Did you write this poem?'

'I – I may have done. I suppose.'

'Yes or no, Mr Youngman? Did you write it?'

'Well, I – I wanted to pay tribute to Bubbles. She was – well, there's been nothing like her for years in the tennis world. I mean, I've been keen on tennis ever since I was a boy. The pater took me to Wimbledon when I was ten. You could do that in those days. It – it wasn't like today, thousands and thousands pushing and shoving and paying the earth to get in. And not all to see the tennis. You know, a clergyman was arrested for indecent assault there not so long ago. Clergyman, pressing up against schoolgirls leaning over a fence. What would my father have said? Letting down the cloth, giving way to . . . to all that.'

Here it is. The ever-hovering cloud. But why did

he bring up that case from the past? Because he couldn't help it? Because of what some Wimbledon experience of his own a year ago, two years ago, has triggered off in his mind? Something he's been striving to blot out?

Right. Go in.

'And you, Mr Youngman, did you visit Wimbledon last year?'

A long, perhaps fearful, pause.

'Come on, you've been following Bubbles Xingara round the tournaments for years, haven't you?'

'No. No, that's not true. I hadn't heard of her until she began to get into all the papers and they said what a little beauty she was. Thought I'd drop down to Eastbourne and see her then, and, when I did, I knew she was just wonderful. Wonderful.'

'And then you took to following her wherever she went. Yes?'

Had he, the bouncy little old man, pestered Bubbles? Pestered her once too often? Tried perhaps to seize hold of her and give her a kiss? Been treated to some stinging put-down? And then, the Leven at dawn . . .?

'No, no,' he said. 'Dare say I'd have liked to have gone wherever she went. Oh, I would have done. I would. Yes, indeed. But couldn't afford it, couldn't afford it. Fare to America, all that. No, no, had to be content with whenever she happened to play in England. Exhibition games, Eastbourne, and then I'd get myself a ticket for the whole of Wimbledon.'

So, not quite such a persistent worshipper? And, worse, he's slipping away from me. Change course.

'But you're not at Wimbledon now, are you, Mr

Youngman? Because something's happened to Bubbles, hasn't it?'

Little Angus Youngman took a faltering step backwards, allowed himself to sink into one of his scuffed leather armchairs.

'Poor Bubbles. Poor little kid.'

Wait. Is this it after all? The beginning of the cough? Those tears forming in his blue, blue eyes?

'Yes, poor Bubbles, as you say. Poor dead, murdered Bubbles. Now, why don't you tell us all about it? All about it, everything. Just tell us.'

'Tell you?'

He looked up.

'Mr Youngman, just what happened down by the Leven?'

'I – I don't know. You mean where Bubbles was murdered? But how should I know anything about that? Anything more than was on the television, in the papers?'

'There's one very good reason why you might know more about it. Isn't there, Mr Youngman?'

'Reason? What reason?'

'Why don't you tell us, Mr Youngman? Why don't you?'

'I – I don't know what you mean?'

'I think you do. Weren't you there? There by the river at Adam and Eve House?'

'No.'

The word shot out of him as if an internal spring had been triggered.

'You were at Adam and Eve House when Bubbles was killed, weren't you?'

'No. I said no. No, I wasn't. I – I've never been there. I didn't know that was where she – where

Bubbles lived till I read it in the paper the day after she was killed. I didn't. I didn't.'

'But you wrote to her, didn't you? You wrote while she was still alive? This.'

She pulled out the second plastic wallet and pushed it in front of his face. He stood for a long moment staring at the first of the three sheets of the chaotic outpouring. It seemed almost as if he was failing to recognize what it was he was looking at. But then he spoke.

'Yes. Yes, I sent that to her. I'm so pleased she saw it. You see – You see, I loved her. Yes, I loved her. I – I know I'm much too old for her. People would think it's ridiculous, but I did love her. I loved little Bubbles more than I ever loved anyone in my life.'

She looked down at him as he shrank sprawling back into the big leather chair.

Very different from *Maybe it's because I'm a gentleman*. And what does that tell me?

A sudden descent. What does that tell me? It tells me that, however little strength it may have taken to drive that smooth spike into Bubbles Xingara's neck, the feeble creature in front of me now is very unlikely to have done it.

As I should at least have suspected – the thought came tumbling at once into her head – if I hadn't been thinking with half of myself about something else. About Anselm.

No, don't dodge.

What I should have remembered was that this screed here in my hand was sent, not to Adam and Eve House, but to Bubbles care of the Lawn Tennis Association. Didn't he just confirm that? *I'm so pleased she saw it*. So this silly, shrinking old man never knew where Bubbles lived until he heard it on TV. After her death.

Yes, damn it, damn it, damn it. Another wild-goose chase.

It seemed, when Harriet got back to her office in Levenham, as if wild-goose chases of the sort that bedevil every eye-catching major inquiry were to be the order of the day. She had scarcely caught up with her messages when one of the DCs in the Incident Room below rang through to say they had *a weirdo* on an outside line.

'She's insisting on talking to you yourself, ma'am, the Hard Detective,' he said, and then gave a suppressed chuckle. 'Or at least her actual words were *the Firm Detective*. But I guess that's you, ma'am.'

'Right. But I don't want to know. You must have dealt with women like her before. Probably wants to tell me she could lay hands on the murderer by psychic means. Put one of the women DCs on the line, and let her think she's talking to me.'

She put her phone down and turned back to the pile of reports that had accumulated even in the short time that she had been over in Boreham.

But before long there came a tap at her door and, in answer to her sharply irritated *Come*, one of the Birchester WDCs came in.

'It's Johnson, isn't it? What is it?'

Putting an evidently brave face on it, WDC Johnson advanced to the desk.

'Ma'am, I've just been taking a call from the woman you said I was to let think I was you.'

'Well, how did that go? Bark a bit, did you?'

WDC Johnson grinned.

'I think I managed to convey I was heading the team without resorting to anything like that.'

'So why have you come to me now?'

'Ma'am, I'm sorry but – well, I'm sort of sure there's more to this than some crank trying it on. Ma'am, she sort of said, as far as I could make out from all her toings and froings, she was wanting to confess to the job.'

'Oh, come on, Johnson. We've had half a dozen like that already.'

'But, ma'am, there was something . . . I mean, she sounded pretty barmy a lot of the time. But there was one bit that made me wonder if she knew something.'

'So what did she say? Exactly.'

'It was this. I think I've got the words. *I speared her. I had to do it. I thrust the javelin in.* Then she went off on a great rambling spiel about conquering the Evil One. Or something. She was speaking so fast, I couldn't really make it out.'

'A javelin? She spoke about a javelin? You're sure?'

'Absolutely, ma'am.'

Harriet thought.

Not certain just what a javelin's like. Used in athletics. So . . . So, yes, it could very well have the sort of spike that . . .

'You got a name? An address?'

'She suddenly went all shy when I asked her, ma'am. I think she may have cottoned on she wasn't speaking to *the Firm Detective*. To you, ma'am. But she had said something about somewhere called Grainham Hall. At least I think it was *Grainham*. She was gabbling away so fast.'

'No, you're quite likely right. Grainham Hall's a big independent school just north of Birchester. And – And it's got a reputation for its sporting record. So there could well be javelins about. And, what's more, Bubbles Xingara was once a pupil there. Good work, Johnson. Good work.'

'Thank you, ma'am.' And an unstoppable blush.

It might, she thought when Johnson had left, it just might be kosher. Confessions, of course, two a penny. But those few words Johnson quoted. *I thrust the javelin in.* As far as I know there's been nothing in the papers or anywhere else in the media about the weapon being a javelin.

She picked up her green internal phone and got through to the Incident Room.

'Is DI Brent there? Put him on, if he is.'

Damn it all, she had thought, DI Brent – oh, hell, Anselm then – is a senior officer under my command. Just because . . . Just because, damn and blast it, I think I am in love with him. No, just because I am in love with him I can't cease making use of him.

But perhaps it's better if I do it without us coming face to face. That last time, watching him admit to defeat in Marseilles and having to stop myself defending him, was more than enough.

As it was, his voice over the phone, with that touch of Levenham burr, almost undid her. She had to grip hard on the edge of the desk.

'DI. We've had a call from a woman at Grainham Hall, where Bubbles was once at school, you know.'

'I remember, ma'am.'

A steady enough reply. So long as this could be kept to that level.

'She's a confesser, or seems to be. But she may just possibly be the real thing. She said something – I didn't take her pretty confused call myself, WDC Johnson did – about having thrust in a javelin. Presumably one of the ones used in athletics. And that's made me think this ought to be further investigated. You've seen that wound. It could well have been inflicted by something like a javelin. So, listen, she wouldn't give a name, but she did indicate she came from Grainham Hall. Talk to Johnson, get as much out of her as you can. Then first thing in the morning go over there and see if you can track her down.'

'Yes, ma'am.'

The phone at the far end put down. All done in safety.

At home that night as she dropped into her usual chair and took the first long swallow of the whisky-and-ginger John had brought her she told him – she would tell no one else – how wrong she had got it about old Mr Youngman. She kept back, however, not without a pang of conscience, the reason she had not taken into account that the love-tormented scrawlings of the *Angus* letter had been sent to Bubbles via the Lawn Tennis Association in London. Anselm, if he was to be spoken of, must be left to another day.

After all, she argued, John's said more than once over the years since he became the Majestic's chief negotiator and liable to long stays abroad that if in his absence I felt some overwhelming sexual urge I could do what I allow him to do. But, no, if this is different . . . If Aphrodite really has come in on Eros' heels, it's all very much more serious. But sex and love. They're not to be measured in percentages. I can't stick some litmus paper into my head and see whether it comes out blue (swift attack of lust) or pink (in grip of obsessive love).

And, even if it is the coils that can knot two human beings together so blindly, those coils can fall away. Love doesn't always last for ever, never mind what the romantic poets say. If I am in love with Anselm Brent at this moment, it doesn't mean I still shall be in – what? – another moment's time. Or, in a day's time. Or a week's. I don't have to be in love with him for ever. Look at what nearly happened between John and myself at the very beginning. When, after wrapping bloody Aphrodite's coils round and round myself just knowing this sexy chap as *John*, I learnt he was *John Piddock*. I felt the coils loosen then. I swear I did. I can recall the moment now. So maybe when I learn something about Anselm, something however odd, that jars horribly, then it'll all go away.

And it'd be stupid to do a big confession thing to John now if that's going to happen.

But I don't want it to. I don't want it to.

But hardly had she finished her tale about dapper little Angus Youngman when abruptly all the paths seemed to be leading towards just that confession.

'Well, yes,' John had said, 'didn't I tell you the other day that age makes no difference to the omnipresence of the sexual impulse? From eighty down to eight, we're all liable at any moment to be struck down.'

She reacted to that ominous *we're all liable* more sharply than she might have done.

'Oh, nonsense. Eighty I'll concede. God knows, I've just had all the example of that I could want. But eight? No. Never.'

He laughed.

'Exaggerating a bit, I admit. Led away by a piece of alliteration. But up that figure just a little, to, say, thirteen, and you're well inside the target area. I don't know about thirteen-year-old schoolgirls of your time, but I promise you when I was that age the hormones were really throbbing. And not only in me, in every other boy I knew. We none of us could wait till, as the more sophisticated among us put it, we'd got rid of our virginity. We were swept onwards by the cloud of sexuality, about which we didn't have the faintest understanding, on towards that simple generative act it seeks to make us arrive at.'

'Well, to be honest, I don't remember too much about myself at thirteen. I suppose I did know about your *simple act*, though I dare say I may have had friends who didn't. But it's true enough, by the time we'd got to fourteen or so most of the girls at school could think of little else but boys, unless someone held their heads, our heads, my head, firmly down to our textbooks, or perhaps to hockey sticks.'

'Exactly. But how much was ever said in public about that, forty years ago? No, it's really only more recently that the ever-interesting subject – and it's not called that for nothing – has been allowed to come to the forefront the way it has.'

'Well, I wish it hadn't. Think how much more interesting the papers would be if there was something other than the sex-angle to every story.'

'Ah, but, you see, there is a sex-angle to every story. Or – must stop exaggerating – to almost every story. And it's not always so obvious that it gets into print. And even when it did, in the pre-Victorian days for example, it quickly enough got supplanted by a version people were happier with. Nobody – or, well, hardly anybody – wants actually to acknowledge the omnipresence of sex. Altogether too much to cope with.'

'Another John Piddock theory looming into view? You're ruddy incorrigible.'

'No, let me give you an instance. Take the eighteenth century in England. What do we think of it as being?'

Harriet blinked.

'You want me to answer that?'

'Yes, come on. Put your hand up. *Miss, miss, I know. I know.*'

'Well, I don't know if I do. But I suppose I'd say it's sort of elegance. A land of art and elegance. Didn't somebody call it that? You see, I did read books, once.'

'Yes, well, thank you, answer I hoped for. An age of elegance and good manners. But did you know that in London at that time there were as many as twenty-five thousand women prostitutes? In the trade, as it's often put. Because it was trade, and trade of considerable proportions, affecting – and this is my point – the whole economy of the city. Ubiquitous sex. There was a guide to the various women available, names, specialities, the lot. All right, the same thing, more or less, goes on in Birchester today, and most of the other big cities. But in those days London was a much smaller place, and so these activities really affected the whole of society, economically just as much as morally. There were fortunes to be made in the trade. One woman, Moll King she was called, started out with a coffee house, that's to say, a brothel, and ended up building a whole street in a fashionable part of north London. It was known then as Moll King Street. And astronomical prices were paid for sex, as much as twenty guineas. God knows what that would be in today's money. And more. More was paid by one lady of quality, fifty guineas, to be, I quote, *well mounted!*

'John, is all this getting to you? Or what?'

A self-deprecating laugh.

'No, not really. Or only in a strictly intellectual sense. Your virtue is safe, madam. At least for the present.'

Well, yes, she thought. But the trouble is I don't want it to be safe. Not safe from Anselm anyhow. Oh, God. Oh, God, I'd like to be in bed with him. Now, now, now.

She might even have told John then, after all. I could do, she thought. Didn't he once get tangled in Aphrodite's long hair himself? That woman in Delhi he eventually told me about.

But John was clattering on.

'No, let me give you another example. A better one really. Sex between man and woman affecting the destiny of at least one nation. Queen Elizabeth the First. Did you know she was, it's fully come to light recently in a biography by— Damn it, I've forgotten the name. A Professor Somebody. No, wait. I made a note.'

Harriet waited, amusedly patient, while he rummaged in the pocket of his slightly the worse-for-wear summer jacket. Half a dozen tattered and battered pieces of paper, cards and receipts, examined, discarded. Then he hit on what he was looking for, an old envelope.

'Yes. Of course. Starkey, Professor David Starkey. And he said Elizabeth was sexually molested by the married man who was both her uncle and her guardian, Thomas Seymour. Contemporary documents go into some detail. So, guess what effect that had, first, on her, turning her into a woman who distrusted all men. And then, more importantly, that distrust affected the course of national life. She refused to marry, became the Virgin Queen, although old Eros put in front of her various courtiers and at least one foreign prince. And that meant she never did her duty in providing an heir to the English throne. So afterwards what happened? Chaos. Rebellion. Every kind of trouble, and all because of the ubiquitous cloud.'

'Well, I certainly didn't know all that. And I see, yes, it's a good argument for the power of your great god Eros.'

'You should read more. It'd make you less ignorant.'

'Oh, thanks, mastermind. But has it ever occurred to you that a really major inquiry such as the Bubbles Xingara business probably spawns more words than ever Shakespeare wrote? And who has to read those words? Every one of them eventually? Yours truly.'

'Okay, okay. As you know, I'd be the last to denigrate that sort of reading, whether in the end it produces an answer or not.'

'*Or not* may be right in this case. Nothing so doomed to failure as what we call *a stranger murder*. I could be looking for almost anyone in the whole United Kingdom. Or, worse, the tennis world stretches from America to Australia, and Bubbles could have become a target for a really obsessed stalker from anywhere.'

'Don't say the Hard Detective's on the point of throwing in the towel.'

'No, no. Of course I'm not. No, if whoever killed Bubbles is to be dug out of the woodwork, then I'm going to dig them out. But, God knows, it may take a year. It may take even more.'

Depression welled up in her.

And, at once, a secret antidote suggested itself.

# A DETECTIVE IN LOVE

Why not give way to Eros, wrap myself altogether in Aphrodite's coils? Why not, like John's eighteenth-century lady of quality, pay my fifty guineas, or pay whatever confessing to John will cost me, to be *well mounted*. Well mounted by Anselm.

I could. I could risk everything, husband, job, everything. And escape into a life of love.

# Chapter Ten

There came the sudden sound of noisy voices on the garden path outside. The doorbell rang, pealing out under a steadily pressed thumb.

'You know what?' Harriet said. 'It must be the twins.'

'Oh, God. I meant to tell you. Graham rang just before you got back, saying they were on their way. Bringing piles of dirty washing, no doubt, and saying they're due back at college tomorrow or the next day.'

'Thank you, my learned friend. And I suppose now I've got to get them some supper with, like as not, nothing at all in the fridge.'

She pushed herself up, went to the door, unbolted its locks and opened it.

Graham and Malcolm came barging in, lugging a suitcase apiece, and submitted to being kissed.

'Supper?' Harriet asked, realizing only now how their arrival had saved her from blurting out to John what had happened to her.

'Great, Mum.'

She went into the kitchen, opened the fridge, saw a packet of sausages and a large box of eggs.

Oh dear. Done provident John an injustice. Ought to have given him more credit. But now it's exit the Hard Detective, if that's what I still am. And enter the Earth Mother.

Then, as she busied herself with the cooking, she found unexpected and contradictory thoughts slowly marching through her head.

Earth Mother. Well, there's something to be said for that role. Not a role perhaps to give up being a police officer for, but worth combining with being a useful police officer? So, then, is it worth giving up both Hard Detective and Earth Mother to become lost in love? A harder nut to crack.

Okay, I've just been saved from making the decision. By the skin of my teeth. Because I really do think if the boys had come just ten minutes later John would have known everything. And I'd have said something like, *My tousle-headed blond lover weighs equal in the scales to your dazzlingly beautiful Indian lady.* And then would I have said more? That I'm throwing over everything, you John, the twins, all our past life, because I've been struck down by Eros and encoiled by Aphrodite?

I think I might have done. Would have done. I'm caught. Yes, caught.

When the right circumstances come, tomorrow, or next week, or some time next month, I can see myself seizing on them. Seizing on poor unaware Anselm. Crushing him. Crushing him with kisses. Until I have him. Have him as mine.

The sausages had had long enough under the grill. The eggs in the pan, four of them, had just got to the point the twins liked, a little harder for Graham, a little more runny for Malcolm.

She dished them on to the plates waiting on the tray and took them into the waiting appetites in the dining-room.

'Hey, Mum, you should hear the time we've been having down in the Smoke,' Malcolm lunged out.

'Oh, but better is how we got the cash for it,' Graham broke in, spluttering with laughter.

'You're going to tell us,' John said. 'So tell us.'

'We sold ourselves,' Graham claimed.

'No, no, we did better than that,' Malcolm announced. 'We sold a whole lot of future little Grahams and Malcolms.'

'Yes. Our future offspring, in great gobbets of spunk. We joined the sperm donation thing at Uni. And got paid per ejaculation. How about that?'

John looked over at Harriet.

'What we were talking about,' he said. 'The thunderous pressure of the sexual urge. So powerful that, apart from whatever these young men may have been doing in various beds, they still have enough of the urge to procreate, little though they realize that's what it is, to make them rush off to do it into test tubes. They think it's only to earn a bit of extra cash, but it's just that urge, implanted in them, to perform that almost momentary act.'

Perhaps he's right, Harriet thought. And what does Earth Mother feel about her little boys being so boastful about their sexual energies? Heaven knows, heaven knows.

And then, again, a picture of Anselm came into her mind, vague in outline but potent. Christ, she thought, that's what I'd like. What I want, want, want. Anselm's spunk in me, deep, deep inside me. Oh, God.

What shall I do when I see him next? Tomorrow. What shall I do tomorrow?

\*

But next day in her cramped little office at the top of
Levenham police station it was not Anselm, DI Brent,
she saw but Handy Andy, DI Anderson.

'Morning, ma'am. Got a bit of news for you. Good
news, I think.'

He smiled down at her, white teeth flashing wide.
*I'm a good boy. Don't I deserve a kiss?*

'I could do with good news, DI,' she said, her voice
a cold shower. 'Let's hear.'

'Oh, well. Well, it's this. I was over at Adam and
Eve House yesterday evening, and—'

'What were you doing there? I don't remember
tasking you with anything that would take you there.'

He grinned.

'More of a private visit, actually. You know there's
a permanent police presence there.'

'Who do you think ordered it, DI? Before you even
joined the team.'

'Yes.'

He had the grace to look a little sheepish now.

'Yes, ma'am. Of course.' The uncharacteristic look
faded rapidly away. 'Well, the fact is last night one of
the Levenham WPCs was over there, and I thought she
might like a bit of company.'

'Are you telling me you went there with the object
of making sexual advances while she was on duty?'

That plainly came as a shock.

'Er – no. No, ma'am. That is, I just wanted to keep
the poor girl company. It's no fun doing that sort of
duty.'

'It's not meant to be fun, DI. And I don't want to
hear you've been doing anything of that sort again, not
while you're under my command. Understood?'

'Yes, ma'am.'

She could see him making up his mind to turn and leave.

'You said you had some information for me, DI. If it's relevant to the inquiry let me hear it.'

'Yes, well, I think it is relevant. Or it may be. You see, while I was there I also talked to Fiona Dipcock. Sorry, ma'am, Diplock.'

'I warn you, Mr Anderson, you're in a fair way to being sent back to Birchester, and with a disciplinary charge to speed you on your way.'

'Yes, ma'am. But all the same I think you'll be glad to know what – ' he paused, meaningfully – 'what Miss Diplock told me. What I got out of her in the end.'

'I'll be the judge of that.'

'Yes, ma'am. Well, what she said was this: a few days before Bubbles was killed she apparently had some sort of a row with someone who accosted her down by the boathouse there, just where she was murdered in fact. Fiona didn't have any details. Apparently she hadn't been very interested in what Bubbles had told her. Wasn't all that much love lost there, I think. Fiona, who doesn't think much about anybody but herself, says she never thought about it again. Until something I was telling her about major inquiries like ours jogged her memory. Bit of serendipity I was chatting to her really.'

Oh, no, you don't, Handy Andy, she thought. You're bloody lucky I've let you get away with as much as I have. You needn't think I'm going to congratulate you on a smart piece of work. More a smart-arse piece of work.

'Right. You did well to let me know this. I think I'll go over to Adam and Eve House later on and have a word with Miss Diplock myself.'

She pushed back her chair when Handy Andy had gone, stood up and began to pace up and down the cramped office.

Yes, a stranger to that wide lawn at the big old house, whoever Bubbles' killer might be, but more than likely they had not been entirely a stranger to Bubbles herself. Something she had done, quite unconsciously perhaps, had possibly in that mysterious way – like . . . like the sudden unexpected sight of a tennis player's calloused hand – set off in someone's mind a powder trail of obsessive longing . . .

To and fro she paced. Up to the room's single dust-powdered window, opened as much as it would go this stifling day, away back to stare at a calendar on the far wall, *Compliments of Levenham Chamber of Commerce*. Turn and stamp up to the window again.

But that incident, whatever it was, something perhaps sharper than that exchange with a cheeky fan that Anselm told me he'd read about – at Eastbourne, was it? *Who's your boyfriend? Who's yours?* – might have triggered an obsession with Bubbles. And that might . . .

Too many *mights*? Well, perhaps. Or perhaps not. But some such incident might have led whoever it was to track Bubbles down to Adam and Eve House, find out that she went for her early-mornings runs and then accost her. And Bubbles might well, at such a time as that, have felt a spit of temper, dealt with the intruder as vigorously as she was said to have dealt with Pierre le Fou.

And then . . . Then afterwards she may have been, if only for a day or two, worried or upset or even simply amused by whatever it was. And might, casually, have mentioned it to Fiona.

Up and down again. Dusty window, calendar, window. Puff of sluggish air coming in. Turn and tramp back.

But what if this person, smarting under that rebuff administered when they had had a lover's hopes of success, Eros' imperative answered as eagerly as it was put . . . What if they had returned to the Leven at dawn that day with murder in mind.

Up again to the window and its faint waft of slightly cooler air.

So if . . .

Down below in the street a noisy band of boys dressed in sports gear was going by, blocking most of the pavement, shouting and shoving and pretending to threaten the occasional passer-by with the oars from the kayaks which three or four of them were holding perched upside-down over their heads. Two teachers shepherding them paying little attention.

Discipline, she thought momentarily, why will nobody enforce it? Even here in Levenham they could do with some tough policing. All right, it must be near the end of term and some high spirits to be expected, but to let that mob go noisily by . . .

Train of thought about what Bubbles might or might not have told Fiona finally interrupted, she wondered for a moment if Anselm's nephew – what was his name? Yes, Jonathan – was one of the mischief-makers. Or would the lad, destined for the police, take after his big uncle? Be naturally law-abiding? But, in any case, Jonathan didn't seem to be in the boisterous procession, though she thought she had seen, trailing behind, his lumpier friend.

Boy who scrunched up my autograph. Cheeky bugger.

Then, of course, her picture of Anselm swam suddenly into pulsating view. She suppressed it hard. Cling on to peace of mind as long as it seemed to be there.

When Harriet got to Adam and Eve House she took Fiona Diplock out to the big lawn at the back. It was in any case a more comfortable place to be than anywhere inside. If June had been a dry month, July was proving even hotter, reducing the Leven beside the house to a mere thread of slow-running water as darkly green as the heavy enervated foliage of the syringa bush at the corner of the old house. The grass of the lawn that had been biscuit-coloured in June was now almost shrivelled away. The heat-baked house even appeared to be somehow shrinking in on itself.

But there was another and better reason to be out on the lawn. In the patch of shade beside the old boathouse, almost at the exact spot where Bubbles, Fiona's friend or perhaps secret enemy, had been killed, it might be possible to get out of her more than she had said in idle conversation with Handy Andy. If idle conversation was all that had taken place between him and his *Miss Dipcock*.

After a little chat, about of course the weather, Harriet began.

'I asked if you could spare a few minutes because of something Detective Inspector Anderson told me you had said to him.'

Do I detect a hint of a blush beneath the tan on that smoothly blue-eyed, carefully pink-lipped face?

'Oh, yes? What was that?'

'You said, if he remembered your conversation correctly, that some time before Miss Xingara was killed she told you she had had some sort of a confrontation with someone who had come up to her as she finished her morning run.'

'Oh, yes. I believe I did mention that. And when it came to mind – I can't remember what brought it back to me – I did wonder if I shouldn't have told some police officer about it earlier on. But—'

A girlish giggle that hardly sat well with the cool-as-mint personality she generally presented to the world. A hint of something unresolved lying there beneath? A glint of guilt that her relations with generous little Bubbles had not been all they might have been? Or guilt even that she had occupied a place in Bubbles' stepfather's mind that rightly belonged to his wife?

'But what, Miss Diplock?'

Touch of sharpness needed here.

Now Fiona Diplock did blush, a deep flush coming up under the tan and the red of the day's heat.

'But – well, you see, I couldn't have told one of you if I had totally forgotten about it, could I?'

'And you had totally forgotten? Totally? It didn't come to mind now and again, and you decided not to mention it?'

'No.' Something not far short of a shout of denial.

'Very well. If you're certain of that.' Keep her disorientated. 'So perhaps now you should tell me everything you remember Miss Xingara saying to you about the incident. Everything.'

'Yes, yes. I will. I'll try. But she only spoke about it once, and it was quite a long time ago.'

'Nevertheless, you should be able to recall a good deal, if you concentrate, about something so relevant to the terrible thing that happened—'

She broke off. Swung round. Pointed with deliberate drama to the place where on the day of the murder that hideously bright blue tent had stood.

'That happened there.'

She saw, with a glint of pleasure, Fiona Diplock go noticeably paler for one brief moment before her face resumed the flush the hot day had brought to it.

'Right. Now, as much as you can remember.'

'Well . . . Well, Bubbles just sort of mentioned it one day. It was— Yes, I'm sure you're right, or . . . And – Inspector Anderson was. Yes, probably about a week before – before poor Bubbles . . .'

'Go on.'

'Well, she said that she had just come in from her run, and – and she was anxious to get into the boat-house, have her shower there and wait for Peter – that is, wait for Mr Renshaw to come down and take her blood pressure, as he always did, and then to suggest what work she should do on the machines.'

'Good. You're recalling something at least.'

For an instant she wondered if she should seize the opportunity to find out if in fact Peter Renshaw had been detained that morning in Fiona's bed. But, no, the details of this dawn confrontation down by the river were what counted. Something might lead to the very person who had come to this very spot a few days later. With, in all probability, a javelin.

And Fiona seemed ready to go on.

'Well then, Bubbles said, this person— She never actually mentioned whether it was a man or a woman. I think all the time she just kept saying *they* and *someone*. She said this person suddenly came up and I don't know . . . I expect asked for her autograph. People were always doing that. And then, I gathered, somehow a real argument developed. Bubbles said something about giving the person, whoever it was, a bloody good kick, or something, knocking them to the ground. I expect Bubbles thought it was a hell of a cheek, when she must have been covered in sweat and needing to get indoors, for someone to ask her to sign their damn autograph book.'

Abruptly Harriet thought of the day when Anselm had asked her if she would sign his nephew's autograph book. Which had she chosen, the green page or the pink? And Anselm? Had he by then realized, even subconsciously, that she had a special regard for him? Felt she would be willing to do almost anything he might ask?

Oh, God, *a special regard*. That's hardly what I felt even then. And not in any way what I feel now.

She knew then that it had all come rushing back, had filled her to capacity. Love. Aphrodite, the enchanter, in full blazing light.

Oh, God, I love you, Anselm. I love you, love you, love you.

# Chapter Eleven

Little else emerged about the dawn encounter. It was, Harriet thought, an oddly mysterious affair, with even the identity of the other party, man or woman, tauntingly vague. But tauntingly vague it all remained, even though she had pressed Fiona hard.

She had gone as far as she could. Pressing too hard, she had long ago learnt, is apt to produce an obstinate silence. The really hard detective knows when not to be hard.

Did I even let myself forget that with Fiona, she asked herself. And, worse, was that because my mind had, suddenly, shot off to . . .? To Anselm, Anselm, Anselm. If I'd been paying more attention, would I have succeeded in easing out of the recesses of Fiona's memory a word or two extra about what Bubbles said? And would it have helped?

The terrible thing is it might have done. Has love ended what might have been my chance of resolving the case? Love that overwhelming whatever. If I'd been doing my job as I ought to have been, would I at this minute be driving away from Adam and Eve House with perhaps just one detail about Bubbles' murderer that could lead to a positive identification?

Well, perhaps not.

Perhaps that early-morning row in the mists rising

from the river – and it may not even have been as serious as a full-blown row – was no more than a minor, half-forgotten incident in the life of a busy, happy tennis star. Quite likely the secret of who brought that life to a sudden unthinkable end lies somewhere else altogether. Like in the mind of a woman at the school where Bubbles once was?

She put her foot down a little harder on the gas pedal.

At once a new thought came into her head. All right, over in Levenham there may be news that the weird telephone caller wanting *the Firm Detective* is something other than a run-of-the-mill compulsive confessor. It may be she's ready to confess, in accurate terms. But who is it who's going to be there in my office with that news? Anselm is.

And what'll happen when I see him? Is it possible, really possible, that instead of saying coolly, *Well, Mr Brent, what did you find out over there at Grainham Hall?* I'll rush up to him, wrap my arms round him, kiss him till my probing, loving tongue can go no further into him?

In one instant my whole career thrown away like – like that dirty scrap of paper with my signature and *Join the Police* which that boy got rid of so dismissively?

She found her foot had eased back on the gas.

Love. Bloody love, what a puzzle it is. Think. How can it be I have these feelings for Anselm, be-damned-to-everything feelings, and yet in bed at home with John, back on the nights when I've not been too exhausted, we made love. And it wasn't at all any duty-bound coupling.

How was it, too, I felt not the slightest jolt of disloyalty to my feelings for Anselm then? That equally

I never felt for an instant *This is deceiving my husband even as we embrace?*

Yes, the desk sergeant at Levenham said, DI Brent had come in. Just five minutes ago. He was in the Incident Room.

Harriet felt a lowering of relief. Surely in front of all the detectives busy at monitor screens or with ears clamped to telephones or perhaps sitting back with a coffee she would not give way completely. In the Incident Room, if anywhere, she could meet Anselm and contrive to behave as if the Hard Detective was merely asking DI Brent how his inquiry had gone.

But she still felt a tautening of all the muscles in her abdomen as she thrust open the door.

Anselm, DI Brent, thatch of untidy fair hair, flowerpot-ruddy face, four-square frame, everything that was at instant call in her mind, was standing there with a mug in his hand beside her own table at the top of the room. Handy Andy, DI Anderson, was sitting nearby, looking up at him with a broad grin.

'Oh, come on, Saintie,' she heard him say, 'la Dipcock must have sent something down to your apparatus. She's a hundred per cent come-on, despite the don't-touch-me look.'

*Saintie*, she thought at once. So that's what Handy Andy has taken to calling Anselm. Trust him to seize on that link with St Anselm's Church to mock at someone who could be a competitor.

She walked up to them. With steps that she forced herself to make, not relaxed, but perfectly normal.

'Well, DI,' she said to Anselm, 'any joy at Grainham Hall?'

Anselm gave her a plainly hangdog look.

Oh, God, she thought at once, he's failed somehow.

It'll be another pretty well useless affair like the Marseilles one. And I've stupidly made him own up to it bang in front of cocky Handy Andy. Oh, my poor Anselm.

Her first quick reaction proved right.

'No, I'm sorry to say, ma'am, I just got nowhere over there.' An exasperated sigh. 'I've never met such a stuck-up, la-di-dah lot in all my born days. I dunno, but somehow they made me feel like – well, as if I was not fit to set foot indoors without wiping my boots.'

*You got nowhere? Nowhere?* The Hard Detective in her wanted to snap out And the love-struck woman? God knows what she wanted to say. To offer comfort? To fold him in her arms?

But she said nothing. Waited.

'I did get to find out who our caller is, all right,' Anselm stumbled on. 'But that was all. She's a Miss Mackintosh. Miss Prudence Mackintosh. She was a sports teacher at the school till a few years ago. Still lives somewhere near, it came out. But when I asked for the address they just wouldn't tell me. *Oh, no, no, officer* – just as if I was no more than a stupid constable – *we can't give out addresses just like that.'*

Down at the nearby table she saw Handy Andy raise his dark eyebrows till it looked as if they would slide off the top of his head.

Oh, why, why did I let my Anselm in for this? I could have asked him to come up to my office. Most natural thing in the world.

But – But in there, with the door closed, what might I have done?

'And you left it there, DI?' she said, forcing herself at last to speak as she would to an inefficient probationer.

Anselm flushed, a sudden heated scarlet.

'No. No, ma'am. 'Course not. I repeated to them that I was a police officer, Detective Inspector I said. Told them I was fully entitled to have that address. And – And they just looked at me. Lady who said she was the Bursar, something like that, and her assistant. *I think we would need to speak with someone of more authority before we release confidential information.*'

'That's bloody nonsense, DI.'

And then because she could not, with Handy Andy sitting there looking pleased, say anything that might seem to be letting Anselm down lightly she went on, 'Bloody nonsense, and you know it.'

But this only made Anselm put himself in an even worse light.

'Yes, ma'am,' he said in a mutter, 'I do know it. I did know it. But – But, well, I just couldn't outface those two stuck-up cows, and there it is.'

And now Handy Andy, inadmissibly, put his oar in.

'Like me to pop over there, ma'am? See if I can't knock some sense into them?'

She knew she should round on him and put him firmly in his place. It was what she would have done in similar circumstances at any time. But would that be too obviously coming to the defence of her shorn lamb? No. No, a lamb treated as DI Brent had been treated by a fellow officer could rightly feel entitled to some defence.

But this isn't *DI Brent*. It's Anselm, the man I'm through and through in love with. And won't Handy Andy, sex expert, be able to seize on even the smallest indication in the way I defend his fellow officer? Add it to other tiny signs he's noticed? Be put within inches of my secret?

'Yes, DI,' she said, turning to him. 'Yes, I think you might well do that. Get over to Grainham just as soon as you like.'

She turned and left the room.

Handy Andy returned from Grainham Hall just after six that evening. He brought with him, under arrest, Miss Prudence Mackintosh, aged seventy-two, former tennis teacher under whose guidance Bubbles Xingara, twelve, had quite suddenly become a potential Wimbledon winner.

'Yes, boss,' he said. 'Piece of cake really. Bursar there at the school gave me her address, no trouble. Didn't even have to say I was a DI. So then I went round there and the old duck treated me to a cup of tea, Darjeeling, and straight away coughed from here to kingdom come.'

Harriet could not but be bitterly conscious how much more effective Handy Andy had shown himself than socially overwhelmed Anselm. But she fought to conceal any glimpse of that feeling.

'Very good, DI,' she said. 'So we'll have her down to an interview room and get it all on to tape.'

She didn't add, *And then with any luck we'll have resolved the case.* Something prevented her. The last nail in Anselm's coffin?

Instead, almost without thinking, she abruptly added one thing more.

'I think I'll have Mr Brent sitting in. He may have some useful input.'

Had Handy Andy challenged this, she would have been hard put to say what input Anselm could possibly have. After all, he had done no more than go over to the smart school where Bubbles had begun her upward flight, and there be turned away as a clodhopper not fit to talk to a former teacher, much less question her. He was hardly going to have anything worthwhile to say as Prudence Mackintosh's formal confession to killing Bubbles Xingara was recorded.

But she had said he should be present, and Handy Andy had scarcely manifested a hinted disagreement.

Oh, God, she thought, he's just filed away one more piece of evidence against me. Perhaps the last piece. Does he know for certain now that Harriet Martens, the Hard Detective, darling of the media, has absolutely blotted her copybook in falling absurdly in love with an absurdly naïve and absurdly countrified subordinate?

Prudence Mackintosh was led in. An elderly stubby little woman, if still with something of sprightliness in her step. Square face untouched by any make-up, grey hair cut short and firmly brushed into order. Softly grey eyes, contriving to be watchful and – Harriet thought – open a little too wide, with surely a touch of wrought-up excitement in them. Mouth, however, held rigidly straight. White blouse, an amber necklace just showing at its neck, pleated grey skirt, 'sensible' shoes.

'Please, sit down, Miss Mackintosh,' she said. 'I understand from Detective Inspector Anderson here that you wish to make a statement about the death of Miss Bubbles Xingara. But first I must ask you if you wish to have a solicitor present, your own or one we can find for you.'

'What I have to say will be simple enough. I wish to con—(

'No, Miss Mackintosh. I gather that the statement you want to make to us will be about a very serious matter that may affect your whole future. So, once again, may I suggest that you should have a solicitor.'

'Unnecessary.'

Harriet sighed.

'Very well. Now I am going to ask my colleague, Detective Inspector Brent, to state, for the benefit of these recording tapes, one of which will be sealed and handed to you or your representative, the time and place of this interview together with the names of the people present. Go ahead, DI.'

While Anselm was working his way through the preliminaries she asked herself why she had given him the task rather than Handy Andy. Is it as a mere sop to his pride? To give him some part in what's going to be a competitor's triumph? Or is it in fact to punish him? For failing to be the man I wanted him to be?

No telling. Love buggering up all rational thought.

She came to herself realizing Anselm's voice – that slight burr that sent through her a trickle of beating joy – had fallen silent.

God, have they all been waiting for me to begin? No, perhaps only seconds have gone by, if that.

She leant forward across the table and looked Prudence Mackintosh full in the face.

'Miss Mackintosh, what is it you have got to tell us about the death of Miss Bubbles Xingara?'

'That I killed her.'

So here it is. The confession. The end of the case.

And, the thought sprang at once into her mind, the thought she should not have been having, it could be the end, too, of my – what will it have been? – my temporary acquaintance with this not very forceful detective, DI Brent. Oh, yes, magistrates' court to come, the trial, too, in due course, probably in Birchester, bound to be noisy and nasty demonstrations outside, best place for it. But at those Anselm will be no more than a figure on the periphery. The man I have come to love. That I still love. Love despite shortcomings I would despise in myself. My Anselm. Anselm of the thick-skinned right palm.

Once more she brought herself to concentrate on the sturdy little woman with the square face and complacently resolute look.

'Very well,' she said to her, 'you tell me you killed Bubbles Xingara. So, first of all, why? Why did you do it?'

Here was a question which, it was at once plain, Prudence Mackintosh had decided she was not going to answer. Mute of self-malice.

'Look, Miss Mackintosh, it's not enough for us, the police, to go to the Crown Prosecution Service, and say here's a cast-iron case for bringing someone to court for murder. We have to show them we have something more than those three words you spoke just now, *I killed her*. All right, a jury cannot be asked to convict on evidence of motive and nothing else, and I shall shortly ask you for an account of what actually happened on the morning of June the twentieth last. But we need to back up such facts as emerge with a reason for you committing this act. This terrible, appalling act.'

Still the set expression. The stating, *I've told you I killed her, that is all I have to tell.*

Once more into battle then. To say the same thing, over and over again. Until she breaks.

But unexpectedly Handy Andy on the other side of her leant forward.

'It was love,' he said. 'It was love, wasn't it, Prue? You loved Bubbles when she was a schoolkid, and when she waltzed away from you that love of yours turned to plain and simple hate. Didn't it? You can tell me. I know all about things like that.'

Yes, Harriet thought at once, you do, sexual expert, know about that sort of thing. You must have had dozens, scores, of girls hate you after you'd got what you wanted out of them. And no doubt you're right about *Prue*.

*Prue*, how dare you call her that, you crude bastard? But the crude bastard had got it right.

'Yes, I loved her, she was the light of my life.' It came pouring out now. 'Why didn't she stay at Grainham? She could have learnt just as much from me as from that beastly, stupid American coach she was given. Cacoyannis. What does some horrible Greek know about tennis? And he was sacked by Bubbles' stepfather, wasn't he? I've followed every word about my Bubbles. Of course I have. But that stepfather was no better. A man like that knows nothing about coaching. Nothing.'

'All right.'

Harriet – Harriet in love, far now from being the Hard Detective – could bear it no longer. The twistedness of that shutter-straight mouth once that the key had been turned in the lock. The tears welling up into the soft grey eyes. Ready at any instant to tumble down the squared-off face, to splash on the worn and chipped surface of the table between them.

'Miss Mackintosh, I'd like to come now to the actual circumstances.'

'Yes, yes. All right, I'll tell you. I'll tell you everything, every single thing that I did that morning. If it helps to bring justice down upon me. Yes.'

And the tears did now pour blubberingly out. And, yes, splash on to the table.

'Do you want a break, Miss Mackintosh? Time to recover yourself a little.'

Safe to let her have some moments off the hook, now that those words *I killed her* were on the tapes. What was to follow would be no more than confirmatory evidence.

'No, no. No, I must tell you now.'

'If that's what you truly want.'

'Yes. Yes, you see, when I heard that Bubbles had bought Adam and Eve House, a place I once knew well – I used to go to tea there as a child, you know, and I love the romantic story of how it got its name – I decided the time had come to punish her. For leaving me when I loved her so much.'

She took in a deep breath, returned to the charge.

'I had read in the Levenham paper that my Bubbles went running every morning as soon as it was light. So I went over there, to the other side of the Leven, and I watched and watched. It didn't take me long to get to know that she – that she finished her run all on her own at the old boathouse. Oh, we used to have such fun in the old days when there were two boats in there and we played pirates.'

A silence.

'But you did something more than play pirates on June the twentieth?'

'Yes. Yes, that was the day I chose. I had prepared. I went over to the school and took away one of the javelins from the pavilion, a woman's weight one. Then

I got into my little car and I drove to the place on the road from Levenham that's nearest to the river. You know, in the old days we teenagers used to walk out to that very place at dawn on St Valentine's Day and make our way down the meadows to take part in a ceremony that had been held year after year since the Middle Ages. I expect they've forgotten all about it now. All boys and girls want nowadays are those terrible sex-mad films and loud music.'

Yes, Harriet thought, she must have parked that car no more than a quarter of a mile from Adam and Eve House. And we didn't get a single report about it. That's what's made this inquiry so difficult, the expanse of almost deserted farmland we've had to cover. And the car was on the opposite side of the Leven to Adam and Eve House, so maybe inquiries weren't pursued as they might have been. On the other hand, a car there at that very early hour could quite easily not have been seen by a single soul.

Right, enough of days gone by. Some facts now that can be checked. Evidence.

'Miss Mackintosh,' she said, 'what precisely did you do on the morning of June the twentieth last?'

'I was telling you. I was telling you everything. You said you needed to know. I was telling you. I left my little car and I carried the javelin down to the river. I waited. At last I saw Bubbles coming back from her run. I waded straight across the river. I didn't care. And then I said to her, *You went. You left me. It was wrong. Wrong. Cruel, cruel. How could you?* And I killed her. I had to. I had to, you know.'

'Thank you, Miss Mackintosh.'

For a moment she sat in silence, looking at the tear-stained face of Bubbles' murderer opposite her.

'What happens now,' she said eventually, 'is that you'll have to go down to what we call the Custody Suite, where, in front of the custody sergeant, Detective Inspector Anderson will formally charge you. Finally, in all probability, the custody sergeant will say you are to be detained until you are taken to the magistrates' court tomorrow.'

It was not DI Anderson but DI Brent who spoke then.

'No,' he said.

Harriet turned to him sharply.

Christ, has he suddenly gone soft or what?

She almost clutched hold of his arm and said, *Anselm.*

He sat there, seemingly startled at the sudden word that had come from him. And then, swallowing fiercely, he brought out a few other words.

'No. She didn't.'

'She didn't what?' Handy Andy snapped out.

Anselm seemed to take courage.

'Miss Mackintosh did not do what she said she did,' he announced. 'She did not wade across the river to kill Bubbles Xingara. She couldn't have done. There was so little water in the Leven that morning you could have crossed it in a single stride.'

# Chapter Twelve

Handy Andy, the man who had arrested poor, wretched Prudence Mackintosh and brought her in, tied to his chariot wheels, to make her statement confessing to Bubbles Xingara's murder, was quick to round on her.

'You lied to us. You no more murdered Bubbles than you flew to the moon. There's such an offence as wasting police time, you know. You could go to prison for that, if you're so keen on putting yourself behind bars.'

It went on for about a quarter of an hour, pound, pound, pound.

Harriet let it happen. Prudence Mackintosh deserved some punishment after all. Anderson could be let do his worst, or best. Before long he would have Prudence Mackintosh admitting in her own words that she had never crossed the trickling Leven and killed Bubbles. Perhaps she would even say out aloud that she had felt she ought to be held guilty of killing the girl she saw as having betrayed her love. Confessers confessed for reasonless reasons like that.

So I can allow myself to think about the man on my other side, sitting still there in seemingly sullen silence, not even chewing at a pencil.

What about Anselm? What do I feel about him now?

And it is feeling. Oh, yes, it's that. Am I feeling again that I can love him? Did I really ever feel that his failures could somehow make him into a person I did not love? Was that last defeat out at Grainham Hall the one thing that might, in an instant, have hurled me out of love? Was it like all those years ago hearing John's surname was the slightly ridiculous *Piddock* and it so nearly being love's death-blow?

But how do I really know what I feel? Christ, if this were simply a matter of working out by logic what must have happened when one villain killed another, it'd cause me no trouble at all.

But feelings . . . Feelings. And, worst of all, feelings of love. They're a marsh, a wild wide stretch of ominous, over-vivid green. Not a single safe foothold.

No, stop this. Stop it. For God's sake, I'm a detective. I'm sitting in an interview room opposite a woman I was on the point of allowing to be charged with murder. I must pay her attention. I must pay attention to Handy Andy. Probably making almost as crass a mistake in questioning that poor deluded woman the way he is now as he did when he arrested her.

She almost shook herself into awareness.

And saw at once, looming up, a possible serious flaw in considering Prudence Mackintosh innocent. That javelin she had spoken of with such conviction. Of course, she had spoken with equal conviction of wading across the Leven. Damn it, I was a fool not to have spotted that at the moment she said it. Didn't I look down at the river that first morning while Bubbles' body was lying under that sun-glaring blue tent? I took in then how small a trickle of water was flowing, little more than would float a paper boat. I should have remembered.

But the javelin. The moment Prudence Mackintosh said the word what I saw once more was that single, circular wound in Bubbles' throat. Circular and, as Professor Polk implied, so clean that only microscopic analysis would reveal any tiny traces of anything transferred to it. So, if Prudence Mackintosh's confession was all in her mind, how could she have known the fatal wound was such as a javelin would make?

But, if love-racked Miss Mackintosh didn't thrust a real javelin into Bubbles' throat, who did? If she didn't deliver that blow, how did she know it was a javelin that made that wound? We've told no one. No one. Not a single bloody journalist. I'm certain of that. It's why I've been keeping the media at bay.

So can Anselm be wrong after all?

She swivelled round and looked at him. He was sitting there, silent as if he had been turned into a wooden carving.

What is he thinking? That his sudden last-minute triumph is not what it seemed? But how can it be wrong? Prudence Mackintosh said she waded. She made a point of it. But the Leven was truly that day only the smallest of trickles.

But there's this: Prudence was once a games mistress at Grainham Hall. Almost certainly she would know about any javelins there. If they actually had them. No, wait. One thing clear: victim of her obsession with Bubbles, she would have read every column-inch about her in every paper she had got hold of. And, yes – I must get this checked and double-checked – I do seem to remember that in the early days some of the papers at least made great play with the wound. It sharpened up the story beautifully for them, the life-full body with its delicate skin (all except the palm of the right hand, which none of them ever mentioned: I'd have remembered) and the savage wound that pierced it.

Harriet thrust herself forward.

'One moment, DI,' she said to Anderson. 'There's something I want to know. Miss Mackintosh, tell me, is javelin-throwing one of the sports taught at Grainham?'

The tears halted. A half-concealed sniff.

'Of course it is. I taught it to the girls myself. For two years running I was English Girls champion.'

So my doubts not as valid as I had begun to think. And – another thing – Prudence Mackintosh would know, if anybody did, just what sort of a hole in the ground a javelin makes. So she could have worked out that a javelin had to be the weapon used, and incorporated one in the confession she felt driven to make. The confession that was her substitute-killing of the girl who had rejected her love.

'Miss Mackintosh, one more thing. You spoke about a javelin. Now, if all you told us originally was not what happened, how did you come to tell us Bubbles was attacked with a javelin?'

'But – But she must have been. Don't you in the police even know that? What else could have made the wound I read about?'

Yes, the final doubt settled. But wait. Something more. Now, thanks to Miss Mackintosh, it looks as if, paradoxically, we have a strong idea what the mysterious weapon was. All but certainly a javelin.

But, if it is, where did it come from?

Answer plain, if dispiriting. From anywhere. From anywhere in the whole of bloody Britain. Or even at a pinch from abroad. Taken to use that early morning at Adam and Eve House, and then, since it wasn't found in all the searches round the house, almost certainly cleaned to the point where there were no visible signs of blood and quite likely put back in place. Useless to make any hunt for it then. Only when Bubbles' murderer is under questioning, perhaps in this very room, will we possibly lay hands on the weapon and find, with a good deal of luck, those microscopic traces that can be presented as evidence.

Prudence Mackintosh was released at nine. Handy Andy, tasked with making doubly sure the confession he had extracted was indeed a tissue of imaginings, had reported that a call to Grainham Hall School had confirmed there were in the pavilion six women's-weight javelins and six men's-weight, kept naturally under lock-and-key. None missing. Nor had any been, they could vouch for it, on June the twentieth. He had obtained, too, the rules-laid-down specifications for athletics javelins, 600-gram for women, 800-gram for men. Finally by simply consulting Professor Polk's pathology report he had learnt that the diameter of the clean-cut, single-thrust wound was significantly larger than the maximum diameter of the javelin Prudence Mackintosh had claimed she had used.

'Thank you, DI,' Harriet said. 'But you realize what this means?'

'Yes, ma'am,' Handy Andy replied, with no sign of remorse over that over-hasty arrest. 'Means we're up shit creek again.'

'If you choose to put it that way, yes. But down in the Incident Room, as you well know, there are even at this time of the evening, four or five officers still going through the computer records. One of them may, at any moment, come up with something that starts us off again. And there's even something I want you to look into yourself. One thing Prudence Mackintosh said has lingered in my mind. She was denouncing anyone else who had had a hand in Bubbles' career, and she mentioned Bubbles' American coach, a *horrible Greek* she called him. Now, what I want to know is this: if Peter Renshaw took over as coach, in what circumstances did this Cacoyannis leave? Prudence Mackintosh mentioned a row, a dispute, something like that. It could be there was some bad blood there. Maybe there's nothing in it. But I want it looked into. So have another word with Peter Renshaw in the morning, right?'

'Okay,' Handy Andy said.

Once again she was tempted to come back with *Okay what, DI?* And once again, in the interests of harmony among the team, she let the *ma'am* go.

Handy Andy sent off duty, to pursue no doubt some conquest or other, she still had work to do. Work that, she trusted, would absorb her enough for no thoughts to intrude about the aborted interview and how in the course of it Anselm Brent had run a switchback in her mind from outcast lover to fully re-instated one.

So it came as something of a shock – she even wondered if she was falling prey to some hallucination – when an hour or more later, going out to her car in the soft star-pricked darkness of the late July night, she saw a shape down at the far wall of the car park, a shape that had become embossed on her mind. Anselm's broad-shouldered back in, as almost always even on a warm summer's night, his heavy tweed jacket.

She stopped and looked more carefully.

Yes, he was sitting hunched unmovingly on the low wall, looking out into vacancy.

Leave him there? Or – Jesus, how I want to – go over and ask him whether he's all right, what he's doing out here at this time of night?

She walked across, footsteps all but noiseless on the blotchy tarmac.

Once standing beside him, unnoticed she believed, she could not stop herself reaching over and, putting her hand on the worn tweed of his jacket, giving the hunched shoulder beneath a slight affectionate pressure.

Anselm's reaction came as a complete surprise. She felt his whole solid body shudder as if a charge of electricity had run through him.

And then she realized that her approach had not gone unnoticed. He had been aware of her. He must have been. Aware of the heat of her body as she stood at his shoulder, aware of her arm coming round him. So, when at last she had succumbed to the desire to give him that affectionate squeeze – affectionate, no, by God, more than that, more, more, more – his whole body, which she had thought of as slumped inertly, had reacted in that judder of tension released.

'Anselm,' she brought out past contracted vocal cords, 'what is it? Why were you sitting here like this?'

'It's – It's – '

He turned and looked up at her.

'I – I – I let you down,' he said. 'I wanted to earn your – your respect. I – I wanted to give you back what you – what you've given me.'

And then suddenly he reached round and seized her free hand.

She felt, with a flood of pity and gushing–outwards

love, the faint remains of ribby calluses – little tennis played since June – all across his palm.

Oh, God, she thought. He wants me. He's known all along what I have felt for him. That's what he means by wanting to earn my respect. He knows, and – and perhaps he loves me, too. And I love him. Oh, Anselm, Anselm, Anselm, Anselm.

They stayed there in the heavy summer darkness, her hand in his.

The minutes passed. The classic picture of two lovers under the stars remained.

Slowly her mind moved onwards. Everything is changed now, she told herself. While this, all this, was, as I thought, entirely within myself, nothing outside was affected. But now, now that the sexual link has been acknowledged, acknowledged by the roughness I can feel against the back of my hand, the cloud of sex, John's overhanging cloud, has enveloped us, invaded us. We are within its influence. Our freedom of action, the little we had of it, has gone.

We must do as Eros impels us, what Aphrodite has ensnared me for.

Then a flicker of rebellion. No. No, John must be wrong. He's been theorizing to the point where he can believe nothing else. He's wrong. Yes, of course, Anselm and I have abruptly been betrayed into simply letting sexual impulses run from one of us to the other back and forth. But that's a common enough happening, hardly more important than the twins' joyful boasting about selling their sperm. Put a woman and a man together into any tightly confined situation – the terrible chestnut of the stuck lift – and it's as likely as not they'll experience some sexual interest in each other.

But is that really John's hair-coiling Aphrodite? Can't I, as the anti-drugs ads put it, *Just Say No?*

God, it would lift a clamping burden if I could. If I could say, or pretend, or convince myself, that what has just happened doesn't really count. That it's a feather, something that rests on us for a moment and is blown away. Then we'd be free of all the things Aphrodite's thrall brings with it. Free of what John talked about once, about how people didn't realize how the sexual attraction of male to female, or female to female, or male to male, permeated aspect after aspect of everyday life. Queen Elizabeth the First, and the fate of nations. All that.

And that's what we – all three of us, actually – will escape from if I can just say to Anselm – if I can just call him *DI*, and say I'm doing no more at this moment than feel a passing lech towards a close subordinate whose handling of things I have come to admire. If I could cease to be so aware of feeling, feeling with this acuteness, the slight remains of those calluses against the skin of my hand.

So try? Try and perhaps succeed in avoiding untold complications, complications that could be the end of both our careers. A promising officer in a country force finding his career driven on to the rocks, and . . . and the Hard Detective ruined as a softy.

'Listen.' No, I can't say *DI*, and I won't, won't say *Anselm*. 'Listen, you seem to be in some sort of trouble. Is it because over at Grainham Hall you made a mess of getting hold of that mixed-up, deluded woman? Or thoughts of what happened in Marseilles?'

Suddenly the hand holding her own was jerked away.

Was that it? Did what I said, the cold touch of sage

advice, do it for me? Send him scuttling back to where he was before, a country detective inspector pleased to be working under a big-city detective superintendent with a reputation, the media-hailed Hard Detective? And no more than that? He's hardly committed himself. That hand that reached over to mine, it could have been in error. A mistake in the dark.

But, no. No, it wasn't. And for me it wasn't just a shove from brooding Eros. No, it was Aphrodite, and it was Aphrodite for him. I know it. Aphrodite swirling round him the long inescapable tresses of her hair. Enfolding him, holding him. Capturing him. It was.

'Yes, I was sitting here thinking about all that, Marseilles and the mess I made of things over at Grainham Hall. But I—'

'No, listen. Who made a mess of things there? All right, you could have brought in Prudence Mackintosh more quickly. But look what happened when Anderson got hold of her. We damn nearly had a major scandal on our hands. And we would have done, only you were on the ball. I never noticed that discrepancy about the amount of water in the Leven, but you did. You did, and you saved our bacon. So you've nothing to be ashamed about, nothing at all.'

'Yes, I have.'

'Why? What is this?'

'I – I haven't come up to your expectations. I'm not the sort of chap you should – you should, well, like. No, more. You should go for.'

The end of all evasion. Yes, now it was out. Now it had been said. Now Anselm had said it. Anselm, Anselm. Yes, he knows. He knows Aphrodite has entwined us together in the coils of her hair.

And what am I to reply? How am I to answer? With

a lie that he won't believe? With a lie that'll hurt him, hurt him deeply?

No.

'Oh, my dear. My darling. That's not so. All right, when it seemed you'd done badly at Grainham Hall, yes, I felt a momentary disappointment. But it was only momentary. A minute afterwards – or, well, certainly from the moment you spoke up in the interview room, my feelings for you were back to where they were when . . . When, to tell you the simple truth, there by Bubbles' body you showed me your hand with that thickened skin, looking so ugly and yet so – damn it, yes, so sweet. Then I wanted you, and I've wanted you from that moment on, though I've been stupid enough to try not to show it. Oh, Anselm, Anselm.'

Then her hand was grasped again.

And the kisses she had seen herself giving him that evening when the twins' unexpected in-and-out-again visit had stopped her confessing all to John were hers to give.

# Chapter Thirteen

No, I don't think so, Harriet in the darkness of Levenham police station car park had said to Anselm. Two senior police officers, clothes thrust aside, making hasty and writhingly vigorous love on the gritty tarmac where any late-night passer-by might see them, it was not anything the Hard Detective could contemplate. Even the back seat of her car, waiting there on its own, had about it an aura of scrabbling come-and-go sexual contact that repelled her. And, equally, if a little better, a return to her top-floor office and locking themselves in there seemed still sordid.

One last long kiss, and Anselm walked off towards the house he shared with his widowed mother, his brother's widow and her son, the future detective Jonathan. Harriet stood there until the last sound of his heavy brogues clunking away was lost in the quiet of the Levenham night.

She turned away at last and headed for the car. But then . . . Then she found she was dancing. To music in her head, a bright swirling of joy under the stars above, she was dancing. Across the potholed asphalt of the parking lot she danced as if she were at a disco, on a stage even. *I'm in love, I'm in love*, the words sang out in silence. *I'm in love and he loves me. He loves me. I'm in love.*

But at last, when her capering steps had brought her to within a few feet of her staidly waiting Volvo, she brought herself to a halt, stood for a moment stock-still, took in a long, deep breath and, shaking her head, as if to fling the nonsense into the night like a dog emerging from water, got in and drove carefully off towards Birchester and home.

Yes, she thought sober now, what I've been caught up by, what we've been caught up by, Anselm and I, is absolutely John's Aphrodite embrace. It's not in any way snatching, eyes-open, at half an hour's sexual excitement or even half a month's. It is a significant part of my life. Of Anselm's life.

John, the very thought of him pushed at once an urgent question into her mind. Am I going to tell him what has happened? I could, of course. Didn't he tell me all about his affair in New Delhi? And that was certainly something more than any casual encounter with a whore in Brazil. Was it on a par with what has happened between Anselm and myself? Well, to be honest, yes, it was. What John and that Indian lady experienced for those few months is what Anselm and I are experiencing now.

With the Volvo humming through the dark towards the faint dome of light on the horizon that was Birchester, she nevertheless found an unaccountable reluctance to be as open with John as he had been with her when he had come back from saving the mighty Majestic some enormous sum in India. She tried to work out why.

But by the time she had reached the outskirts of the city and needed to pay more attention to her driving she had still reached no conclusion. Was it because what she felt for Anselm was something more than she had ever felt for John? Was it not just love but a yet more slavish submission to the power of sexual attraction? Was it a grand passion, one of those affairs, more common in novels than in life – or, she asked herself, less acknowledged in life than in the safety of fiction? – that bring happy ruin to those who are in its grip.

No answer as she parked outside the house. No answer as she strode up the path to the door. No answer as she put her keys in the locks, turned them, pushed the door wide and called out, 'It's me.'

But, no sooner had she declined John's offer to cook her an omelette – a canteen meal taken at her desk still heavily with her – and accepted the drink he poured for her, than, almost against her will, she said something in response to a casual question that she knew might well lead into the sort of conversation in which a confession could take its natural place.

'Well, we had a fine demonstration today of how, as you like to think, the sexual cloud can send a shrivelling lightning-bolt into the most unexpected of places.'

'Oh, yes? Can it be after all that you're coming round to agreeing with one of my theories?'

She laughed.

'You may well think so when I tell you how the quiet life of a retired games-mistress at Grainham Hall School has just collapsed all round her. She would be – I won't tell you her name – the last person anybody would think of in terms of sex, one of nature's spinsters, podgy face, muscular frame, make-up of any sort seen as appallingly frivolous.'

'Oh, I'd have my reservations about not thinking in terms of sex for anybody whatsoever. But go on.'

'Right. She rang us up with a long garbled outpouring, more or less implying she had killed Bubbles Xingara, and, though what she said had many of the marks of the compulsive confesser, there were things in it that led me to send – '

She came to a full stop.

To send Anselm Brent? Should I say that?

'I'm sorry, sudden thought about something else. Where was I? Ah, yes. So I sent one of the Greater Birchester Police officers, a DI called Anderson, to talk to her, and he was so impressed with what she said about her motive that he arrested her on the spot. Then when we had questioned her for some time and were convinced by what she had said about being in love with Bubbles ever since she had been a star pupil at Grainham Hall, and were on the point of actually charging her, another of the DIs, a fellow called – '

Again she broke off.

No, Anselm's name must not be said aloud. It'll bring ruin. One day perhaps I'll embrace that, embrace ruin. But not yet. Not yet.

'Well, it doesn't matter who. The thing is that, just when we thought we'd heard exactly how Bubbles had been killed – with, of all things, an athletics javelin – a fundamental inconsistency came up in what she'd said about the actual circumstances. And it turned out to be a wholly imaginary murder. After a bit of setting her straight, she eventually agreed she hadn't done anything. Now, doesn't that just tell you what the power of – would you call that the work of Aphrodite? – what it can do.'

'Oh, yes,' John said. 'Yes, I'd call that the coils of Aphrodite all right, though I dare say the poor lady had never even kissed little Bubbles, much less taken her to bed. But, you're right, the oppressive cloud, it weighs on everybody more or less, and Eros shoots out of it and Aphrodite follows sometimes in his wake.'

*Sometimes.* She thought for a half-second. Was he saying you could be exempt from those enwrapping tresses? And, more, that somehow some people are safe from Eros' thunderbolts?

'Weighs on more or less everybody? *More or less?* Is the great theoretician of the sexual impulse rowing back a bit now?'

John grinned.

'Of course I am. You can't really have thought what I said applied to absolutely everyone. No, look at it this way. Belief in God. Almost everyone all over the world believes in God, or at least in a band of gods. But here and there you can find the odd genuine atheist, someone exempt. As I see it, just as there's a looming cloud of sexuality there's a cloud of belief in God. Or, perhaps a cloud isn't the best image. Let's say, more simply, that in the human mind, whether it's in Britain or America or India or anywhere, there's a built-in tendency, a very strong tendency, to believe in a Deity. We need to. Almost all of us, even if in the ordinary way we hardly think of it. But it's there, and in moments of, say, real distress or, worse, danger we pray. Moments of great joy, too.'

'You're right. Yes, we do. Even avowed unbelievers. Like you, you old heathen.'

John smiled, with, she thought, a tiny touch of complacency.

'And the same thing,' he said, 'applies to the sexual impulse. It's in our minds, fixed there, whether we like it or not. A part of them. A part of each one of us. All right, the occasional, very occasional I think, individual is free from it. But everyone else has got it embedded in them, and from time to time it exercises its power. It goes spreading like the fine roots of an immense tree into every cranny in the earth below. Right down to the depths of your sad games-mistress.'

Right down into me, Harriet thought. Into me and into nice, cheerful, fundamentally innocent Detective Inspector Brent, quiet stalwart of the Leven Vale Police.

But can I, after all, possibly enrol myself among the few exceptions, the genuine sex-atheists? Of course I can't. How, if I was one, did I come to marry John? To bear him twin sons? To make love with him as happily as we did, say, on that June morning just after he'd got back from Brazil? As we have often since?

But does this mean that I've got to tell him, here and now, that the impulse has spread down to the finest roots in myself, and in Anselm?

I don't know why, but I can't. Not now. Not at this very moment.

'Well, I've had quite a day, and I ought to be over in Levenham promptly tomorrow. So . . .'

John looked at her.

'Off to Bedfordshire?'

'And, I'm sorry to say, Sleepfordshire. Straight away. I'm bushed.'

It was not Sleepfordshire straight away every night, however, nor every early-waking morning, as the weeks went by and the hunt for Bubbles Xingara's murderer dragged on. But neither was it arriving with Anselm at John's *simple generative act*, precautions or no precautions.

Harriet found a hundred reasons to put off the moment. And Anselm, in the car on the way to see some witness, pulled over to the verge in some quiet spot, for all that his desire was frequently demonstrably evident, was too much Handy Andy's Saintie to press her.

For one thing, she found she had decided that until she had told John the truth she was somehow debarred from making a total break. And am I really going to wreck my career, she asked herself almost every day. I'm certainly not going to try and have my cake and eat it. To have Anselm as a hole-and-corner lover, in daily, hourly, danger of discovery – *Hard Detective in Country Love Nest*, the *Daily Dirt* headline – that would be beyond my strength.

And, in my inmost heart, don't I still want above everything the career I've given all my working life to? And it's not just the career I want. I don't, in fact, care one little bit if I never get to be a Chief Constable or yet higher, the first woman Inspector of Constabulary. But I do care to be someone who's doing their share, more than their share even, to set what is right firmly on top of what is wrong.

Then there's the daily grind of the case. I want to be the one who resolves it, the one who gets Bubbles' murderer into court. And into prison after that. All right, I've scorned the media's *Hard Detective*. But only because the name was given me by journalists wanting a catchy headline. To be a Hard Detective itself, that's another matter . . . It's something to be proud of, and I am.

So am I going to toss it all away? And, incidentally, bring Anselm's decent career in Levenham to a nasty, sticky, media-smeared end?

I may not be able to hold out against that. But I'm going to hold out as long as I can.

And yet . . . Yet. Yet.

Yet I'm in love with Anselm Brent. And I can't help it. I ought to be decisive, hard. I ought to take steps never to see him unless there are other people present. And I could contrive to do that. But I'm not going to. They mean too much to me, these occasional moments we get together. *Alone in a world for two.*

Oh, God, dear Anselm. Still finding himself even in those moments sometimes calling me *ma'am*. And me not daring to point it out. Careful of him. Like a doting mother, for Christ's sake. And I don't want to be any sort of mother to him. I want and want and want to be his lover.

And I don't, not at this time. Not yet.

What if some sharp-eyed cynic, like Handy Andy Anderson, happens to see us at the roadside somewhere when I'm holding him so hard to me I can feel the very beating of his heart? Or, what if Handy Andy – he's had clues enough already – gets to guess in some other way, in any of our hundred betraying moments? Well, he can go to hell. I love Anselm Brent, and that's what means most to me.

Oh, God, why am I in such a tangle?

A knock at the door of her office, now mercifully cool as yet another of the rainstorms that had marked out August swept down.

'Come.'

It was Handy Andy, as if he had emerged from the mangled web of her thoughts.

'Think I've got a bit of a lead, ma'am.'

'We could do with one, DI. Take a seat. Mr Tarlington was on to me yesterday. Wants to cut back financially. So, unless we can show him there are active leads we're following, you may find yourself back in Birchester working on small-time wages hold-ups. So what have you got?'

'It's that man Cacoyannis. You remember I didn't really get anywhere talking to Peter Renshaw weeks ago when you tasked me with finding out how he actually got the push.'

'Yes. Yes, DI.'

'Well, it occurred to me yesterday I might still get the lowdown on that, not from Renshaw but from the lovely Fiona.'

For a moment Harriet was inclined to say something sharp about *the lovely Fiona*. But she let the rebuke go unsaid.

'And . . .?' she asked sharply.

'And yes, there was a row, a hell of a row, when Caco went. Seems he'd got to think he could do anything he liked with Bubbles. You know the way a tennis coach gets to have so much influence on all aspects of a player's life, especially of course when the player's a young girl, that they often feel they're theirs for the taking? And with a little piece like Bubbles, who could blame anyone?'

Yes, Harriet thought. John's theory again. A whole life re-directed, or perhaps only potentially re-directed, by the power of Eros.

'But Bubbles wasn't the sort of person you could manoeuvre like that,' she said, letting her much suppressed sharpness have free rein. 'So, what actually happened?'

'Yeah. Well, whatever the strength of it, Caco somehow came unstuck. Got booted out. Literally, I gathered. And Peter Renshaw took his place. I dare say in more ways than one.'

'Any evidence for that, DI?'

Something in her tone brought Handy Andy to a stop.

'Well, no, ma'am. No. But I just thought . . . Well, it's quite likely, isn't it?'

A few weeks earlier Harriet would have stamped on that *likely*. But now she saw life through John's eyes, felt his cloud of ubiquitous sexuality weighing down everywhere. So, she thought, yes, in theory Peter Renshaw might have attempted – yes, even while spending his nights in Fiona Diplock's bed – to make his stepdaughter into his sexual plaything.

But, damn it, there's been no sign of it. Nothing at all.

'Look,' she said, 'what I want to know now is whether Cacoyannis was in this country around the time of Wimbledon. If we can be definite he was in America then – I suppose that's where he works now – we can cross him off. But if not, then you were right to come to me with this, DI.'

'Well, shouldn't be too difficult to find out about him,' Handy Andy said cheerfully. 'I mean, if he was over here, it'd be for the tennis some way or another. A few inquiries at Wimbledon, or maybe elsewhere, down at Eastbourne, should do the trick.'

She thought for a moment.

A chance to get rid of this sex-fixated snoop for a couple of days or more?

'Very well,' she said. 'Go down there. To Wimbledon, or down to Eastbourne, and see what you can find out.'

'Yes, ma'am.'

The prospect of a run down to London and its fleshpots bringing out, for once, the fully respectful *ma'am*.

*

Handy Andy took his time about his inquiries, pleading by phone that with Wimbledon, reverted now in rainy August to no more than an unusually large local tennis club, he was finding it hard to locate witnesses. But Harriet had plenty of other lines of inquiry to have followed up or to initiate, even if none of them looked on the face of it very hopeful. There were still a good many of the e-mails, faxes, letters and – mostly yukky – cards that had been sent to Bubbles to be subjected to the often time-consuming process of checking out. There was a former practice partner of hers in America, one Jo-Ann Parash, from whom she had parted not on the best of terms, according to Peter Renshaw, who appeared to have given up on the tennis world but had still to be located and alibied in case she had been in England at the crucial time. There was, too, an unsatisfactory report from one of the Birchester police stations about a man working on a roof in the city at the time of the murder who had – the details were unclear – failed to come to work on the day after the murder, or had left work the day before. That ought to be gone into. And no one had yet been able to trace Bubbles' father, the little spoken of Pablo Xingara, long ago vanished into total obscurity, perhaps even into death.

Plenty to be done. Plenty to see had been done. And any one of the tasks she gave out might be what in the end would lead to the person who had thrust into Bubbles' throat that full-size javelin, wherever it had come from, wherever it was now.

And, pushing insistently into her mind, there was Anselm.

Each day her attitude towards him seemed to differ. On one day she would be determined, never mind the fact that she loved him, that if he swam into her head at some moment when she had ceased to concentrate on the matter in hand, whether it was allocating tasks to her team or the mundane events of daily life, brushing teeth, checking the fridge, getting petrol, she would thrust that image out.

The next day she might find herself deciding, from the moment she hauled herself out of bed, that she was going to contrive, at whatever cost, to see as much of him as she possibly could. To see him alone, even if it was for only five minutes while she knew no one was likely to come knocking at her office door.

But, she would think then, there are those who do not need to knock, or who give the door the most perfunctory of taps. Handy Andy the prime example there, which made his prolonged London trip all the more of a blessing. But what if, when she was stroking Anselm's cheek with the back of one finger as she loved to do, the door opened and Mr Tarlington, tight in his braided uniform, red ears sticking shootingly out, was standing there?

But on the very worst days – or are they, she often asked, the very best? – she would defy all doubts, summon *Mr Brent* up to her office on the flimsiest of excuses, be ready standing there when he knocked, as he always did, to push him back against the door, banging it reverberatingly closed. Then she would seize him by both arms and kiss and kiss him for as long as breath held out.

# Chapter Fourteen

It was not until September the first that Handy Andy at last came in to report. But when he had told her what he had learnt she found herself thinking that every day of his prolonged stay away might have been worth it.

'Yeah, took me some time to gather up the gossip. All the top players are far away now, pulling in the dollars up and down the States. But I did eventually find guys who had heard what was being said when they were here. Girls, too, natch. Amazing what you get to hear sometimes between the sheets.'

Oh, yes, Harriet thought. Trust you to trick yourself into believing getting a girl into bed is the only way to learn anything from her. Still, I suppose that's how you cope with the thunder-heavy cloud above you. Perhaps that's the answer, too. Let Eros have his way. On any and every occasion. Only it isn't. Going along with that will bring big trouble to you one day, Detective Inspector Anderson.

'And what precisely did you learn?' she had asked, her voice cold.

Handy Andy was unfazed.

'For one thing,' he said cheerfully, 'everyone I talked to was absolutely clear that Bubbles was never in the tennis lesbian camp. So one line of inquiry the less. But, more important, I managed to learn a good deal about friend Cacoyannis. Apparently what my little Fiona had gathered, stuck away there in Adam and Eve House, was a hundred per cent correct. Old Caco did attempt to rape Bubbles. She took it badly, and came out with it all to Mummy's boyfriend, as he was then, Peter Renshaw. Who, to his credit, beat Cacoyannis up good and proper before sending him on his way back to California. Someone told me you could date what had happened to Bubbles by a sudden falling-off in her form. Seems she lost early in the Austrian Ladies Open at Kitzbühel to a girl far below her in the rankings.'

'Very good. You've got Cacoyannis with a heavy grudge against Bubbles, caught out by not being able to keep his hands off. But have you got any more than that? A grudge wears away with time, you know, even one as deep as his might be.'

'Ah, but I have got more. I've got the bugger back in this country shortly before Wimbledon this year. He was seen skulking around at Eastbourne, out of a job and making the odd quid or two selling gossip to any journalist who'd pay attention. And, from what I heard, that wasn't many. So, look at it this way: here's a man with a really heavy grudge, against Peter Renshaw, against Bubbles. His career as a coach wrecked by what Renshaw, if not Bubbles, told people about him. Broke. Acting like a scavenger on the fringes of the world in which he once featured pretty high in the pecking-order, coach to a real rising star. And he was here certainly in this country just before the murder. I've got inquiries in with the Immigration people, find out when he left. But I'm willing to bet it'll turn out to be the day after the murder or the day after that.'

'We'll see. But if he was in this country then, I'm going to have a word with him. If I have to go to the States to have it.'

It took a good deal longer than Harriet had expected for the Cacoyannis line to begin to look as if it was going to bear fruit. No one in the Immigration Service, swamped by an outcry in Parliament about the huge sums international criminals were making bringing in refugees from Eastern Europe to work as prostitutes, appeared to have time to deal with the inquiry. Something to tell John, Harriet thought wryly. More support, as if it's needed, for his thesis about the widespread economic effects of Eros.

Even when at last there came confirmation that Cacoyannis had left the UK, not at all as quickly as Handy Andy had been willing to bet, on July the first, there were still long delays. In America it took the FBI, working at Harriet's request, a considerable time before they were able to locate Bubbles' former coach.

Understandably enough, Harriet thought, when at last the positive report came through. Cacoyannis, it turned out, had dropped down so far from his former job as coach to rising star Bubbles Xingara as to have landed up as a barman. His only remaining link with the world of tennis was that he was working in the famous casino at the tennis club at Newport, Rhode Island. A casino, her FBI contact told her on the phone, that was not in fact a gambling place.

'You know what it is?' he said with the suppressed glee of someone about to unwind a dirty story. 'It's a *casino* in the old Italian sense. In other words, it was once a good old-fashioned whorehouse.'

Harriet produced the bark of a laugh that was expected of her. Ubiquitous sex popping up once more.

'Yes, ma'am, that's what it was. But then, when things began to get a bit respectable, some guy who'd been thrown out of the nearby gentlemen's club, for getting a pal to ride his horse through the bar I believe, bought the place and the land around it and opened it up as his club, complete with tennis courts. So now there's the International Tennis Hall of Fame there. I guess, if you come over, see this Cacoyannis guy, you'll love to spend an hour or so looking over that.'

'I dare say I would. I'll let you know what I decide, and thanks for all your help.'

She saw herself, momentarily, wandering round that tennis museum endeavouring to forget the palm-roughened club player she had left behind. And at once she felt a wave of longing for Anselm that almost brought her to tears as she sat at her desk, her hand still on the phone she had just put down.

A quietly respectful tap at the door.

She lifted up her head, drew the back of each hand rapidly across her eyes.

'Come.'

And it was Anselm himself.

'Just a quick word, ma'am, if I may. It's about that roofer fellow from over in Birchester. Seems he—'

'Shut the door.'

'Yes. Yes, ma'am.'

He took a pace inside, turned and quietly closed the door behind him.

To find his arms pinioned, Harriet's hot breath warm in his right ear.

'Now,' she said.

'Now? Ma'am, what – what, Harriet?'

'Now. Now, you fool. Christ, don't you want to? You're not always so slow off the mark.'

'But – But—'

'Now, I said. You're always making sheep's eyes at me when I say *Wait*. Well, now . . . Now, now, now, I'm not saying *Wait*. I'm saying it's now.'

All thoughts of the need to have told John about the situation had flown from her mind. Aphrodite's hair was twined fast around them. Eros had descended at his chosen moment.

Without stopping for Anselm's consent or even a sign that he was ready, she plunged her eager fingers down to the flies of his ever-ordinary grey trousers, seized the tab of the zip, ripped it to the bottom, tore open the little hooked catch above, yanked down trousers and shorts.

Plainly she had not heard the quick rap at the door, if there had been one. But what in the next instant she became aware of was that the door had been pushed wide open, almost banging into Anselm, his trousers down to his knees, and that Handy Andy, Detective Inspector Anderson, was standing there, a slow smile beginning to spread across his clean-cut tanned face.

'Get out.'

She must have spoken with such force, the force she was accustomed to use to suppress any street yobbo who tried it on with her, that Handy Andy at once took a step back, crestfallen.

She pushed Anselm aside, sent him stumbling, hog-tied by his trousers, and slammed the door closed.

For a moment or two she stood there, breathing heavily while Anselm contrived to right himself and haul up his heavy trousers.

'God, I'm sorry,' she said to him at last. 'Christ, I don't know what that clever sod's going to make of this. And it was all my fault, all my fault. You know what my husband believes? He has a theory that sex lies at the root of almost every happening, good or bad, in the world. The overhanging cloud, he calls it. Well, God knows, this has just proved how right he is.'

'Look,' Anselm said, carefully zipping up, still pale from shock. 'Look, if . . . Well, if it'd help at all, I'd gladly put in my resignation.'

'No,' she said. 'No, listen. If I had any doubts about loving you before, about whether I should love you, whether it was somehow wrong to love you, then they've gone now. Every single one of them.'

'No, you listen. That bugger's going to go round the whole place, round the whole of Greater Birchester Police as like as not, telling everybody what he saw. Making out it was worse than it was, if I know anything. And I'm not going to let that happen to you. Be made a fool of in front of everyone who'd built you up as the Hard Detective, the one who set the example of how a police officer should be. No, it's the only way to deal with it, saying it was my fault. He won't be able to deny it. He hardly had time to see what was what, only that I was there with my pants half-way down my legs. If I say I was – '

He came to a halt. A blush rose up on to his cheeks that, at the height of the crisis a few minutes earlier, had actually gone pale almost as paper.

'Oh, Anselm. Anselm, darling. I know what you were going to say. You were going to tell people you initiated the whole business. That you were – oh, God, how is it they put it? – *attempting my virtue.*'

She laughed. She could not help it.

'Oh, Anselm, my dear. Oh, Christ, you're so sweet, and so good. Damn, damn, damn it, I don't deserve you.'

She gulped down something. A tear? A choking in her throat?

'But you weren't attempting my virtue, were you? The boot was altogether on the other foot. And I'm certainly not going to allow you to make a martyr of yourself. Damn it all, you're a good copper. A place like Levenham, like the whole of Leven Vale, needs someone like you. Someone with persistence, determination, someone who's not going to let crime go undetected if there's anything he can do about it. So, no. Whatever we do about what happened when you came in just now, it's not going to be dealt with by you resigning. Or, for the matter of that, by me resigning. I know my worth. And, this is something I wouldn't say to anyone else, I'm a bloody good police officer. I'm the famous media-created Hard Detective, and I'm damn well going to stay that way.'

She walked back over to her desk, exhausted. Slumped down. Sat in silence.

Then she lifted up her head.

'No, I see what can be done now. First of all, you are going on leave. You've been working seven days a week ever since you were called to see Bubbles Xingara's body, there beside the little trickling Leven, and you bloody well ought to have some time off. So, two weeks' leave, starting today. That's an order. And I'll tell you what I'll do myself. Just before you came in, I'd had a call from the FBI. They've found this fellow Cacoyannis for us. He's working as a barman in Newport, Rhode Island. Well, someone should question him, and I'm damn well going to do it myself.'

She gave Anselm a smile, or a show of one.

'And with any luck, with both of us off the scene, and Anderson enjoying himself being in charge of things here, there won't be too much fall-out.'

'But – But, well, are you sure?'

She smiled again, more easily now.

'No, not sure. Certainly not perfectly sure. But more or less sure, perhaps. Come here and kiss me.'

He took a step towards her, stopped, looked over at the door.

She laughed.

'Okay, here's the key. Now, come on. But a kiss and no more, all right?'

It was a kiss and no more. But Harriet made sure it was a lingering one.

# Chapter Fifteen

Too early, Harriet had realized, for the much-praised glories of New England in the Fall. But there was pleasure here in Newport all the same. The hoped-for but always doubted pleasure of the loosening of Aphrodite's entwining hair. Two days away from quiet Levenham and amid the glare and hustle of America at its busy and bustling best, she found she was able almost all the time not to think of Anselm, and that she was thinking of John only to compare his accounts of his business trips to the States against her own first-time impressions.

Whether or not this was her true state, she did not dare investigate. Enough that, for the time being at least, it seemed she was free of those long pale-golden tresses. If this was an illusion, well, it was one worth cherishing for the peace of mind it gave, if for nothing else.

Only once or twice her mind went back to Levenham and that outwardly comical scene when the thunderbolt from ever-hovering Eros had smashed through some narrow gap in her defences and Handy Andy had burst in on herself and trouserless Anselm. But when the, in fact, not-so-comical sight came back to her she quickly told herself that this time-out, away from it all, was the last opportunity life was giving her to escape.

If it was an opportunity.

And now, accompanied by unabashedly handsome, life-glowing FBI Agent Fernandez – 'Ma'am, call me Chuck' – who was making no impact at all on her sexually, she was walking along Newport's Bellevue Avenue, as bright and hustle-bustling as she had expected America to be.

'Okay, here we are,' Chuck Fernandez said, pointing to a canopy stretching out over the sidewalk on the other side of the street. 'According to my information one Michael Cacoyannis should be on duty in the Horseshoe Piazza bar inside there right now.'

Harriet felt a slight tightening of her muscles.

Was she at last about to confront the man who had gone creeping across the fields towards Adam and Eve House in its calmly rural setting that June morning, nearly three months ago, carrying with him a long, 800-gram javelin. But where had an American ex-tennis coach got hold of such a weapon? And how had he hit on the notion that something as silent would be his best way of putting an end to Bubbles Xingara's life and getting away with it?

Chuck Fernandez cheerfully pushed open the Casino's heavy entrance doors.

Harriet felt as if she had stepped from up-to-the-minute Bellevue Avenue, all sleek shiny cars smoothly manoeuvring past each other and shops with names like Fotomat, into the world of a hundred years before. A long, ornately built piazza looked on to a tennis court of the smoothest, lushest grass that might have been tended and cared for over the years by the gardeners of an English cathedral close.

'The Hall of Fame court,' Agent Fernandez murmured in church-interior tones.

'Yes,' Harriet said.

'What you see round it is the canopy of the Hall of Fame restaurant, a place of fine dignity, together with the Casino administration and the Hall of Fame itself.'

'Yes.'

Harriet stood in respectful silence for a count of fifty. Then she turned to Chuck Fernandez.

'And the bar?' she said.

'Through here, ma'am, and I doubt if at this hour there'll be many drinkers there, if any.'

The bar was as long and as glinting and as bottle-backed as Harriet had expected, and, as Agent Fernandez had forecast, it was empty of drinkers. Only behind it there stood, forearms resting on the polished surface, the man who must be Michael Cacoyannis. Big-built, dark hair cut short, shiny with some oily preparation, close-shaved cheeks almost black, pudgy mis-shapen nose, a heavy-lipped, sensuous mouth, eyes mistily brown under thick tangled eyebrows.

Harriet marched over to him, aware of Chuck Fernandez dropping a pace or two back.

'Michael Cacoyannis?'

An immediate look of wary suspicion, a gathering-up of his whole thick frame.

My English accent, Harriet thought. So has he reason to be wary of someone from England demanding his name? Is there something he did in England not so long ago that makes him suspicious of anyone from there?

'I asked: are you Michael Cacoyannis?'

'What's that to you, lady?'

'This.'

She thrust her warrant card under that pudgy nose.

'Detective Superintendent Martens, making inquiries concerning the death of Bubbles Xingara.'

Now the wary look was altogether evident on the dark face.

'Look, this is America. You ain't got no business here.'

'Oh, yes, I have. I'm making an authorized inquiry.'

'Anyhow, Bubbles Xingara ain't anything to do with me.'

'Nonsense. You were her coach for three years. Until you were dismissed for attempting sexual intercourse with her.'

'Attempting sex – hey, that's a damn lie.'

'No, it's the plain truth. You attempted to rape Bubbles Xingara. She told Peter Renshaw. And he punished you in his own way and saw that you were dismissed.'

'That yellow-belly. He couldn't punish a damn fly.'

'Nevertheless he gave you enough of a beating to make you leave the country pretty damn quickly.'

'If I was kicked out as Bubbles' coach, then what the hell was I going to do in lousy Limeyland?'

'So why did you go back there?'

'Who says I did?'

'The Immigration Service officer who examined your passport when you arrived, just before the tournament at Eastbourne. And his colleague who inspected it when you left confirms that you did so within a few days of Bubbles Xingara's death.'

'You accusing me, or what?'

'I am asking you some questions. Depending on the answers you give, I shall ask Agent Fernandez of the FBI here to detain you to await extradition. Or not.'

'The hell you will.'

'One more reply of that sort and you'll be on your way to a cell. Now, where did you get hold of the javelin?'

A look of incomprehension on the dark close-shaved face in front of her.

But genuine incomprehension? Or, if he had in his mind at this moment a picture of himself creeping with that silent weapon towards Adam and Eve House, the quick necessary attempt to pretend he had not understood?

'What the heck are you saying, you— Javelin? What's a javelin?'

Surely he must know. Like many liars, going too far?

'Don't tell me someone into sports like you doesn't know what a javelin is.'

Then a slowly appearing look of recognition. Genuine, or put on?

'Oh, yeah. Yeah, one of them spear things they have in athletics. Never had any use for that sort of fancy sport, me. But I know what you mean. A javelin, yeah.'

'So, where did you get hold of the javelin you used?'

'Hey, yes. I remember. What I read about little Bubbles when she was killed. Didn't they say it was a stabbing with some sort of spiked mystery weapon?'

'And you are saying now that you were not the man who used that javelin?'

'I was not.'

'Very well, so where were you on June the twentieth?'

'That's weeks and weeks ago. How the heck should I know where I was then.'

'I take it that means you deny being on that day at about the hour of six a.m. in the vicinity of Adam and Eve House, home of Bubbles Xingara?'

And at last the implacable questioning began to show results.

'Look, lady, I never touched a hair of her, not even when I thought she'd open her pretty little legs for me. That boyfriend of her mother's had no right to do what he did to me. I shoulda sued the guy.'

'But you didn't. You went running back here and you went over and over what he'd done to you till you could think of nothing but getting your revenge.'

'No.'

'Yes. And you thought you could get that revenge not by meeting Peter Renşhaw in fair fight. You're too much of a damn coward for that. But you thought you would kill the girl who, if you'd been man enough not to give way to your lust, would have brought you fame and respect as the coach who made her World Number One. Yes? Yes?'

Then tears came. The big misty brown eyes suddenly filled with a watery gloss. There was a crudely noisy sniff. And down the black-haired cheeks there rolled two glutinous rivulets.

For a moment Harriet began to doubt that this was the murderer of Bubbles, there in front of her on the other side of the long, gleamingly polished bar. But she thrust the thought away. Questioning a suspect should leave no room for even a flicker of doubt.

'No. No, I never,' the big ex-coach snorted.

'You never what?'

'I never went near that place. Yeah, I read in the

paper she lived in some house called Adam and Something, but I never found out where it was. And I never had no intention of going there. I went over to England when I heard there was a chance of getting to coach some other English girl who was playing her first Wimbledon. And that was all. When she wouldn't have nothing to do with me, I quit.'

'You expect me to believe that? You expect me to believe you didn't go down to Adam and Eve House on June the twentieth last very early in the morning carrying an athletics javelin, and that with that weapon you didn't kill Bubbles Xingara?'

'I didn't. I didn't. I was never near the place.'

More tears, or sweat perhaps.

'All right, prove to me you weren't.'

'How can I? How can I prove – hey, wait. June twenty, you said.'

'You know very well when Bubbles was killed.'

'But I wasn't there. June twenty, I was in Paris, France. That's where I heard Bubbles had been killed, murdered. I remember now. See, there's this guy I was buddies with, and I thought he could maybe fix me up with some work. French guy, I hired once to be Bubbles' hitting partner in California. You gotta have a guy for that with a girl who knows how to hit like Bubbles did. Make her even tougher. That's what.'

'Never mind all that. You're saying that on June the twentieth last you were in Paris meeting with Bubbles Xingara's former practice partner. Are you going to give me his name?'

'Too right I am. Henri Jouve, that's what he's called. You go to France, talk to him. He'll tell you where and when we met that day, and the day before. We talked about Bubbles then, natch we did. Lady, I could not of been in England then, and I never was at that Adam House. You'll see.'

Harriet turned round.

'Agent Fernandez, can you detain this man while I make inquiries by phone to Paris?'

'Sure can. Ask me, he's dreamt up all that stuff. You sure had him running then, ma'am. Guess I know now why, when I was assigned to assist, they told me you were called the Hard Detective back there in England.'

It was not easy to make contact with Michael Cacoyannis' buddy, Henri Jouve. First, Harriet had to phone Greater Birchester Police to talk to Inspector Franklin, expert in things French. Then she had to wait while Franklin made his own inquiries with his friends in the Paris police. Then Franklin had to wait while they made their inquiries about Jouve, whose address Cacoyannis had said he did not know, or would not give.

But Harriet, despite having nothing to do for a week and more – she never did visit the International Tennis Hall of Fame – found she had begun to manage wholly to avoid evoking the image of Anselm, trouserless or trousered. Perhaps, she allowed herself to think once or twice, the whole thing had been some sort of hallucination. Perhaps she had never really been struck down by love, but only under the terrible power of Eros had tricked herself into feeling caught in Aphrodite's net.

Whatever the reason she was at least grateful that no haunting image came to her, awake or asleep.

Then, when she was beginning to think her time in her characterless motel must be brought to an end, the phone in her room rang just after two a.m. She was not asleep. A day doing almost nothing had left her all too wakeful. But she was half-dozing and the sharp sound of the phone sent her shooting upright on the much too big bed.

'Yes? Yes?'

'Is that you, Miss Martens?'

She recognized Inspector Franklin's incurably formal voice.

'Yes, it's me.'

'Inspector Franklin here, ma'am.'

'Yes, yes. What is it? You've heard from the Paris police?'

'I have indeed, ma'am. And they've been most helpful.'

'Inspector, what did they say?'

'Ah, well, yes. Not good news, I'm afraid.'

'What sort of not good news?'

She was managing, just, not to shout.

'Well, it seems, ma'am, that this fellow Jouve does corroborate what your fellow, Cacoyannis, has claimed. Apparently Cacoyannis was in Paris on the date in question. My friends in Paris tell me that they pressed Jouve very hard and he couldn't be budged. He even produced some supporting witnesses. I don't know if you'll want to go over there and check for yourself when you get back here from America, ma'am. But, if you want my opinion, I'd say it wouldn't really be worth your while.'

'No,' she managed to say. 'No. I don't think it would be. And thank you, Inspector. It all must have caused you a lot of trouble.'

Why am I going to these lengths to thank the pompous idiot, she asked herself.

'No, no, ma'am. It was a pleasure, a pleasure indeed. I always welcome the opportunity to speak my little bit of French, you know.'

'Yes. Well, thank you again.'

End of my stay in safe-from-love America. Safe for me at least.

But what will happen back in Levenham, where Anselm should have returned from the leave I sent him on before eventually I was able to set off for America? What will happen when I set eyes on him again? Or, no, not on Anselm. When I set eyes on Detective Inspector Brent again, will he be no more than Detective Inspector Brent? Or will he be what he was before I left?

# Chapter Sixteen

*Back to Square One.* Harriet had always hated that much-used cliché. Clichés in general she distrusted for their woolly masking of the truth, and she did her best not to succumb to them. But *Back to Square One*, with its unthinking acceptance of defeat, was her real *bête noire.*

So it was all the more bitterly ironic that, as after a quick check in her office she entered the Incident Room on the morning after her return from America, and saw Anselm Brent, standing looking over WDC Johnson's shoulder at whatever was on her monitor, those words should at once come slap into her mind.

And, cliché or no cliché, the fact was that for her at that instant the words were absolutely true. At the mere sight of Anselm she had in a single mind-altering flash reverted to the state that had begun to set in when she had stared down at his muscular palm with its blotches of puffy yellowy-white calluses that now distant June morning. *Back to Square One.*

She forced herself to take a deep inward breath.

'Well,' she said loudly for the benefit of the whole room, 'I've got some bad news for you.'

At once Anselm turned to face her, a look of drowning apprehension on his broad face, manifesting itself in a sudden withdrawing of his forget-me-not eyes.

Good God, she thought, he cannot be thinking I am about to tell him, in front of all the people here, that I am going to end the affair between us?

But that's what it looks like. Thank Christ, the poor devil's standing where no one else can see that expression.

Quickly as she could she made the announcement she had begun with her *some bad news*.

'As you know, I went over to Newport hoping to bounce that man Cacoyannis into telling me the truth about what happened there by the river at Adam and Eve House. And I failed. Or, rather, I found he had a solid alibi – one or two details still to check – for the twentieth of June. He was far away from Adam and Eve House. In Paris.'

Mercifully the general outbreak of disappointed groans and murmured curses created enough noise for Anselm's look of stony incomprehension to pass unnoticed.

Harriet thought for a moment.

'So we must redouble our efforts in every other direction,' she said loudly. 'I'll be holding a briefing – ' she glanced at her watch – 'at ten, sharp. But first I'd like to hear about something that was nagging at me all the way on the flight back. Wasn't there a man who suddenly left a job in Birchester just after the murder? Working on a roof, was it? Mr Brent, will you come up and tell me where that particular inquiry's got to? If anywhere?'

She was pleased to see then that her summoning Anselm to her office had not produced any exchanges of grinning, behind-the-hand looks. So Handy Andy

Anderson, not present in the room, must have decided to refrain from telling everyone about what he had seen when he had flung open the office door that day, two weeks and more ago.

Nevertheless it was with a forced bravado that she ushered Anselm into the office in front of her and then firmly closed the door behind them.

She went across towards her desk, feeling, to her fury, her legs actually seeming weak beneath her. Anselm, Anselm.

She pulled back her chair, sank down on to it.

What to say?

To come straight out with, *Anselm, my darling, my darling*? Or make one more effort, useless though it must be, to get back to the calm unthinking state of those nights in the faceless motel in Newport? Deny what I feel, now at this instant pulsing and pulsing through me, take up that excuse for bringing him up here and ask about – who was it? – yes, that missing roofer?

She found she was gripping, with sweat-sticky hands, the edge of the desk in front of her.

One deep breath.

'Your leave go all right?'

Neither one thing nor the other. But perhaps the best way to do it.

'No.'

Anselm shot out the word as if it was a gobbet of filth he was flinging at her.

'Anselm. What – What is it?'

'What is it? You can ask that? It's love. Fucking love, that's what it is. I'm in love with you, Harriet. In love, in love. Did my leave go all right? Of course it didn't. What did I do, all day and half the bloody night too? I thought about you, thought about you. I couldn't think of anything else. I still can't think of anything else. Christ, I'm a grown man and I can't do anything but – but behave like some stupid mooning teenage girl.'

She jumped to her feet. The chair behind went rocking back till it struck the wall. She ran – or was it tottered? – round to where he was. Folded him in her arms, hugged him with all her force.

But then, as she stood bent awkwardly forward, up on her toes an inch or so, painfully reaching to his greater height, there came to her like the slow tolling of a death-bell the thought that she must give him up.

She must give him up. She hardly knew why the decision had come to her, when as soon as she had seen Anselm she had realized that her time away in America had not in any way had the effect she had both hoped for and hoped against. Two minutes, three minutes ago she felt absence had done nothing to break the hold the thunderbolt of Eros and the clinging toils of Aphrodite had caught her in. And now, still wrapped in those soft clamping tentacles, she was thinking with all the force she could summon up that, clamped, caught, or not, she must give Anselm up.

He was a decent man. A good police officer, doing his job in the proper way. He had a solid future ahead of him, keeping the Queen's peace as they said, making the world about him a better, safer place for those in it. But Eros, bloody, bloody Eros, had ruined it all. The infection that he had caught from her. Yes, she began to see, it was because through her, through her absurd love for this man in so many ways different from herself, so much more simple in his outlook, so unstrivingly better, he had become as much in thrall as she was herself. She could not let someone she felt for so intensely, so intimately, endure such crippling punishment.

No, if by telling him I no longer love him, by telling him that monstrous, unbelievable lie, I free him, then I must do it. I must do it even if I have to endure that punishment myself for all the days, the weeks, the months, even the years, to come.

Oh, John, John, she thought, how right you were. Yes, everywhere around us, everywhere all over the world, Eros waits, ready at any moment to poison anyone he chooses. Oh, yes, there are, here and there, people guarded somehow from those bolts of lust, the love-atheists, the truly chaste. But for all the rest of us, for me, for Anselm, Eros is there and when he has struck, there waiting, too, is Aphrodite and her encircling miasma.

And her coils must be broken. Or, if they can't be, and in me they cannot be, they must somehow be ignored, blotted out, expunged from the stricken mind.

She released Anselm, took a step backwards.

'Listen,' she said, forcing dryness and hardness into her voice. 'The inquiry, Bubbles' murder. What I told everybody down in the Incident Room just now is a fact. Now that Cacoyannis is out of it, the inquiry is bogged down, going nowhere. And it's got to move on. I asked you about that man, that roofer, whatever he is. Has there been any progress there while I've been away? Do you know?'

'What – What?'

'Mr Brent.' She forced herself to use the name, though it was like pouring down her rejecting throat a black, bitter dose. 'Mr Brent, I asked you what you know about that roofer who disappeared so suddenly from his job within hours of Bubbles' death.'

'Yes.'

He shook his head, as if he was casting off some thick enshrouding wrapping.

'Well? Well?'

'He . . . He's just been identified. Ma'am.'

'Identified? Then who is he? Speak up, man.'

'Name of Brewer, ma'am. Grant Brewer. WDC Johnson was telling me when you came into – '

A blank, wall-hit stop.

She knew at once that into his head there had come the sight of herself coming into the Incident Room, light grey suit with calf-length skirt, plain white shirt buttoned to the neck, her customary working clothes in the cooler months of the year. What she sometimes called to herself her *go-thither* outfit. And into his head that sight had lodged itself.

But it must not be allowed to stay. He must, Anselm must, *go thither*.

'Well, DI, what was it Johnson was telling you? Are you going to let me in on the great secret?'

The brute sarcasm did the trick.

'Sorry. Sorry, ma'am. I was – no, this is what Johnson said. She said they'd learnt that this Grant Brewer had worked at Adam and Eve House. Not recently, but shortly after the Renshaws, or Bubbles, bought the place. It needed a lot of repairs, especially to the roof. But that had come to an end and this fellow Brewer got other work. In Birchester. And then – it was his foreman there who eventually thought it was odd enough to be worth reporting – when at their meal-break up on the roof they were working on they heard the news of Bubbles' death on the radio Brewer suddenly scrambled down to the ground and never came back.'

'And has he been seen again now? Anywhere? Or is he totally lost to sight?'

'I – I was asking Gilly Johnson, ma'am, when you came – '

Once more Anselm came to a full halt.

She could almost see what he must be seeing again in his mind. Herself. The woman who had so often kissed him, who had in the end suddenly torn down his trousers, been on the point of making ferocious love to him. The woman, it seemed, for whom he was now deep drowned in love.

She pulled herself into a rigidly upright stance.

'Then you'd better get down to the Incident Room and find out what else Johnson's got hold of, hadn't you? I'll be down again for my briefing at ten, when I've had a look at all this stuff on my desk, and I'll expect a full report.'

The Hard Detective issuing orders.

When Harriet went down again to the Incident Room for her briefing Handy Andy was there. But she got from him, she saw with a lifting of relief, no look of amused complicity.

Well and good.

Up on the platform at the top of the room, she gave her team, noticeably smaller now than it had been at the beginning, a rapid review of the current situation.

'And eliminating Michael Cacoyannis,' she concluded, 'was not the only setback I ran into in the States. The FBI had also found Bubbles' former practice partner, Jo-Ann Parash, and established an impregnable alibi for her. Well, not sure that *impregnable* is the best word. The wretched girl had got herself pregnant by someone or other, had tried to get an abortion and on June the twentieth was in hospital. Nor has the FBI had any success in locating Bubbles' father, the mysterious Mr Xingara. They couldn't even tell me whether he was in America or had slipped over the border into Mexico, or gone almost anywhere else.'

She looked round the room. The faces that a month before had still been hunters' faces were, for the most part, no longer so. They were the faces of the dulled. No wonder inquiries into the roofer had been pursued so half-heartedly.

'Christ,' she barked, 'somebody come up with something. Oh, I know there are more than a few still to check from all those thousands of e-mails Bubbles got. But unless something a bit harder turns up we shall all still be here at Christmas. Or, in fact, I may not be. I've just had a memo from Mr Tarlington saying he wants to discuss with me how practical it would be if from now on I ran the inquiry partly from Birchester. So it may come to you sending me Christmas cards. Try one of those terrible, multiple-signature teenager cat-picture cards we've filed away saying *We love you, Bubbles*.'

She got her laugh with that. Well, a laugh's better than the apathy sucking them all down.

'But, damn it,' she snapped. 'Christmas is not so far away now. So let's have some suggestions that lead somewhere.'

'Well, ma'am,' placid Sgt Wintercombe boomed. 'The trouble is we're no longer getting the co-operation we might from other forces. There's an e-mail I was looking at last week, one from someone who at least doesn't sound like a teenager. So it could be our man.

No proper name, of course, only some silly nickname, but your electronic wizards in Birchester, if I may say so, have done nothing so far about tracing him. At the start of it all they were getting back to us over an inquiry like that within twenty-four hours.'

'Very good, Sergeant. I'll personally put a bomb under them. Anything else?'

'Ma'am,' WDC Johnson said. 'There's this chap Brewer, the roofer. We have made some progress there.'

'So I understand from Mr Brent. Any more come in since first thing this morning?

'Yes, ma'am.'

'Yes. Good. Let's hear.'

'Well, ma'am, after Brewer's foreman eventually told us about him suddenly quitting his job, where incidentally he was getting high wages – he's fearless on heights, they told me – inquiries since have turned up an odd fact. A pretty suspicious one, in fact. You see, Brewer, who, the foreman said, was a bit of a loner, had been due to go to Spain on holiday in the second week in July, all paid for and booked. But on the afternoon of the murder, not next day as we first thought, he turned up at the travel agency wanting to transfer his booking to the first available flight. When they told him the sort of fare he was on didn't allow for that he tried to cancel. But he was on a cheapo flight and wasn't allowed to hand it in so near the departure date. So then he simply let that go, and booked whatever flight they had, leaving at once. And in fact on June the twenty-first he left.'

'Never to return?'

'Oh, no, ma'am. Eventually he came back, flat broke, to Birchester, and yesterday through a Job Centre we traced him.'

'He's still in Birchester now, far as you know?'

'He is, ma'am. He's got a new job, on another roof, and he's back in his old digs. I went there and made a few discreet inquiries. He seemed to be well settled in, so I didn't do any more. But I did make a PNC check.'

'And what did that magical national computer have to tell you?'

'One conviction, ma'am. Indecent assault, three years ago.'

'Yes, not much necessarily. But all the same, it makes him look worthwhile, perhaps more than worthwhile. Where can we find him now? Does anybody know?'

Again it was WDC Johnson who answered.

'Yes, ma'am. He should be in Birchester, up on the roof of a building going up in the Moorfields area.'

'Right. We'll go and see him straight away. Let's have some action.'

The Hard Detective went across to Birchester accompanied by DI Brent. Little though either of us, she had decided, will welcome the other's proximity. But, if Anselm is to be broken from his bondage at all, it has to be by thrusting him, however painfully, into a situation of normality between us or at least of outward normality.

So she had him there in the car, sitting in front of her, next to WDC Johnson, who was driving. To sit within touching distance, she felt, would be asking too much of herself. But she permitted no brooding silences to fall.

'You've neither of you spoken to this man Brewer?'

'No, ma'am,' Johnson answered promptly. 'He was in Spain when we got to hear about him.'

'And you, Mr Brent? You don't know him, know of him, as a local?'

A moment's pause before an answer came.

'He's not a local to me. From Birchester, they say.'

'Did either of you talk to that foreman of his who reported him going off like that?'

'He went to his local PS in Birchester, ma'am, whichever was nearest to the building being put up in Chapeltown,' Johnson said. 'I understand Mr Anderson went over and saw him afterwards. But I never heard what he found out, if anything.'

'And you, Mr Brent?'

Again a tiny pause before he brought himself to speak.

'I was on leave, ma'am.' Another pause. 'As you may recall.'

She did not let the half-hidden resentment affect her. Relentlessly she went on forcing him to answer whatever questions she could think of. As well as making hapless WDC Johnson provide more snippets of almost useless information.

It had begun gently to rain, the first signs perhaps of autumn. Behind her jerkily forced questions and comments she heard the swish of their tyres as an increasingly obtrusive background.

Then at last Johnson pulled the car up.

'This should be it, ma'am.'

'Right, you'd better stay here. Mr Brent, I'd like you to come with me.'

Face thunderous, Anselm opened the far-side door, stepped out into the damply wetting drizzle.

Yes, she thought, he knows damn well what I'm

doing, and he's hating it. But I'm going to go on doing it. Being hard with him. Being hard with myself. Fighting off, if it can be fought off, the sullen cloud above us. As sullen – she glanced upwards – as the actual rain-cloud there.

The building, apparently yet another office block, was only three-parts finished. Inside, she found a carpenter at work and learnt that there were men on the roof and that Grant Brewer was one of them.

'Can they carry on in this weather?' she asked, by way of thanking the man for his help.

He laughed.

'Well, they do. But I'm glad I'm a chippie, that's all.'

They went on, up flights of bare concrete stairs, following his directions. Eventually they came to the top floors where the outer walls had not yet been put in place. A chilly wind blew in a little of the fine rain.

'Must be almost there,' Harriet said.

Anselm grunted.

Should I stop here while we can, she asked herself. Have it out with him again?

No, it'd be no use.

'Right, up we go.'

In a minute more they had emerged through a small doorless doorway on to the roof itself. In front of her, blurred in the misty rain, Harriet saw a panorama far down below of a large part of the city. She felt a lurch of disquiet. Heights never much to her taste.

Quickly she looked round at her immediate surroundings. They were on a narrow area of the freshly installed leads. Behind them there rose up bright new, yellowy-brown unweathered timbers, awaiting their covering, in row after row reaching to the peak of the future roof. Perched at intervals at the very top were three men hammering home the remaining cross-beams.

She turned to Anselm.

'Which one's Brewer? Do you know?'

'No idea.' Two sulky words.

'Right, we'll find out soon enough.'

She lifted her head and called up.

'Grant Brewer? Mr Brewer, we're police. We'd like a word.'

None of the hammering men appeared to have heard.

'Too windy, I suppose,' she said to Anselm. 'We'll just have to climb up nearer.'

For a moment she had considered sending him up on his own. But her long-engrained habit of never as a woman officer failing to do what was asked of a male officer prevailed.

It was not really difficult to use the cross-bars of the unclad parts of the roof as a sort of ladder, although from time to time as she somewhat laboriously climbed she felt one or other of her feet slip on the rain-wet wood.

Half-way up, with Anselm sullenly following her a foot or so below, she paused and thought of calling upwards again. But it seemed pointless. They could hardly talk to Brewer, let alone subject him to questioning, leaning as they were against the slope of the unfinished roof.

She drew in a long breath and started off again. Nearing the crest she saw that the three roofers were now looking down at them. But she waited until she had managed to get astride the heavy top beam, finding herself next to two of the roofers who were working close together, with the third some fifteen feet away at the far end of the long ridgepiece.

Damn this skirt, she thought savagely as she made efforts to hoick it up enough to be able to sit in reasonable comfort, though she had to take care not for an instant to look downwards.

'Which of you is Grant Brewer?' she said as soon as she was settled.

For a short time, perhaps only ten or twenty seconds, there was no answer. Then the man nearest her replied.

'That's him. Along at the end. Grant, you silly bugger, answer the lady, whoever she is. She's come all the way up for a chat, you cunt.'

'I'm police,' Harriet said briskly, adding as Anselm came scrambling on to the ridgepiece in front of her. 'Detective Superintendent Martens, and this is Detective Inspector Brent.'

'The law, is it? What you done, Grantie?'

From the far end of the wooden structure that was to be the roof chubby-faced, curls-crowned, vacant-looking Grant Brewer produced a few strangulated words.

'It wasn't me. It wasn't. I never.'

'Talk to him, Mr Brent,' Harriet said to Anselm. 'Shove yourself along towards him. I can't even see his face properly with you between us.'

Anselm, after a moment, began to move forward along the ridgepiece. And at once, from the awkwardness with which he set about it, Harriet realized that, if she was unhappy about heights, he was yet more so.

She felt an upsurge of the feeling for him she had tried so hard to suppress.

Tell him to stay where he is? Try to get myself past

him and along to that damn idiot at the end there? But, no. If I have my duty, Anselm equally has his.

She watched him shuffle himself bit by bit onwards, and concentrated with all her force on stopping the physical fluttering of her stomach muscles.

At last he got to within four or five feet of the curly-haired silent youngster at the far end of the roof, leaning easily forward with his feet on a cross-bar. The picture of outward confidence. But then suddenly, as Anselm slowly shuffled nearer, he shot bolt upright and stood there swaying from side to side.

'No,' he screamed.

He turned and looked down at the streets far below, and Harriet at once knew what he was intending to do.

'Catch him, hold him,' she yelled.

Grant Brewer began to launch himself forward, a chubby balloon. Anselm took a desperate lunge in his direction, foot slipping and scrabbling on the wet wood of the beams.

He was in time.

For a little the two of them wrestled together, Anselm with one hand round the would-be suicide's leg, the other clutching scrabblingly at one of the half-installed timbers. Abruptly losing all fear, Harriet swung herself along towards them, reached high and gripped Brewer by the sleeve of his leather jacket. Digging her fingers fiercely in, she hauled him back.

# Chapter Seventeen

With the aid of Grant Brewer's two fellow workers, they
succeeded in getting him to the ground, a hopeless,
quivering jelly. Bundled into the back of the car, with
this time DI Brent in the rear seat, they drove at speed
back to Levenham. Beyond the purr of the engine and
the swish-swish of the tyres as the rain still steadily
soaked down, only Grant Brewer's occasional sobs or
snorts broke a long silence.

When they arrived Harriet was not surprised to see
a long trail of snot hanging down from the boy's right
nostril.

'Take him to Interview Room One,' she said. 'I'll be
there in five minutes.'

Five minutes she still needed to sort herself out.
However much in the car she had tried to think, she
had been defeated in part by Brewer's sobbing and
even more by Anselm's stubborn, folded-in refusal to
open his mouth.

She ran up to her office, turned her key in the door,
ignored the pile of messages on the desk and plunged
her head into her hands. Fiercely she tried to work out
whether her decision about Anselm had been in any
way altered by the danger she had put him in there
on the roof, by his sudden courage in overcoming it.

Oh, God, she found herself thinking, it has, it has.

How could I have pretended, deceiving myself even, that I would be able to thrust aside love. Love infusing me, infusing him with its all-powerful – what?

But, when she tried to think just what it was she felt occupying every cubic centimetre of her body, every cell in her brain, all she could label it as was *fumes*.

Yes, I'm poisoned by love's fumes. And Anselm is equally poisoned. Think what happened in this very room when I tried to tell him, half-persuading myself it was the truth, that a few days in brash, busy America had brought me to my senses.

And then . . . then Anselm spat out those bitter words, *It's love. Fucking love . . . I'm in love with you, Harriet*. And I knew, I felt, he was as gripped in every way as I was. Yes, oh, yes, I knew what you'd been feeling, my darling, my darling, my own darling.

At last, heaving herself upright with hands spread wide on the surface of the desk in front of her, careless whether their sweat would mark the papers under them, not knowing even whether she was pressing down on papers or on scattered paper-clips or ball-points, she made for the door.

I said I'd be down in Interview Room One in five minutes, and I shall be. I shall.

But she had to hold on to the stair-rail as she made her way below.

Interview Room One, where she had questioned Old Rowley and later Prudence Mackintosh, was occupied. Two Leven Vale officers were there, dealing with a youth who had committed the decent, ordinary crime of taking and driving away. Grant Brewer, who was awaiting interrogation about a crime, wholly, she thought with a jet of bitterness, in the dark realm of Eros, she found in Interview Room Two.

At its door she gave herself a moment to take a good look at him. Still pale as could be under his damply curling crown of black hair, he was looking now a little more composed. No longer was he shivering and sobbing as he had been in the car, nor was that trail of snot stuck to his right cheek.

Did he recover enough to wipe it away, she wondered. Or did WDC Johnson provide in womanly fashion a tissue? Certainly Anselm did not look as if he had come to the snotty young man's rescue. Where, when questioning Old Rowley back in June, he had leant forward and by his look alone impressed on the aged layabout that no lies, no slippery evasions, would help him, now he was just sitting there, an inert presence.

Yes, she said to herself. Yes, I can pull him out of that sink of despair now. And how easy it could be. Give him the least flicker of a sign that all my stiffness and withdrawnness was mere pretence, and in an instant, like some tropical plant touched by the first rains, he'll be back to his old self. I know it. Whatever difficulties he may see in our path, they'll look like so many red-and-white plastic traffic cones to be knocked over and left uselessly rolling.

And, yes, yes, yes, I feel that, too.

She pulled back her shoulders, went across and took the chair between Anselm and Johnson, looking at neither of them even for a moment but straight ahead at wretched Grant Brewer.

'Right, Mr Brewer,' she said, once the preliminaries for the tapes had been gone through, and the dopey young roofer had shown awareness enough to decline the offer of a solicitor's presence, 'tell me, why did you go back to work at all on that morning of June the twentieth?'

The unexpectedness of the question plainly sent a judder of confusion through the fat, pale-faced man-boy. As she had intended it should.

'I – I didn't.'

'For God's sake, man, don't think it's going to help you to talk nonsense like that. Your foreman on that Chapeltown job told us just what time it was when you upped and left. It was after your meal-break, about midday. You'd been working there all morning.'

No answer.

'Mr Brewer, I'm asking you again. Why did you stay on that job until after you'd heard the news on the radio of Bubbles Xingara's murder?'

She thought she was still going to be faced with blank, uncomprehending silence. But before she put her question for a third time the chubby young roofer muttered a reply.

'Knew what they'd think.'

'What they'd think? And what was that?'

'That I'd done it. Killed her. Because of what happened that once. What they called *indecent assault.*'

'Well, now, Mr Brewer, I'm going to ask you straight out: did you on that day in June, the twentieth, assault Bubbles Xingara, take a javelin and jab it into her neck?'

Grant Brewer slowly shook his head from side to side. There was in his big, soft brown eyes a look of some animal, a cow perhaps, faced with an object it was unable to get its brain round.

'Javelin,' he said at last. 'I been wondering . . . Please, what's a javelin?'

Christ, no, Harriet said to herself. First Cacoyannis makes out he didn't know what a javelin was, though he soon enough agreed he did, and now this clumpy fellow's making the same claim.

'*What is a javelin?*' she echoed him. 'You're actually asking me what a javelin is?'

But could this be the clever answer of a clever murderer? Was this apparently dully podgy youth capable of rapidly winding back down the trail of logic? Of working out that, if he could convincingly claim not to know what a javelin was, he could not possibly have used one to kill Bubbles Xingara?

But, no. No. All my training tells me I'm dealing with someone who, if he uses logic at all, uses it only to plot out his existence one or two steps ahead.

'So you didn't know that what you took to Adam and Eve House that day was something called a javelin?' she said. 'Javelins were spears back in the Roman times. Now they're just thrown in athletics, to see who can make them go furthest. But you, you didn't have to throw the one you'd got hold of, did you?'

'But I didn't do it. I didn't.'

'We think you did.'

Suddenly she thought of the piece of evidence, or of semi-evidence, hearsay, that she had extracted from Fiona Diplock when at Adam and Eve House she had taken her out down by the boathouse. There had been little to it. Just that Fiona under pressure had recalled something more than Handy Andy had learnt about her half-forgotten conversation with Bubbles. Bubbles, she had said at last, had gone as far as to knock down, or kick over, the person, male or female never actually specified, who had angered her.

'We think you went early one morning in June, a few days before Bubbles Xingara was killed, down to the Leven by Adam and Eve House, and waited there for her to come back from her run. And then . . . Then what did you do? Did you try to kiss her? And she – what? – gave you a good kick, sent you sprawling, showed you all too plainly she didn't want anything of that sort. So you came back later, carrying a javelin you had somehow got hold of, even if you just thought it was a long stick with a sharp point. And, because she hadn't let you make love to her, you thrust that long weapon – did you think it was your prick, Brewer? – deep into her throat. Were you aiming for her mouth, Brewer? The lips she wouldn't let you kiss? Were you? Were you?'

'No, no, no, no. No, never. Never. I wasn't there ever. I didn't do that.'

'You expect us to believe you? When, as soon as you heard Bubbles' body had been found, you dropped everything and tried to get out of the country? You really expect us to believe you weren't there at all at Adam and Eve House?'

'I was there.'

Ah, at last. At last the cough.

Yet, even as the triumphant thought bloomed in her mind, she felt an inkling of doubt. A tiny question mark in one corner of the page. Something not quite right. Perhaps it was the sudden picture of Grant Brewer walking towards the murder scene carrying that long, eight-foot, pointed spear. Hard exactly to see.

Brewer, opposite her, sat blinking.

Then, with a curious dipping of his head somehow like a swimming bird gathering up a floating morsel, he spoke again.

'I was there. But not down by the river. I was never down there. It was when she first came to the house, when she bought it, and I was working on the roof. An' . . . An' she was nice to me when she met me going up and down. She spoke to me. *Morning, Grant*, she said.'

He seemed to think he had told them enough, and Harriet began to feel that perhaps he had. Or perhaps not.

'So it was then that you fell in love with her?'

Oh, Eros, Eros, she thought, how many others have you hurled down to their deaths, or to the living death of a life sentence?

'She was lovely. She smiled.'

'And that was all? She smiled for you?'

'I never did it. I never.'

Now, she abruptly realized, they had arrived at the last chance. The boy had denied being at Adam and Eve House when Bubbles had been murdered, and certainly it looked somehow unlikely that someone, who in all probability had never known what a javelin was, had carried one there and killed her with it. More, he had said, not unconvincingly, that his whole relationship with Bubbles lay in responding to her careless smiles. But wasn't the boy, even now, doing what any murderer would do, as long as they could keep it up? Deny everything, time and again.

So, one last banging-out attempt.

'Right. Out at Adam and Eve House, when you were working there, Bubbles smiled for you. She smiled, and you smiled back. But that wasn't enough for you, was it? You wanted to make love to her, didn't you?'

'No. No, I couldn't. Me . . . and her. I – I'd never – I couldn't make myself even talk to her, could I?'

And then she saw it. Grant Brewer might be daring up on the high roofs of buildings, but that was the sole daring he could rise to. He hadn't had the courage to speak so much as a word when carefree Bubbles, flashing by, gave him one of her cheerful smiles, the smiles she bestowed on everyone.

'So,' she said, almost wearily, 'you in fact seldom even exchanged a word with Bubbles Xingara?'

'No. No. How could I? With her? Bubbles?'

'And you weren't at Adam and Eve House early one June morning when Bubbles was coming back from her run, and you didn't accost her then?'

'No, I couldn't of. I – I wouldn't of dared.'

'The first you heard of Bubbles' murder was when, up on that roof in Chapeltown, the radio was on at your meal-break—'

'Yes, yes. Then. Then, and I – I had to go. Get away.'

'And you did not, on the morning of June the twentieth last, go to Adam and Eve House carrying an offensive weapon, namely one athletics javelin?'

'No. Never.'

The simple total denial. And believable now.

Back in her office, Harriet refused to let herself think again about Anselm, even though there had been no opportunity to indicate by a touch of a hand, or the quickest of looks, that his time of exile was at an end.

She sat down and began to go through the messages and memos she ought to have dealt with earlier. She saw the task as anaesthesia. Sooner or later she would have to decide what to do about Anselm. But not yet. First must come the fact that, once more, her inquiry was back to the bogged-down state she had snarled over at her briefing.

But the first sheet of paper she picked up – it was, yes, oily with the sweat her hands had planted on it when she had forced herself to go down to question Grant Brewer – turned out to be a message from the Leven Vale Chief Constable.

*Detective Superintendent Martens. Please see me at your earliest convenience.* And a squiggle of initials.

She felt a flush of shame. A request from a much senior officer, in such definite terms, ought not to have been neglected.

She picked up her phone and asked Mr Tarlington's secretary whether he was free to see her.

'Oh, yes, Miss Martens. Yes, he's been waiting for you.'

She hurried down to her car, drove the short distance to Leven Vale Police headquarters in an old mansion about a mile out of the town. Mr Tarlington, in uniform as always, sitting upright, dwarfed by his desk, face set, sticking-out ears redder than ever, gave her a sharp look through his perched-on rimless glasses.

'Ah, Miss Martens. Yes, I wanted to see you. A matter, let me say, of some immediacy.'

'Yes, sir? I'm sorry. An urgent interrogation.'

The eyes behind the glinting spectacles lit up.

'It's brought a result?'

'I'm afraid not, sir. It was a young man, a roofer, who abruptly left his job the moment he heard about Miss Xingara's death. However, under pressure he proved to have been simply scared, because some time ago he'd had a conviction for indecent assault and he had been working at Adam and Eve House when Miss Xingara first bought it.'

'Nothing to it then? You're sure?'

I wouldn't have told you if I hadn't been sure, would I?

But all she said was, 'Yes, sir.'

'Very well. Now, what I wanted to see you about was this: I had a meeting yesterday with my Police Authority, who were yet more concerned than myself at the rate of expenditure on your inquiry. We have already well exceeded our budget for the whole of this year, and there are still three months to go. I've been looking at the figures for overtime expenditure. Frankly, they're horrifying. They have to be reduced, Miss Martens. Drastically reduced.'

'I understand your concern, sir, and your Police Authority's. But the fact remains that Bubbles Xingara was a nationally known figure, an internationally known one. The public expects a result, and goes on expecting one. Not a week passes, as you must very well know, without some reference in the press somewhere to her murder. To be blunt, a reference as often as not to our lack of progress. I attempt to keep expenditure down. Of course I do. But in a situation like this every line of inquiry has to be traced to its very end.'

'Yes, yes. I know. I know all that, Miss Martens. But the fact remains the Leven Vale Police cannot afford the demands you have been making.'

He produced a smile that was more like a grimace.

'You know, sometimes I find myself wishing that it had been one of my officers who had first come across that body and that he had had sense enough to carry it across the Leven and dump it in Greater Birchester Police territory. Only a few yards away.'

'I understand, sir. But let me point out you have had a great deal of assistance from our side. There's not only myself but DI Anderson, a very experienced and efficient officer, as well as almost half the team of detectives deployed.'

'That's as may be, Miss Martens. That's as may be. But, say what you will, my Authority is demanding that less be spent.'

'So what do you propose, sir? Specifically?'

Put the ball into his court – as powerfully as the Brit with the Hit had ever done.

Mr Tarlington looked down at the desk in front of him. And then looked up.

'Well, what I have had in mind for some time, Miss Martens, is this. That . . . That you should return to Birchester – I've had a word in fact with your Chief Constable – and take up purely administrative duties there, so that you can still exercise a general supervision over the Xingara investigation. We will, of course, retain DI Anderson, an officer as you say of impressive efficiency, in day-to-day charge here.'

Handy Andy, Harriet thought. Shouldn't have put in that anodyne *experienced and efficient*. Only true on the surface. I've always thought Anselm, despite his failures, the better man. So, put his name forward? Give him the boost he deserves, and I'd like him to have?

But, no. No, I can't be seen to be favouring him, not when Handy Andy's there with his tale of trousers-down all ready to spill.

'Very well, sir,' she said out loud. 'If that's your decision.'

The Leven Vale Chief Constable must have heard the note of something like anger under her terse reply.

This was, in fact, much more of a step-down than the vague idea about her working from Birchester which he had earlier put forward.

He shifted to left and right in his high-backed chair.

'Of course, Miss Martens,' he said hastily, 'I see you still as very much in the driving seat of the inquiry. Your work with us much appreciated. Much appreciated. The Hard Detective, you know.' His twisted teeth appeared in a sort of grin. 'It goes without saying, absolutely, that you must be available to come back at a moment's notice should any strong new lead emerge.'

'Thank you, sir.'

# Chapter Eighteen

What was my first thought, Harriet said to herself, looking back, when I heard that, in effect, I was to be taken off the inquiry? That I had to all intents and purposes failed with it? Anselm, I had thought at once. I'm to be taken away from Anselm. Will I ever see him again? Will I? Is this after all the end of everything?

Then, immediately, she had pulled herself together. Of course, she could see Anselm, if she wanted to. And she did. She did. She was not being banished from some fairy kingdom; she was being sent back from Levenham, to Birchester, not much more than twenty miles away. There would be nothing really to prevent her driving over to Anselm. She could make the journey inside half an hour. She could make it every single day.

She let a wry grin distort her face.

*Administrative duties*. In other words, not much to do. There would be plenty of chances to get hold of Anselm, put him in her car and drive ... Drive to somewhere where they could make love, make love as often and as freely as they could ever want. Why not? Eros rules, OK.

And at the same time a parallel thought slid into her mind. Now I'll see more of John. That'll be nice. Long chats in the evening, gossip about life at the nerve-hub of the mighty Majestic. Those stuffed pockets of his yielding more scraps of the wisdom of the ages, hastily noted down. I shall even be able to relieve him of some of the household duties he's been so good about doing while I've been spending almost the whole of every day in bloody Levenham.

And the twins'll be back for Christmas. We'll be able for once to have a full family gathering. Must look out that pudding recipe I clipped from *The Times* all those years ago.

Then, like a deep gong stroke heralding some final ending, she found her mind abruptly filled with the poised heavyweight thought that, her Aphrodite-tangled love for Anselm blotting out everything else, it blotted out, too, the Christmas pudding. It blotted out John's learnedly stuffed pockets, the twins' careers at university. It was going to shatter the whole structure she had lived in for twenty years and more. She had been wedlocked. That was it. Wedlocked. And a hammer blow was going to send that lock flying into fragments.

Now, if she put herself wholly into Anselm's keeping, as she wanted to do, as she desired with all her force to do, she must tell John what had happened. Make her confession.

And then . . . Then it would all be over. Oh, yes, perhaps she would be at home over Christmas, would even make that pudding. But the Christmas feast would be no more than a pale mockery, however much she enjoyed John's company, however pleased she was about Graham and Malcolm's progress. If she loved Anselm the way she did – and she did, she did – then it would mean the ending of a whole long period of her life.

Eros. Eros, that mighty god, would have had one more triumph. No, he had had that triumph with her. Among the millions down the long ages he had brought into the arms of Aphrodite, senseless victims, she, too, ranked.

A twisted and ugly triumph, as twisted and ugly in its way as when someone, driven surely by the sexual demon within them, had killed bright, happy, admired Bubbles Xingara.

Then back to her had come the realization of what Mr Tarlington's bland gratitude really meant.

Am I now never to be the one who finds out who killed Bubbles Xingara? Who among all the hundreds and thousands out there had had the opportunity to wield that long, sharp-pointed javelin?

Has the Hard Detective's time come to an end? Was I at last up against something too hard for me?

No, damn it, I was not. If I'd been allowed more time, extra resources, I would have found that killer. It might have taken me months more. It might have taken years more. But hard work would have done it.

Someone approached Bubbles Xingara that cloudless morning in June and thrust a javelin into her throat. That was a fact. That there was a someone. And that fact would have left other facts in its wake. All right, all the searches at Adam and Eve House had found nothing, and it was almost beyond the bounds of possibility after the passing of so many months that anything now could be found. But there were other facts than those generated by that one brutal fact of the killing itself. There was the fact that, first of all, someone had got hold of the javelin. Then there was the fact that they had actually committed the murder, and that they were a person, a real human being moving about in the real world. Someone, somewhere, would have seen them in the aftermath of that killing behaving out of character. And, although what they may have seen might have meant nothing to them at the time, at some future point something about that person's behaviour, perhaps when they were once again struck down by dread Eros, would be markedly different. Then that someone would perhaps begin to ask why they had changed, and at last speak out about their misgivings.

So I could have detected it, if I had been allowed to stay a hundred per cent on the case. Hard work, hard detecting, would have brought Bubbles' killer to light, eventually. If I had been permitted to work hard.

But now, now, what will I do? Call up Anderson from time to time and ask how things are going? A fat lot of good that will be.

And, worse, am I soon even going to be as much on the case as I will be sitting in some backwater office at Greater Birchester Police headquarters? Because I am in love with Anselm Brent. The pillar-cloud of sexuality will be enveloping us. So twist and evade as we may, it is more than likely that before long someone in the media will get to learn about us, and both our careers will be over. Then where am I likely to be in six months' time? A former detective superintendent who once had a triumphant career and who, copybook blotted as they put it, is now – what? – someone summoned when a new police series is coming to television to *advise*? Someone whose name can be used as bait in an advertisement for an anti-burglar device? Someone ekeing out a sort of living alongside club bouncer Anselm Brent.

So better now to make that confession of mine to

John? To act before he sees those headlines? To say that, like many and many another, I fell foul of the great Eros, that I'm caught in Aphrodite's softly steel-meshed net?

The best-laid plans of mice and men, as the poet Burns is always ready to remind us, John said with a wry grin that evening, gang aft a-gley. When, as a preliminary to what she had stiffened herself to confess, Harriet had told him she would soon be working back in Birchester, the last thing she had expected was that he would have equally surprising news for her.

'Well, you know our masters, mine as well as yours so it seems, think nothing of changing the course of our lives with the briefest of warnings.'

'What? What's this? Your masters have exploded some bombshell under you, too?'

'They have. Another Indian one, you might say. It seems our people out there have got themselves into a jam again. And, as the one who was able to sort them out last time, I'm being sent there.'

'And where exactly?'

'Oh, New Delhi, of course. That's where our office is, after all.'

'So . . . So, well, will you be seeing your beautiful widow, Mrs— What was her name?'

'I've a feeling I don't need to tell you.'

'No. You're right, actually. Burnt into my mind, sort of. Mrs Kamala Singh.'

'Correct. And, no, I don't know whether I'll see her or not. If she gets to hear I'm in Delhi, and the news goes whizzing round in her sort of circles, then she'll certainly expect me to call. And I suppose I will. Probably. If only because it's the polite thing to do. But, of course, I'll have no intention of – what? – stoking old fires. But that's something that'll be rather out of my hands, whether I go to see her or not. You know my theory, as you choose to call it, about that grim old god sitting up there, Eros by name.'

Then she saw that, after all, her opportunity to make her long-withheld confession had come.

'Yes,' she said, rather rapidly. 'Yes, I know all about your theory. You've repeated it to me often enough. But now, curiously, I don't at all feel like calling it a theory.'

'No? What do you call it then? A nonsense?'

'No. A fact.'

'A fact?'

He sounded genuinely surprised.

'Yes, a fact. The existence of all-powerful Eros, looking down at us wretched human beings from within his thunderous cloud. I believe in him now all right, and in your foam-born Aphrodite. You see, I'm one of their victims.'

John sat up in his chair.

'I've been going to tell you for quite a long time. But then somehow for a little I thought there might be no need. And now I know that there's every need. John, dear, I'm in love. Head over heels, to use the beastly cliché, in love.'

For a moment John sat there, silent.

'So who is it?' he asked at last.

She took a gulp of breath.

'A man called Anselm Brent. I may have mentioned him to you casually, I forget. He's a DI in the Leven Vale force, one of the officers on my team. And I don't still quite know how it came about – well, yes, I do. It began when I saw his right hand, the palm of it. It was clustered with calluses. He was showing it to me because, as we were both looking at Bubbles Xingara's body on the morning she was murdered, I had exclaimed about her hand. It was calloused, too. I had no idea what that might mean. And DI— And Anselm told me it was the result of hours of tennis practice and play. He's a keen player himself. So then he showed me his own palm, and – and that was it. I was lost.'

'Yes, I see. I see how it could happen. Our old friend Eros loves to try that sort of trick, make some tiny circumstance set off an explosion of sexuality. I'm sorry he chose to try it with you, though. And even more sorry if, as you seem to have been saying, it's more than a sudden dart of lust, even of dart after dart. If it's Aphrodite at work, I'm very sorry. But what's happened has happened, I realize that.'

'Oh, yes. It is worse than Eros. It is Aphrodite as well. I've tried to throw those tresses of hers off, if that's possible. I tried. There were times when I thought I'd never need to tell you. More than once I thought I'd cast it all out of my system. When I was in America I thought being in a different world, if only for a short time, had done it. But then, the moment I stepped back into the Incident Room at Levenham and – and Anselm was standing there it was all back again in an instant. I – I'm obsessed with him. Obsessed.'

They had said no more that evening. In the same way that Harriet had contrived, even when her feelings for Anselm were at their most intense, to live an ordinary life with John, they both felt now that, once the admission had been made, no more need be said, nothing need be altered, until the moment came when a decision on their future had to be made.

So, in the short time before John had to leave for India, it was the simple routine of ordinary life. It was breakfast in the morning, cereal on Mondays, Wednesdays and Fridays, grapefruit on Tuesdays, Thursdays and Saturdays. The necessity over of being in Levenham by eight every day, it was croissants in bed with the papers on each Sunday, and, yes, after a while sex, and it was as delighting as ever. There were, too, pleasant evenings sitting out in the garden while the light and the good weather still just lasted and reading or idly chatting. It was every now and again the telly.

But they both knew that she was no longer truly John's, that her whole loyalty was Anselm's. So she had had no hesitation, on the morning after her avowal, as soon as she got to Levenham in summoning Anselm.

He stepped into the office, looking suspicious and rebellious.

'It's all right, you fool,' she said.

'All right? But—'

'I've told my husband about you. About us.'

He stood there, silent. She thought she could see beneath the ruddiness of his cheeks a pallor setting in.

'But what's he said?' he choked out at last. 'Did he— he didn't hit you or anything?'

She laughed.

'No, John's not the hitting type. Or at least not with his fists, though he can use words to some purpose when he wants. And I suppose if he'd wanted to last night, he'd have made me feel a total louse. Squashed me. But, no, he understands what can happen to someone when, as he likes to put it, old Eros strikes and Aphrodite, goddess of love, follows in his wake. When, as he quoted to me from some book once, the fucking leads to kissing. He knows it's inescapable then.'

'Don't think I understand.'

'No need to. The key's in the door, lock it and come here.'

Then Eros finally and ferociously had his way. And if anyone tapped at the door and waited for her answer she didn't hear them.

The weeks went by. John had left for Delhi a fortnight after he had told her about the job, with no decision taken about what was going to happen. Harriet mastered the elements of the Forward Planning brief allocated to her at Greater Birchester Police headquarters, and, as she had forecast, found frequent opportunities at weekends and sometimes in mid-week to snatch Anselm from his home and even from the Incident Room at Levenham police station. They existed in a daze of sexual fulfilment, making love sometimes out in the open while the weather still held, and in the chill of late autumn in her own home, regardless of the risk of noticing neighbours.

Not that, Harriet felt, she would have anything to worry about if some busybody in their street did write to John in Delhi. Their arrangement stood, thanks to John's seemingly infinite tolerance. He had said before leaving that until she wanted to make some definite move he was happy to let things stand.

'And Mrs Kamala Singh?' she had dared to say, if with a hint of a smile.

'We'll see. We'll see.'

And so it had been left. Every two or three days a

fax from Delhi chattered on to her machine at home. A chattering of inoffensive chat. And she replied in the same vein, news of the twins at university, mild complaints about the dullness of her present work, an occasional mention of the Bubbles Xingara investigation, though there was little about it to be said.

When I do have a major decision about us to tell him, she said to herself once, it'll have to be a letter, a Dear John indeed. Unless he's back home before that point arrives . . . Or unless I get a Dear Harriet from him.

At headquarters at her borrowed desk most of the time she simply sat dreaming, dreaming about when she could see Anselm next. Occasionally she forced herself to pay attention to the papers in front of her – damn it, I'm being paid to do this: must do it right – but always, at the back of her mind, was the thought that this time-out from reality was bound to be brief. The headline *Hard Detective in Country Love Nest* would appear sooner or later. So she did not hesitate to take every risk there was, dragging Anselm uneasily in her wake.

Her phone seldom rang with official calls from Levenham. DI Anderson was too proud in his new reponsibility to do more than give token compliance to his instructions to keep her fully informed. Once he did ring to say there had been a development. Yet it was no more than that Pablo Xingara had at last been traced. To Mexico. Where he had died from cirrhosis of the liver. One week before his daughter had been killed.

Then just after the New Year she got another call.

She had gone tramping into headquarters on the Tuesday after the second Bank Holiday of the extended period of revelry. She had been still fuzzy with the Christmas and post-Christmas cheer which her sons, swift consumers of whatever alcohol was on offer, had insisted on, and which had done little to lift the depression she had experienced on account of a self-imposed vow that she and Anselm were not to meet over the holiday. She had, in fact, attempted to avoid all forced jollity by offering to do any duties that would free another senior officer. But the Assistant Chief had firmly told her that after her long stint over in Levenham she deserved the break. So she had given up the attempt, and had done her best to entertain her sons without telling them, as she and John had agreed, what sooner or later was going to happen.

As soon as she had got in her phone rang, Anderson's voice came, overloud, into her ear.

'Harriet.'

The sod, was her immediate reaction. Now she had been pushed aside in his favour, any attempt at the respectful *ma'am* had been dropped. She felt like giving him a trouncing he wouldn't soon forget.

But that *Harriet* had been loud with excitement. Something new, and important?

'Yes, what is it?'

'We think we've found him. This time we've got him.'

# Chapter Nineteen

The man they had homed in on, DI Anderson excitedly told Harriet, was 'a big computer nerd. Don't know his name yet. Our licensed police hacker, old Sgt Downey, hasn't traced him right down so far. But he has broken into the fellow's files, and guess what he's found there.'

'Tell me.'

'One hundred and sixty-seven pictures of Bubbles Xingara. And, listen to this, her address at Adam and Eve House, got from some Internet file almost as soon as she had bought the place.'

'Yes,' she said. 'Yes, this does sound likely, very likely.'

Then, for the first time for weeks, she felt her old instincts begin to revive.

John had once teasingly quoted – reading from an old luggage-label he'd used – a Dickens dictum as applying to her, *There is a passion for hunting something deeply implanted in the human breast*. It had remained in her mind, partly because of how aptly it referred to herself, the hunter, and more because of that luggage-label. Now, again, she acknowledged its relevance.

'Yes,' she said. 'More than likely. Much more. So why haven't we got a name?'

'Easily enough explained. Apparently the computer our target uses isn't his own. It's one of dozens, maybe hundreds, at what used to be Birchester Technical College, some sort of university now. Cheeky sod, all right, making use of one there. But I suppose he doesn't want his old mother at home booting up and finding pix he's doctored to show Bubbles in intimate contact with some unknown male's private parts.'

'He's got that sort of stuff?'

'Well, no. Not actually, as far as Sgt Downey's told me. But I wouldn't be surprised if Downey hadn't filed away something of the sort for his personal collection.'

Downey, she thought. No, I don't think so, not from what I know of him. But, then, why not? Eros could have descended on computer-fixated Sgt Downey as well as into anyone else.

'We'll give Downey,' she said sharply, 'the benefit of the doubt. But why hasn't he found just which computer at that place belongs to this man?'

'Well, there's been the long holidays, you know.'

'Yes, I do know. And I know, too, that Bubbles Xingara's murderer ought to be caught. Right, I'm going over there now. Let's try what a little straight investigation can do. Enough poncing about with bloody electronics.'

'But – But, ma'am, isn't that – Well, isn't it taking a risk? This chap, whoever he is, might get wind of something. And then . . . Well, we could lose him.'

'I wasn't born yesterday, DI. Meet me.'

She did not wait for Anderson at South Birchester University, out beyond Boreham. If what he had told her was right, then the man who had down-loaded 167 pictures of Bubbles Xingara as well as getting hold of her address well before it became public knowledge, could well be the one who, on June the twentieth, had stealthily approached Adam and Eve House in the stillness of early dawn and had then used, in all probability, a javelin to kill her.

The University was a big place, bigger than she had imagined, a massive new building, already after the holiday break busy with students going here and there, the hum of heavy machinery rising up from its deep basement.

She approached a sharp-faced, bespectacled woman radiating a repressive look behind the reception desk.

'Detective Superintendent Martens, Greater Birchester Police. I'm looking for the IT Department, if that's what it's called.'

'We have at least three departments that come under Information Technology. What exactly do you want?'

Don't come the scientific queen with me, madam.

'If I knew, I wouldn't be asking you, would I? Haven't you got anyone who would be able to tell me about all three?'

'Well, yes, I suppose we have,' came the subdued reply. 'If you take a lift to floor four, you'll find someone there who may be able to help you.'

*May be able?* Better be.

The lift that let her out at the fourth floor led directly to an office area. She approached a bright-looking young black woman at the nearest desk, tapping away at her keyboard.

'I want to talk to your cleverest computer expert.'

The young woman at the keyboard gave her a grin.

'Then that'll be Dr Mortimer. You can't get much cleverer than him, so they tell me. I'll buzz his secretary for you. Who shall I say it is?'

Harriet did not hesitate.

'Dr Mortimer won't know me,' she said. 'I'm just here to make some inquiries. You can say the *Evening Star*.'

'Right-oh.'

Little Miss Bright Eyes looked gratifyingly impressed to be assisting someone from Birchester's biggest-selling paper. And, Harriet thought, it shouldn't be difficult to put the blame on her for a misunderstanding when it became necessary to show Dr Mortimer her warrant card. If a bit unfair.

She began to regret her ruse a little when her innocent victim phoned through with a distinct touch of urgency. The press not to be kept waiting. And DI Anderson had still not arrived.

Ah, well.

Dr Mortimer, she thought as she waited, whom you cannot get *much cleverer than*. Begins to look like a very good bet indeed. A computer scientist too clever for his own good, choosing to keep his secret file of Bubbles pictures right under the noses of his almost as clever colleagues. Anyone, too, would need to be more than ordinarily clever to defeat Sgt Downey. Reputation for being able to worm his way into any set of computer files outside government security.

But the clever man's secretary seemed to be taking her time.

When eventually she did appear she came as a bit of a surprise. Somehow Harriet had been expecting either another bright and pretty young woman like the one she had just been talking to or a would-be dragon like the receptionist in the entrance hall. Dr Mortimer's secretary fitted neither of these pictures. She was a glamour puss. The old-fashioned expression came popping up in Harriet's mind the moment she saw her. A mass of blonde hair down past her shoulders, full-lipped mouth generously red-painted, and pouting too, wide blue eyes behind thickly blacked eyelashes, big breasts pointing outwards, it seemed, to each corner of the universe, and long, long legs encased in gleaming tights, or even stockings.

Not at all what you would expect in a technology establishment.

Then, before the creature had had time to say, *Dr Mortimer will see you now*, the doors of one of the lifts opened and a ruffled-looking DI Anderson burst out of them.

'Ah, there you are, ma'am,' he said. 'Glad I found you.'

Harriet sighed quietly.

Dr Mortimer's glamour-puss secretary might not be surprised by a reporter from the *Evening Star* being addressed by a colleague as *ma'am*. But the young woman at the nearest desk certainly looked sharp enough to have cottoned on to the presence of the police. Would she, once the glamour puss had led the two of them away, phone quickly through to Dr Mortimer and warn him?

She might, bright as she was. Or she might not.

Then an idea came to her.

'You know,' she said, 'now that you're here, Mr Anderson, I think I'll leave. No need for two of us to worry Dr Mortimer with what's after all only a routine inquiry.'

She trusted Handy Andy, at whom she directed as meaning a look as she could without betraying the farce, would realize what his mistake had been and act accordingly, and that Miss Bright Eyes would get the

message. Some query about a road accident, whatever . . .

In case Anderson failed to pick up the hint, she
marched over to the lifts, pressed the *Down* button,
was rewarded by having one set of doors open at once,
stepped in past them and in a moment was swished
away out of sight.

Down in the entrance hall she sat on one of two rather
the worse for wear black leather-look sofas and waited
to see what Handy Andy would find out.

Her wait seemed to be lasting longer than she had
expected. She had been keeping an eye on the signs
above the lifts, but a good many minutes had passed
before at last she saw the number *4* light up. She
watched it eagerly. But the light remained where it
was.

Was Anderson taking special care ushering into the
lift a man already under arrest? Or, perhaps more
likely, had he left Dr Mortimer and was standing with
the lift doors propped open making a date with the
glamour-puss secretary?

But at last the *4* changed to a *3*, then to *2*, to *1* and
finally to *G*.

Handy Andy stepped out of the lift's opening doors,
alone.

She rose to her feet and started out towards him.
Only to see him check abuptly at her appearance.
Plainly, he had not expected, cocky bugger that he
was, to find he was not totally trusted.

'Well, DI?'

'No go.'

'What d'you mean *no go*?'

'What I say. I got it out of him in two minutes that

he's got all those pix of Bubbles. Always a good sign when they start to sweat. Thought I was home and dry. But, no, the little bunched-up fifty-year-old sod's got a gold-plated alibi for June the twentieth.'

'You're sure? Despite all those pictures, that address?'

'Yes, ma'am, I am sure. The bugger was away at a conference. In France. At Aix-les-Bains. He left on June the nineteenth and didn't come back till the twenty-first.'

'He couldn't have flown back that evening, June the nineteenth? Or . . . Or perhaps he never even went?'

'No. I checked with the secretary, that piece. The evening after he left she had to ring him. He'd forgotten to take some papers. I don't know what. But she said he was there, definitely. And he couldn't possibly have got back here in the time. Aix-les-Bains is pretty far south, you know. He'd have had to have managed to hire a bloody private plane, and even then . . .'

'I suppose you're right, DI. Ah, well, it's just one more good lead that's turned out to be a no-no. It's what you can expect with an inquiry like this. There must be people all over the country, all over the world even, harbouring sexual fantasies about poor little Bubbles Xingara. In the end we'll get on to the one it was.'

'Or we won't.'

'No. No, DI, we will, if it takes another two years. If we go on investigating every lead that comes our way, we'll get him in the end. That's good policework, and good policework is what produces a result.'

*

But it was only in the car driving back towards head-quarters that Harriet saw what had been wrong. She had been thinking, not for once about Anselm and their next meeting, but about Handy Andy and his sexual antics, his co-operation with many-thunder-bolted Eros. And suddenly she had a mental picture of him standing by the lift gates on the University's fourth floor chatting up the *piece*, as he had called her.

What if, she asked herself with a lateral jump, despite the difference in age between Glamour Puss and fifty-year-old hunched-up Dr Mortimer, she's his mistress? Handy Andy would not have been able to believe it, would never have taken the possibility into account. But it was a possibility. Eros could strike, didn't she know it, anywhere at any time. Hadn't John spoken to her once about eighty-year-old Saul Bellow and his new young wife, mother now of his child?

So, when Handy Andy had checked with Glamour Puss that her boss had been at that Aix-les-Bains conference on those dates in June, had she at once, without even thinking, confirmed what he had asked about, even though it was not as he had said. It could be. It could be.

She took a quick glance into her rear mirror, swung the car round in a U-turn and headed back for the University.

Past the would-be dragon at the ground-floor reception desk. Into a lift whose doors were luckily open. Out at floor four. Little Bright Eyes still tapping away at her keyboard.

'Hello again.'

Swift, teeth-shining smile. So no repercussions from that bit of disinformation.

'Look, I'd like a private word with your Dr Mortimer's secretary. Could you get her out here without making a fuss about it?'

'With Violet? Yeah, I could do that. She's always ready for a ciggie.'

'Violet?' Harriet could not help asking. 'Is that really her name?'

A grin and a flicker of a wink.

'It is. But don't try kidding her about it. She really hates it.'

'Thanks.'

She went and stood by the lift she had come up in, leaning inside and pressing the *Wait* button. A nice little interview room neatly standing by.

In a moment glamour-puss Violet arrived, already diving into her open handbag, desperate evidently for that cigarette.

'One moment. Detective Superintendent Martens, Greater Birchester Police. I want a word.'

And, before the long-legged, blonde-cascading, bosom-flaunting creature knew where she was, Harriet's hand was at her elbow and the gates of the waiting lift were closing behind her.

Harriet kept a finger on the *Doors Close* button.

'Now,' she said to her captive, 'I believe you answered some questions earlier today from Detective Inspector Anderson.'

'Thinks a lot of himself, that one.'

Glamour Puss, Harriet noted, spoke with a strong Birchester accent much mangled by attempting something classier. But more important was what she had said about Handy Andy. Clearly he had tried to make that date. And had failed. So had he questioned her with eyes shut? Or, rather, with them fixed irremovably on those stunning breasts? And had she been already armoured against his arrows?

'He asked you, I think, about the trip Dr Mortimer took back in June to a conference somewhere?'

She saw, however quickly it was suppressed, the glint of fear in the eyes behind their fringes of blacked eyelashes.

'Aix-les-Bains,' she answered after an instant, pronouncing all the *S*es. 'That's in France.'

'Yes. That would be the conference DI Anderson was wanting to know about. Did he ask you if there'd been any hitches about it?'

'Hitches? What do you mean *hitches*?'

Oh, yes, she's lying all right. Time to go for it? Yes, I think so.

'You know damn well what I mean. You told Mr Anderson that all had gone according to plan about that conference, didn't you? And it hadn't, had it? Dr Mortimer wasn't there at all, was he?'

'But – But – How did you know? I mean, I may have made a mistake when – when Mr Anderson was talking to me. He didn't seem all that interested in the answer, tell you the truth. So I didn't bother to think all that much about it, just told him it was okay what he'd asked.'

'Well, I am interested in the answer. Very interested. So you will tell me exactly what happened back there in June. Now.'

'Yes, yes. I will. All right. Well, you see, Trevor, I mean Dr Mortimer – oh, well, yes, Trevor, you might as well know it all – didn't really want to go. He said there'd be no one there who knew anything worth tuppence about whatever it was they were going to talk about. So – So, well, he said what I never thought he would. He said, *Why don't we go away somewhere, you and I?* Well, that was it. We went. Down to Cornwall. And, well, we had one hell of a good time. In bed from morning till night, if you must know.'

Ignoring the triumphantly lascivious look all across Glamour Puss's glamoured-up face, Harriet realized that, once again, a good lead had melted away. If this flaunting creature and her hunched-up boss had been in bed together for even half the time she had boasted of, then he could not have been killing Bubbles, Bubbles of the 167 photos, far away at Adam and Eve House.

'But I didn't want to get Trev— Dr Mortimer into trouble,' Glamour Puss went on. 'I mean, the college was paying his fare and everything. So I didn't say nothing to that Inspector Whatsit.'

But Harriet hardly listened to these last wretched details that had led to Handy Andy being deceived. Three tiny words that had come almost carelessly from Glamour Puss's mouth had sent reverberations pulsating up in her mind. *You and I*, And at once all she could think about was how back in June – it had been as she was setting off from Levenham to go to Adam and Eve House for the second time – the words of that terrible old song from the days of the music halls had come back to her in a surge of longing for her newly discovered love-object. For Anselm, Anselm, Anselm. And now she felt them again, with blotting-out urgency.

*You and I, alone in a world for two.*

# Chapter Twenty

In the days that followed, while wintry January turned into a February every bit as cold and windswept, Harriet found she thought of little, night and day, but her Anselm. Her barely renewed grip on the Bubbles Xingara inquiry had been almost wholly loosened again the moment glamour-puss Violet had quoted those three words her boss had said, *you and I*. That day just after New Year she had checked, still duty-bound, with Dr Mortimer that what Violet had told her was the truth. But she had done no more than that.

'Yes. Oh, yes,' hunched-up, grizzled Dr Mortimer had said. 'I did take the ridiculous creature away for that weekend. I mean, she's so – so bloody sexy. And she's taken a fancy to me. God knows why. But you can never tell with sex, can you? And I was trying then to get Bubbles out of my mind, not very successfully of course. It's strange, Bubbles is the one I love, even now that she's dead. And God knows, as far as I can see, I'll go on loving her as long as I live, despite all the fucking I do with that magnificent brainless body that I seem to have been given the freedom of.'

*As long as I live*, Harriet thought. And am I going to go on being in love with Anselm *as long as I live*?

The question echoed again in her head a few days later. It was first thing in the morning. Anselm, heaving himself out of their bed and heading for the bathroom, said casually over his naked shoulder, 'You know what day it is this time next week?'

'What day it is? What d'you mean?'

He grinned at the door.

'St Valentine's. Feb the fourteenth.'

And it came as a little jolt to her that Anselm should know the date of St Valentine's Day. That, plainly, it meant something to him, whereas she had never paid attention to what she thought of as cooked-up commercial anniversaries, Mother's Day, Hallowe'en, Father's Day, Valentine's Day. She wondered now what had put the thought of it into his head. Was he one of the people who made much of the day, an excuse if any was needed for some love-making, or an occasion to parade silly, sexy ads in the newspapers? Certainly he seemed to have the date firmly in his mind. But perhaps in sleepy Levenham some old St Valentine's customs still prevailed, like leaving real anonymous notes when lovers lacked the courage to declare themselves. And, come to think of it, hadn't poor Bubbles-obsessed Prudence Mackintosh said something about some local ritual on that day? Teenagers going down to the Leven at dawn?

Perhaps Anselm is actually plotting to send a Valentine's card to me. Something all hearts and roses, best card-shop style? Or, worse, with some crude sex pun? No, surely not that. His feelings too genuine, surely. But yukky hearts and roses? It's possible, I suppose. I can see him choosing one like that, if he is going to get one. And what am I going to feel when I see it?

And, more, what year after year am I going to feel each February the – what did he say? – yes, the fourteenth, when I get yet one more hearts-entwined horror? If I do, if I do.

Try not to think about it. But the tiniest crack in the seamless pattern of our absorbed life together?

The sound of water from the shower tumbling down the waste-pipe outside.

But didn't John tell me something about Valentine's Day once long ago? Before he went to Brazil, or even earlier? Some little thing he'd noted about it, blurry writing on a restaurant paper-napkin? All part of the great theory about the ubiquitous sex-cloud. That isn't, as I know now, any mere theory.

What was it he said? The original St Valentine having nothing to do with lovers? Yes, that was it. Valentine had got to be the patron saint of lovers only because his feast day was established on the day that had been the old Roman feast called . . . called, yes, the Lupercalia. And, yes, something else. Yes, John's glee about another little fact, that Valentine's feast actually comes one day before the Roman one. But nobody was going to worry about that, he said, not when love, love, love's in question. Or really sex, sex, sex. And, yes, the Lupercalia was very definitely a love feast, a sex one. Another of John's battered little notes to himself, culled from the French reference book – Larousse, wasn't it? – consisted of the two words *Lupercales* and *licencieuses*. Saying it all.

Except, come to think of it, John didn't let that just say it all. Oh, no, I got the full lecture. Starting from the huge profits florists and the manufacturers of greetings cards make out of the Valentine hoo-hah, and then going on to sex in the world of business. Eros multi-national. Hollywood and the whole millions-making film industry largely depending on sex. Then the fashion industry down the ages. And the immense amounts of energy and money scientists have devoted to bringing the ubiquitous cloud down even lower, rubber technology, the Pill, and combating the after-effects of Eros's activities, all the sexual diseases and their cures and palliatives.

Yes, she thought now, and I can add the tennis industry to the list. Don't tell me Bubbles' wealth came just from her ability to hit a ball very hard with that hand made ugly with calluses. No, she got her millions, whether consciously or not because of her vibrant sexuality. Gift of Eros. Who also, surely, gave her the poisoned gift of murder.

'And all based' – didn't John say? – 'on just that single urge to perform, setting aside the piled-up pre-liminaries, the one simple act. Testosterone, in-escapable part of our bodily processes, even the female, urging and urging the discharge of seminal fluids at every possible opportunity.'

It turned out to be, however, a Valentine of an alto-gether different nature that Anselm gave Harriet, early on the morning of February the fourteenth, a day when he was absent from her bed on duty in Levenham. Her phone rang while she was still asleep. No longer was she always up at half-past six, the Hard Detective ready for battle. Now, when Anselm was not with her, she would lie there once she had woken and let herself dreamily think of him. Dreamily, but in vivid particu-larity.

And it was his voice she heard when she muttered a *Hello* into the phone. But he was not murmuring endearments, as shy Anselm had gradually learnt to do over the past months.

'Ma'am. Something to report.'

The inquiry. At once some nerve-tingling excitement came stealthily into her. The Hard Detective surfacing again.

'Right. Spit it out.'

'The weapon's been found.'

'The weapon? The javelin? Was it a javelin?'

'Oh, yes, ma'am, it was a javelin all right. Some teenagers found it, in the Leven. It was at dawn this morning, at a place – it's about half a mile upstream from Adam and Eve House, actually – where youngsters have always held a sort of ceremony on Valentine's Day. Ever since ever. The girls gather on the Levenham side of the river and the boys go round to the other one. Then you've got to wade across, if you can – the river's pretty full this time of year – and snatch a kiss. Or that's how it used to be. Gather they go a bit further nowadays.'

'But you're telling me they've got the javelin, yes?'

'Oh, yes, ma'am, they have. One of the boys tripped on it as he was getting across, three-parts hidden in the mud, and he pulled it out.'

'And you think it is the one, our javelin, the weapon?'

'Well, can't be absolutely certain, of course. I suppose Forensics may find something. But, if it is what we've been looking for all this while and it's been in the river the whole time, it's not going to be easy to recover prints or anything.'

'It's going to be impossible. But that hardly matters. What's important is where it was found. Are you out there now?'

'Yes, ma'am.'

'Right. Meet me at Adam and Eve House. That'll

be the nearest place by road for me. I want to see that javelin.'

Driving at speed, careless of the icy patches on the country roads, Harriet realised that, although it was Anselm she was going to meet, she had hardly thought of him at all after she had taken his call. She knew, too, with the passion for hunting something running strong in her, that when they were face-to-face at Adam and Eve House he would be back to being DI Brent and nothing more.

Parking at the edge of the house's big sweep of lawn, covered now in icy slush, the remains of the last fall of snow, with here and there zigzags of dark cold-bitten grass breaking through, she thought how different it all was from that dawn day when she had first seen it. No cuckoo crazily love-calling now. Scarcely any sound at all in the still winter air. No rich odours of cows from the pastures round about. No more than a few desperately clinging leaves on the bare branches of the big untidy mock-orange. The lavender hedge that before had filled the air with its sweetly acidy scent now little more than a long tangle of dried twigs.

The house, too, now up for sale, was standing emptily bleak, seeming in its cradle of dead, black creeper branches almost physically pale and shivering in the biting cold. And, perhaps most different of all, the Leven, no longer that trickle of water between mud banks deep-cracked by the heat, was a brawling, swirling, fast-flowing stream.

Down beside it there was, yes, DI Brent. He was standing with his burly Leven Vale Police colleague Sgt Wintercombe, who was holding delicately between the fingers of his thickly gloved hands the javelin.

The weapon. Hard to believe now that anything else had been used. Why otherwise would a javelin of all things come to be lying at the bottom of the Leven, not half a mile from the murder scene?

She went over to them.

'Let's have a look, Sergeant.'

She held out her own gloved hands – thank goodness, I had the sense to put on my padded jacket – carefully took the long rust-dappled shaft and began to imagine just what had been done with it almost eight months earlier at this precise place. Bubbles, back from her run, sweat-drenched in the summer heat, standing probably with hands on knees, leaning a little forward, regaining her breath. Then the killer suddenly coming up to her, filled with hate at that earlier sharp rejection Bubbles had told Fiona Diplock about. The humiliating kick or knock-down, whatever it had been. The long weapon aimed, thrust, withdrawn.

And the killer, yes, going back the way they had come. By way of, yes, yes, of course, by way of the river. So, in a boat. No. No, impossible. The Leven in June had been that mere trickle between two dried-mud banks.

So how could . . . No boat. Walking? All the way along the river bed?

No. Too far. Too far carrying that not-to-be-seen javelin.

Wait. I know.

I know now. A canoe. A canoe could, just, have floated on top of that trickle of a stream. It would be deep enough. I can see it now as it was that day. Yes, a canoe.

And I can see something else. Something I never thought . . .

I can see a noisy gang of schoolboys making their way past Levenham police station, carrying twin-bladed kayak oars or with the light boats inverted on their heads. And I can see, too, even that trailing along at the rear was that lumpy friend of Anselm's young nephew. The one who tore up the sheet I'd written *Join the Police* on.

She felt as if she had been invaded, almost as if an alien from outer space had taken her over, by a notion. An idea. Something hazy, not quite in focus. And perhaps something that forcing into focus would send pulsing away to smithereens.

'DI,' she said to Anselm. 'I'd like a word. Go and sit in the car out of the cold. And, Sergeant, take this back to Levenham and get it sent to Forensics in Birchester.'

She handed back the javelin, turned and strode towards the car, with Anselm a yard or so in front of her looking, from the way he was uneasily holding himself, as if he wanted nothing more than to turn round to see her face.

Like Orpheus, she thought, rescuing his wife from Hell on condition he didn't look back at her. But, love-sick fool, Orpheus did. Oh, yes, and this is another thing I owe to one of John's little bits of paper: back from Hell himself, poor handsome Orpheus was so grief-stricken he enraged all the women round by paying them no attention. And, in an orgy, they tore him to pieces. Another victim of deadly Eros.

But Anselm had better not turn round now. Because he won't see his loved one. He'll see the Hard Detective who wants to find out what he makes of the idea, the nebulous idea, that's hovering just outside her head.

# Chapter Twenty-one

Harriet got into the car, fired up the engine for warmth and turned to Anselm as he settled into the passenger's seat, her face fixed in deliberate neutrality.

'Listen, DI,' she said.

Beside her, she saw Anselm change in a moment from would-be soft and eager lover into impassive police officer.

'Listen, I was thinking just now about what exactly must have happened down by the river there when Bubbles was killed. We know for certain now that what killed her was that javelin Sgt Wintercombe is driving off with this minute. And I think I know how the person who used it brought it here, and took it away afterwards. I think it was in a canoe, which is why they were able to go unseen. I think the level of water in the Leven back then would have made such a trip just possible. What do you say?'

Anselm thought for a little.

'Yes. Yes, ma'am. Trying to recollect as accurately as I can, I'd say there was still enough water to get a canoe along then, maybe with it getting stuck from time to time. But possible, yes, if whoever was in it wasn't some big fatty.'

'Right. So a canoe. Or a kayak?'

'Yeah, a kayak would be just as good. I've quite often rowed one, you know, at the Water Sports Centre.'

'Yes, you told me once that you had. Isn't the bailiff there one of your neighbours?'

'George Green? Yes, he is.'

'All right. Now, who in Levenham would be particularly skilled with a kayak?'

Anselm frowned.

'Hard to say, ma'am. There's George, of course. He's pretty good in a canoe, though he's a bit weighty. And there's quite a few blokes might take one out in the summer, for fun really. But I don't think there are any what you might call regular sports users, not outside of the Grammar. The boys there do kayak racing once a week nowadays, so Jonathan tells me.'

'Ah yes. So would he be some sort of expert in a kayak?'

'Jonathan? Yes. Yes, I think that's one of the sports he trains for, though he's not the school champ. That's George Green's son, the lad who tore up your autograph. Remember?'

'Yes. Yes, of course I do. Jonathan's friend.'

'Well, they're not exactly friends, him and Jonathan. Thing is, Gary—'

'That's his name? Gary?'

'That's him. But, you see, it's just because he lives next door but one to us and is much the same age as Jonathan, or a bit older, so they were more or less told they were friends. But I don't think, in fact, Jonathan much likes Gary, even though they sort of muck around together. Kids can be like that.'

'Good, DI. Yes, true enough.'

Yes, she thought, nothing wrong with Anselm's brains, or his perceptions. He could go far in the police.

'Now,' she went on, 'let me put something else to you.'

'Ma'am?'

'Do you remember something I logged some time ago, more details of what I'd been told by Fiona Diplock about Bubbles saying something about how she'd been accosted, or attacked – she wasn't explicit – by someone near the boathouse, just over there, shortly before she was killed?'

'Yes. Yes, I remember. I've sometimes wondered about it. But there didn't seem to be any way of finding out more about what happened then, not with Bubbles being dead.'

'Exactly. But do you remember, too, that Bubbles never said whether this assailant was a man or woman?'

'Yes, I do. Though I don't really see it as a woman.'

'No?'

She took in a breath.

'But do you see it as a boy? As a young male?'

A look of blank bewilderment.

'Yes, a boy,' Harriet said. 'And remember this. On that day when I gave Jonathan my autograph he said to us that the whole school was *mad on her*. Mad about Bubbles.'

The look of bewilderment on Anselm's broad face began to change.

'But you can't . . .' he said. 'Ma'am, are you really saying the person who killed Bubbles was a boy, a boy at the Grammar? It's not – it isn't Jonathan?'

'No, no, of course not. But just think about it. Didn't you say just now that a kayak, or a canoe, could have got along the Leven *if whoever was in it wasn't some big fatty?*'

Anselm thought.

'But who then?' he said. 'How can we find one boy out of, I don't know, a hundred and fifty possibles at the Grammar?'

'I'll tell you how. Or how, if I'm right about all this.'

'Ma'am?'

'Think. When I gave Jonathan my autograph and he suggested to Gary Green, his so-called friend, that he should get one, too, how did Gary react? He didn't want my autograph, did he? He really objected to the whole idea, and, when he'd been more or less made to produce a sheet of paper, he screwed it up in a rage the first moment he could and threw it in the gutter. Didn't he?'

'Well, yes, I told you I'd seen him do that.'

'All right. But I dare say you were too busy then thinking about Old Rowley to take much notice. Yes? But now look again at what Gary did. Wasn't that really very odd behaviour for a boy? Actually to scrunch up that sheet almost at once, and deliberately to throw it in the gutter? Doesn't that actually indicate he was under psychological pressure of some sort? Heavy psychological pressure?'

'What you're saying is – I mean, you really think Gary Green – he's only just twelve, you know – murdered Bubbles?'

'Oh, as to his age, yes. If we're right about that first scene down by the river, this is definitely a sex-based murder. Bubbles was never going to attack someone physically if they were just asking for her autograph. She might tell them to go away, but she wouldn't set on them in a fury. But that's what she told Fiona she did. She either actually kicked them or she knocked them to the ground. And your Gary's definitely within the category of the sexually active. If he was a year or two younger, I might be as sceptical as you. But at twelve he could be well inside the bracket.'

'Yes,' Anselm said slowly. 'Yes, it is about then that you . . . Or a bit later. Start to think about girls, about having sex. I remember all right.'

'So, put it all together. A boy who's sexually active, and who could have tried it on with Bubbles. Then add this: that Gary Green, you said, was the school champion at kayak racing. And, another thing, you said the Grammar's very keen on all sports these days? I'm willing to bet they have some javelins there, just like posh Grainham Hall.'

'You're right about that. I never did it, but I remember there was javelin-throwing even when I was a senior there.'

'Right, what you could do this very minute is call somebody at the Grammar on your mobile. I dare say you know the number.'

'Yes. Yes, I do, of course.'

'All right then, phone and find out if a javelin has ever gone missing there. It's quite likely no one would have reported it to the police. After all, thanks to our policy of keeping under wraps that we believed a javelin was the weapon, no one had any particular reason to link a missing one with Bubbles' murder.'

Anselm phoned, talked to someone who, to begin with, made difficulties, then in response to some sharp words agreed to call back in a few minutes.

'All right, we'll soon see if a javelin went missing in June. You know, I said once it was no use looking all over England for a missing one. But here, if I turn out to be correct, is a missing one right on our doorstep. So, here's what I want you to do as soon as we've had it confirmed that a javelin was missing. Go back to Levenham and have a word with young Jonathan. Find out if he noticed anything peculiar about Gary in the days towards the end of June. Don't press it, but ask. I wouldn't be at all surprised if he says that, now he thinks about it, Gary was behaving oddly then. Probably it didn't last long, though. It'd be my bet that, since Gary's begun to feel we were never going to get near him, he's been doing his best to pretend to himself that what happened never did happen.'

Yes, the poor, wretched boy, she thought. Eros really had it in for him, even at twelve years of age. A Latin tag of John's came into her mind. *Quem Jupiter vult pedere, dementat prius.* John liked it because it was usually mis-translated as *Whom the gods*, not Jupiter, *wish to destroy, they first make mad*. But, she thought, it hadn't been gods who had made sullen little Gary Green mad, it was one god. And not Jupiter. It was a darker deity. Eros.

'You could be right about making yourself forget,' Anselm said with a sudden lightness of tone. 'At junior school once I accidentally broke the wooden handle of a garden roller when nobody saw me. For a day or two afterwards I felt awful. But then I did just what you said. I made myself forget it had happened. I only really remembered years later.'

She smiled at this picture of a haunted young Anselm.

And then she ceased to smile.

The twittering call note of Anselm's mobile was ringing out in the confines of the car.

A short conversation. And the answer exactly what

Harriet had expected. A javelin had been missing from the sports store at the Grammar since some time last June.

But while the little tinny voice had been clicketing on from Anselm's mobile one half of her mind had been pursuing a different track. She had been struck suddenly by the odd thought that it now looked likely the investigation that had begun with an Eros strike here at Adam and Eve House so many months ago was about to end here on Eros' St Valentine's Day. Then she had run on to wondering for an instant whether the police officer sitting beside her had put a wretched Valentine's card in the post for her.

And then she had found a possibility, a wild, unexpected possibility, had opened up before her.

'Right,' she said to Anselm when he had briefly told her that the javelin had gone missing. 'I want you to go straight away now and talk to Jonathan. Then, if he confirms in any way what we think about Gary Green . . . Then I'm going to leave the whole of the rest of the case to you.'

Anselm sat as still as if something scarcely credible had been brought to his ears. Then at last he spoke.

'But you – you're not going to try – you're saying you won't try to get the cough yourself?'

No, she said to herself before giving him her answer. No, Anselm, I realize now this is my last chance to back out. To send you as far away from me as I can. All right, you're as much in love with me as I still am with you. You're besotted. That's the word. The word for me, too. It's all I can do, even at this moment, to keep my hands off you. But I am going to. I am going to part from you. I can't, after all, let your career, your whole life, be ruined because of what all-powerful Eros has done to us. And, yes, I'm going to save myself, too. I'm going to save the Hard Detective. To fight another day. I'm going to part from you, Anselm. Now. Oh, yes, I tried before, and failed. But now this last chance has suddenly come about, and I'm going to take it. To grab it.

'Yes, DI,' she said, forcing herself to speak coolly as if she was issuing an everyday order. 'I'm leaving you to conduct the whole case right up to the juvenile court. I'm bowing out. It's best. I think it's best.'

Anselm, beneath his winter-reddened cheeks, was pale to fainting-point.

Shifting in his seat, he turned towards her.

'No,' she said, her voice hard as the frosted ground outside. 'No, this is the end. The end for us. It's the best way. The only good way.'

She did not add, as she wanted to with all the strength that was in her, as Eros-struck Dr Mortimer did in confessing to his 167 pictures of Bubbles, as obsessed Prudence Mackintosh might have done, as even despicable Mr Youngman might have done, *But I think I'll love you till I die.*

What the Hard Detective did say in her mind, however, was quite simply, *Fuck you, Eros, fuck you.*